Bleeding Violet

More heart-pumping novels from Simon Pulse

Gone
Lisa McMann

Chasing Brooklyn
Lisa Schroeder

The Hollow
Jessica Verday

Swoon
Nina Malkin

Raven
Allison van Diepen

Bleeding Violet

Dia Reeves

SIMON PULSE
New York London Toronto Sydney

SIMON PULSE

An imprint of Simon & Schuster Children's Publishing Division

1230 Avenue of the Americas, New York, NY 10020

First Simon Pulse hardcover edition January 2010

Copyright © 2010 by Dia Reeves

SIMON PULSE and colophon are registered trademarks of Simon & Schuster, Inc.

For information about special discounts for bulk purchases, please contact Simon & Schuster Special Sales at 1-866-506-1949 or business@simonandschuster.com.

The Simon & Schuster Speakers Bureau can bring authors to your live event. For more information or to book an event contact the Simon & Schuster Speakers Bureau at 1-866-248-3049 or visit our website at www.simonspeakers.com.

Designed by Paul Weil

The text of this book was set in Caslon.

Manufactured in the United States of America

2 4 6 8 10 9 7 5 3 1

Library of Congress Cataloging-in-Publication Data

Reeves, Dia.

Bleeding violet / Dia Reeves. — First Simon Pulse hardcover ed.

p. cm.

Summary: A mentally ill sixteen-year-old girl reunites with her estranged mother in an East Texas town that is haunted with doors to dimensions of the dead and protected by demon hunters called Mortmaine.

ISBN 978-1-4169-8618-8

[1. Mothers and daughters—Fiction. 2. Mental illness—Fiction. 3. Dead—Fiction. 4. Supernatural—Fiction. 5. Texas—Fiction.] I. Title.

PZ7.R25583Bl 2010

[Fic]—dc22

2009015006

ISBN 978-1-4169-9866-2 (eBook)

To my mother, Glenda, who always lets me be myself

Acknowledgments

Many thanks to Susan Lynn Byerly Smith for not only being an awesome Alpha Reader, but also for coming up with the title of this book, though I still think *The Other Side of Crazy* is sooo funny (nice try, Ma!). Big thanks to my first agent, Michelle Andelman, for taking a chance on an unknown kid (always wanted to say that!). Thanks to Michael del Rosario for really getting my book and helping me make it stronger, and for understanding that yes, some people—like us—actually do have green veins. And thanks to Valerie Shea, because although I'm a stickler when it comes to word usage, she's way sticklier (and yes I know that's not a word :p). A big hug to my Blueboarder peeps, especially Amy Spitzley, Brad "the Brad" White, and Elaine "Sweetpea" Alexander—three folks who have taken the art of BS to a whole nother level. And Sylvia Nordeman! Thanks for keeping my secret writer life a secret and for letting me vent about all sorts of heinous stuff—you know what I mean . . . shh! Finally, I have to give a special shout-out to my family: the Reeveses, of course; the Costellos; the Mundines; and the Runnelses. Thanks for giving me the space to be as weird as I need to be.

Chapter One

The truck driver let me off on Lamartine, on the odd side of the street. I felt odd too, standing in the town where my mother lived. For the first seven years of my life, we hadn't even lived on the same continent, and now she waited only a few houses away.

Unreal.

Why didn't you have the truck driver let you off right in front of her house? Poppa's voice echoed peevishly in my head, as if he were the one having to navigate alone in the dark.

"I have to creep up on her," I whispered, unwilling to disturb the extreme quiet of midnight, "otherwise my heart might explode."

What's her house number?

"1821," I told him, noting mailboxes of castles and pirate ships and the street numbers painted on them. I had to fish my penlight from my pack to see the numbers; streetlights were scarce, and the sky bulged with low, sooty clouds instead of helpful moonlight.

Portero sat in a part of East Texas right on the tip of the Piney Woods; wild tangles of ancient pine and oak twisted throughout the town. But here on Lamartine, the trees had been tamed, corralled behind ornamental fences and yoked with tire swings.

"It's pretty here, isn't it?"

Disturbingly pretty, said Poppa. *Where are the slaughterhouses? The oil oozing from every pore of the land? Where's the brimstone?*

"Don't be so dramatic, Poppa. She's not that bad. She can't be."

No? His grim tone unnerved me as it always did when he spoke of my mother. *Rosebushes and novelty mailboxes don't explain her attitude. I never imagined she would live in such a place. She isn't the type.*

"Maybe she's changed."

Ha!

"Then I'll make her change," I said, passing a mailbox shaped like a chicken—1817.

How had I gotten so close?

A few short feet later, I was better than close—I was there: 1821.

My mother's house huddled in the middle of a great expanse of lawn. None of the other houses nestled chummily near hers; even her garage was unattached. A lone tree decorated her lawn, a sweet gum, bare and ugly—nothing like her neighbors' gracefully spreading shade trees. Her mailbox was strictly utilitarian, and the fence that circled her property was chin high and unfriendly.

Ah, said Poppa, vindicated. *That's more like it.*

I ignored him and crept through the unfriendly gate and up the porch steps. The screen door wasn't locked—didn't even have a lock—so I let myself into the dark space and sat in the little garden chair to the left of the front door. I sat for a long time, catching my breath. I sat and I breathed. I breathed and I sat—

Stop stalling, Hanna.

My hands knotted over my stomach, over the swarm of butterflies warring within. I gazed at the dark length of the front door, consumed with what was on the other side of it.

"Do you think she'll be happy to see me?" I asked Poppa. "Even a little?"

Not if you go in with that attitude. Where's your spine?

"What if she doesn't believe I'm her daughter?"

You look exactly like her. How many times have I told you? Now, stop being silly and go introduce yourself.

Poppa always knew how to press my "rational" button. "You're right. I am being silly." I straightened my dress, hitched up my pack, marched to the front door, and raised my fist to—

NO. The force of the word rattled my brain. *Don't knock. It's after midnight. You'll wake her up, and she awakens badly.*

"How badly?" I whispered, hand to my ringing skull.

As badly as you.

Uh-oh.

Nine times out of ten, I awoke on my own, naturally, even without an alarm clock, but if I was awoken before I was ready, things could get . . . interesting. And apparently, I'd gotten that trait from my mother.

Cool.

Just let yourself in, said Poppa, his advice rock solid as always. *It's practically your house anyway.*

I crouched on the porch, the wood unkind to my bare

knees, and folded back the welcome mat. A stubby bronze key glinted in the glow of my penlight.

A spare key.

"Only in a small town," I whispered, snatching it up.

I unlocked the door and slipped inside.

A red metallic floor lamp with spotlights stuck all over it stood in the center of the room. One of the spotlights beamed coldly—as though my mother had known I was coming and had left the light on for me.

Aside from the red chrysanthemums in a translucent vase above the sham fireplace, and the red throw pillow gracing the single chair near the floor lamp, the entire living room was unrelievedly blue-white.

Modern, the same style Poppa had liked—

Still likes, he said.

—and so I immediately felt at home.

My hopes began to rise again.

I slipped the spare key into the pocket of my dress as I traveled down a short hallway, my French heels clicking musically against the blond wood floor. I put my ear to each of the three doors in the hall, until a slow, deep breathing sighed into my head from behind door number three.

My mother's breath. Soothing and gentle, as if the air that puffed from her lungs was purer than other people's.

I stood with my head to the door, trying to match my breath to hers, until my ear began to sting from the pressure.

I regarded the door thoughtfully. Fingered the brass knob.

No, I told you. Poppa was adamant. *You need to entice her out of bed.*

"I know how to do that," I whispered, the idea coming to me all at once.

I stole into the kitchen and turned on the light near the swinging door. The kitchen, like the living room, was blue-white, with a single lipstick-red dining chair providing the only color, aside from me in my violet dress.

I dumped my purple bag by the red chair and went exploring, and after I learned where she kept the plates, the French bread, and the artisanal cheese, I decided to make grilled-cheese sandwiches. I took no especial pains to be quiet—I *wanted* her company. I'd traveled more than one hundred miles in three different crapmobiles and an eighteen-wheeler full of beer just to bask in her presence, but it wasn't until I plated the food that she shoved through the kitchen door.

My grandma Annikki once told me that anyone who

looked on the face of God would instantly fall over dead. Looking at my mother—for the first time ever—I wondered if it was because God was beautiful.

I had the same hourglass figure, the same hazel skin, the same turbulence of tight, skinny curls; but while my curls were a capricious brown, hers were shadow black.

Island-girl hair, Poppa whispered admiringly.

I averted my eyes and presented the sandwiches, like an offering. "Do you want any?"

She drifted toward me in a red sleep shirt and bare feet, seeming to bend the air around her. Her mouth was expressive, naturally rosy, and mean. Just like mine. Our lips turned down at the corners and made us look spoiled.

"You broke into my house to fix a snack," she said, testing the words, her East Texas drawl stretching each syllable like warm taffy. "I better be dreaming this up, little girl."

"It's no dream, Rosalee. I'm here. I'm your daughter."

Her hands clutched her sleep shirt, over her heart, otherwise she didn't move. Her oil black eyes raked me in a discomfiting sweep.

"My daughter's in Finland," she said, the words heavy with disbelief.

"Not anymore. Not for years. I'm here now." I reached out to touch her or hug her—any contact would have been staggering—but she stepped away from my questing hands, her mean mouth twisting as she spoke my name.

"Hanna?"

"Yes."

"God." She seemed to recognize me then, her gaze softening a little. "You even have his eyes."

"I know." I marveled over the similarities between us. "Not much else, though."

Rosalee looked away from me, tugging at her hair as if she wanted to pull it out. "How could he let you come here? Alone. In the middle of the night. Did he crack?"

"He died. Last year."

She let her hair fall forward, hiding from me, so if any grief or regret touched her face, I didn't see it.

After a time, Rosalee stalked past me and stood before the picture window. "If he died last year," she said, "why come to me now? How'd you even know where to find me?"

I sat in the red chair, clashing violently in my purple dress. "I stole your postcard from Poppa's desk when I was seven, the month before we moved to the States." I went into my pack for the postcard. It was soft, yellowed with the years. On one side was a photo of Fountain Square, somewhere here in Portero. On the back was my old address in Helsinki, and in the body of the card, the single word "NO."

I showed it to her. "What were you saying no to?"

Rosalee glanced at the postcard but wouldn't touch it. She settled herself against the window, her back to the lowering sky. "I don't remember what question he asked: to marry him, to visit y'all, to love y'all. Maybe all three. No to all three."

I put the postcard away. "When Poppa and I moved to Dallas, the first thing I did was go to the public library and look up your name in the Portero phone book."

I'd gotten such a thrill seeing her name in stark black letters, Rosalee Price, an actual person—not a legend Poppa had made up to comfort me whenever I wondered aloud why other kids had mothers and I didn't.

"I memorized your address and phone number. For eight years I recited them to myself before I went to sleep, like a lullaby. I didn't bother to contact you, though. Poppa had warned me what to expect if I tried. That's why I just showed up on your doorstep—I didn't want to give you a chance to say no."

She regarded me with a reptilian stillness, unmoved by

my speech. "Who've you been staying with since he died?"

"His sister. My aunt Ulla."

"She know you're here?"

"Even our feet are the same."

"What?"

I took off my purple high heels and showed her my skinny feet—the long toes and high arches. Exactly like hers.

"I asked you about your aunt," said Rosalee, still unmoved.

I admired the sight of our naked feet, settled so closely together, golden against the icy sheen of the kitchen tile.

"I didn't even know I looked like you. I figured I did. Poppa told me I did. I knew I didn't look like anybody on Poppa's side of the family. They're all tall and blond and white as snow foxes. And here I am, tall*ish* and brunette and brown as sugar. Just like you. My grandma Annikki used to say if I hadn't been born with gray eyes, no one would have known for sure that I belonged to them. And I did belong to them, but I belong to you, too. I want to know about you."

That Sally Sunshine act won't work on her, Poppa warned.

But it *was* working. As I spoke, Rosalee's gaze remained focused on me, her unswerving interest startling but welcome in light of her antagonism.

"Poppa told me some things. He'd tell me how beautiful you were, but in the same breath, he'd curse you and say you were dead on the inside. So I've always thought of you that way—an undead Cinderella, greenish and corpselike, but wearing a ball gown. Do you even have a ball gown? I could make one for you. I make all my own clothes. I made this dress. Isn't it sweet?" I stood so she could admire it. "I always feel like Alice when I wear it. That would make this Wonderland, wouldn't it? And you the White Rabbit—always out of reach."

"Why do you have blood on your dress?"

Her intense scrutiny made sense now. She hadn't been interested in me, but in my bloodstains. I followed her gaze to the two dark smidges near my waist.

Sally Sunshine and her bloodstained dress, said Poppa, disappointed in me. *I told you to change clothes, didn't I?*

I fell back into the red chair, the skirt of my dress flouncing about my knees, refusing to let Poppa's negativity derail me.

"What makes you think that's blood? That could be anything. That could be ketchup."

"That ain't ketchup," Rosalee said. "And this ain't Wonderland. This is Portero—I know blood when I see it."

I nibbled my food silently.

"Whose *blood* is that?"

Tell her, Poppa encouraged. *I guarantee she won't care.*

"It's Aunt Ulla's blood," I said. "I hit her on the head with a rolling pin."

I risked another glance into her face. Nothing.

Told you.

"And?" Rosalee prompted.

Did she want *details*?

"Aunt Ulla's blood spurted everywhere, onto my dress, into my eyes." I blinked hard in remembrance. "It burned." I fingered the smidges at my waist. "I thought I'd cleaned myself up, but apparently—"

"Hanna." Despite her apathy, Rosalee addressed me with an undue amount of care, as though I were a rabid dog she didn't want to spook. "Did you kill your aunt?"

I ate the last bit of grilled cheese. I licked the grease from my fingers. "Probably."

Chapter Two

"It's no use," I told Rosalee when she unearthed a cordless phone and asked for Aunt Ulla's number. I poured myself a big tumbler of milk and resettled into the red chair. "If telephoning the dead were possible, I'd be talking to Poppa right now."

We are talking, Poppa said, his voice a snug little bug in my ear. *Who needs phones?*

Rosalee, meanwhile, waited with the phone in her hand, as patient as an Easter Island statue that had stood a thousand years and was ready to stand a thousand more, if that's what it took. So I recited Aunt Ulla's number and watched her dial.

If she wanted to find out the hard way, so be it.

Rosalee's finger froze in the act of dialing, and she studied me head to toe, her face taut. "This aunt of yours . . . was she mean to you? Did she hurt you?"

I nodded. "She hurt my feelings."

"*Feelings?*" Rosalee finished dialing, her face relaxing back into its mask of indifference.

"Emotional abuse is just as bad as physical abuse. Worse! You can heal broken bones; you can't heal a broken mind. Not easily." But Rosalee wouldn't hear it. "She's not going to answer."

"I remember how Järvinens are," said Rosalee, disturbingly patient. "None of y'all ever pick up within the first minute. 'People who hang up quickly—'"

"'Never want anything important,'" I finished. She knew us! *I made a baby with her. She couldn't help but pick up a few things.*

"You'll wanna talk to her, I guess," said Rosalee, waiting and waiting for my dead aunt to answer the phone.

"I have nothing to say to her."

"Well, she'll have plenty to say to you, that's for sure."

I shrugged and drank, smugness pouring into me along

with the ice-cold milk as the wind manhandled the sweet gum on the lawn and sent its branches scraping along the house. The wind wasn't manhandling me. My brief day of homelessness had ended with me sheltered and well fed, not by Child Protective Services or a pimp, but by my own mother. How many other runaways could make that claim?

"Ulla?" Rosalee stopped pacing and leaned against the counter. "This is Rosalee Price. Yeah, *me*."

I almost choked on my milk, my smugness evaporating into sour gas. *"She's alive?"*

Rosalee put her hand over the phone. "Sounds like it."

I slammed the glass to the table.

Rosalee slanted a dark look at me but spoke into the phone, "I *know* that. She just turned up on my doorstep."

I heard Aunt Ulla's heated voice all the way from my chair. Rosalee had to hold the phone away from her ear.

When the screaming died down, Rosalee said, *"How* many stitches? Oh. Too bad. Well, what do you want me to do? Burst into flames? I *said* it was bad."

Louder, angrier yelling.

"Don't yell at me. Yell at your niece when you pick her up. Well, you *have* to see her again. She's your family. Don't put

that daughter shit on me! I never even seen her before today!"
Pause. "What? Diagnosed as *what*?"

Panic sent me scurrying out of the kitchen, my pack slung over my shoulder. What was I doing sitting around like the battle was won? She knew about me now. Aunt Ulla was giving her a play-by-play of all my antics over the past year, including the incident from this morning. Rosalee would be more desperate than ever to send me away. I had to move quick and stake out a bit of earth for myself before Rosalee got off the phone.

I found a switch on the wall that lit the living room: one chair and one footstool, but no futon or foldout couch. No couches, period. Down a hallway to my left was a bathroom, a linen closet, an office the *size* of a closet, and finally Rosalee's bedroom, which housed a twin-size bed.

I went back to the living room, worried. One chair in the kitchen, one chair in the living room, a twin bed in the bedroom. It wasn't that Rosalee didn't have room in her life for me; Rosalee didn't have room for *anybody*.

Opposite the front door was a staircase. I went up expecting more of the same antisocial layout, but on opening the single door at the top of the stairs, I discovered a large, empty attic space shaped like the top half of a stop sign. The walls were white and the same blond wood from downstairs covered the floor. A large window with brass-handled casements overlooked the dark, dreaming street.

Such good bones this room had. Such potential. It even had its own bathroom with a shower, sink, and toilet so white I doubted they'd ever been used.

A guest room. Empty because Rosalee clearly didn't want any guests. Luckily, I wasn't a guest.

I was family.

I set my bag on the floor and unpacked: seven purple dresses, purple underclothes, my purple purse, the big wooden swan Poppa had carved for me, and my cell phone. Since the room had no closet, I placed everything on the built-in shelves along the wall opposite the door, including my pills, which took up almost all the top shelf. I put the few toiletries I'd packed into the medicine cabinet. And that was it.

I was home.

We're both home, Poppa agreed, satisfied. He had been waiting to reunite with Rosalee even longer than I had.

I went downstairs and paused for a bit outside the kitchen door. When I heard nothing but Rosalee's sporadic murmurings, I continued down the hall to the linen closet and commandeered several thick blankets and one purple bath towel.

The purple I took as an omen—a good one.

I hadn't packed any nightgowns, so after I undressed and washed up, I wrapped myself in the towel and combed out my hair, which was always a chore. Island-girl hair did not like to be combed.

"What're you doing?"

Rosalee stood in the doorway of the attic room, staring at my belongings on the shelf and at her blankets on the floor.

Staring in horror.

I untangled the comb from my hair and knelt next to the pile of blankets. "I'm nesting."

"Like hell you are! You can't stay here!"

Aunt Ulla *had* poisoned her mind against me.

"Yes, I can." I unfolded the blankets and piled them atop one another. "What you mean to say is, you don't want me here."

"That's right! I don't!"

I sang, "You can't always *get* what you want."

Rosalee stared at me as though she'd never seen anything like me before. "Are you even gone ask how your aunt's doing? Least you could do after what you did to her."

"You said she's alive." I tested the softness of the pallet and found it lacking. I added two more blankets. "What else do I need to know?"

"It took *eleven stitches* to put her head back together. She only just got home from the hospital. You're lucky she didn't call the cops. You're lucky she didn't die."

When I didn't say anything, Rosalee knelt across from me, keeping the pallet between us. A shiny red bracelet encircled her left wrist, a bracelet with an old-fashioned silver key as long as my pinky dangling from it. I wondered what she'd do if I touched her hand, touched her anywhere, to see what it felt like.

"Why'd you hit her?" Rosalee asked.

"Didn't *she* tell you?"

"You tell me."

I stopped fiddling with the blankets. "She wanted to send me back to the psych ward so they could lock me away forever, and I told her I didn't *want* to be locked away forever, but she wouldn't listen. So I had to show her."

I illustrated just how I'd shown Aunt Ulla by miming a heavy blow to Rosalee's head. Then, unable to resist, I brushed my fingertips across the soft silk of Rosalee's cheek. She felt feverish. Familiar. My fingers knew her. "But I wouldn't do to you what I did to her. Forget about what she told you. You don't have to be afraid of me."

Rosalee smacked my hand away as though it were a fly, the key attached to her bracelet jingling angrily. "Even if you were Hannibal Lecter himself," she said, rising to her feet with careless grace, "around here you're nothing special. *You're* the one who should be afraid." She began to pace. "You know your aunt's packing up your stuff as we speak? Says she's either gone ship it all here or to the state hospital."

"Tell her to ship it here."

"Only thing's getting shipped is *you*." Her footsteps echoed in the empty room, exaggerating the distance between us. "You think I aim to be responsible for what would happen to you if you stay in this town?"

"You haven't been responsible for me for sixteen years," I said. "Why should it bother you now? It doesn't bother me."

"I'll drive you to Dallas myself if I have to," she muttered to herself, ignoring me.

"And then what? You come back here and live your life of solitary splendor? To hell with that. I don't care if you don't want me—I need a mother more than you need solitude."

Rosalee stopped pacing and looked down at me, tight-lipped. "What I *need* is to not have to chase after a bipolar-disordered kid."

If she thought that name-calling would put me in my place, she was sadly mistaken. "I prefer manic-depressive," I told her, "if it's all the same to you. It's much more explicit, don't you think? More honest? But really, you can call me whatever you like as long as I get to stay."

"I don't know anything about *normal* kids, let alone . . ." Rosalee waved her hand at me and all my disordered glory.

"There's nothing to know," I told her. "All I have to do is take some pills and everything is jolly."

"Your definition of 'jolly' includes assault and battery? *You put your aunt in the hospital!*"

"I haven't taken my pills in a while," I conceded.

Rosalee stomped to the shelf and snatched up a random handful of pill bottles. "So take 'em now."

She took up her Easter Island stance, so I got up and got the right bottles from the shelf—lithium and Seroquel.

"What're all these other ones for?" Rosalee asked, examining the bottles she'd picked up.

"Different things: depression, insomnia, anxiety, hyperactivity, blah, blah, blah." I held up the lithium. "This one evens me out. And this one"—I held up the Seroquel—"makes the hallucinations go away."

"You *hallucinate?*"

Having her undivided attention was making me giddy. "That's why my latest shrink decided I was manic-depressive. He said it was either that or schizophrenia, and I'm way too charming and rational to be a schizophrene. His words, not mine."

I washed down the pills with water, which I drank straight from the tap in the bathroom. When I came out, I said, "Is that better? Are you happy? Can I stay now?"

"*No!*"

So much for giddiness. "No it's not better, no you're not happy, or no I can't stay?"

"All of the above."

I picked up Swan from the shelf and cuddled her. She was cold and heavy and made of wood, but a girl like me had to take comfort wherever she could get it.

"Why do you want me to leave?" I said. "I'll be eighteen in two years. All the hard work of raising me has been done.

I'm old enough to see to my own needs. You don't have to *do* anything. What's the big deal?"

Rosalee had hidden her arms behind her back so I wouldn't get the idea that I could cuddle with her, too. "You wouldn't fit in here." She sounded desperate. "I keep telling you. A girl like you could never learn to adapt. And why would you want to? You think you're crazy now? There's things in this town that'd drive anybody—What the hell's so funny?"

I could barely hear her, I was laughing so hard. "Let me get this straight: You want me to leave because you don't think I can *adapt*?"

"I *know* you can't."

Was she serious?

I was biracial and bicultural—a walking billboard for adaptation. And what did she expect me to adapt to? Fishing in the crick? Baking pies from scratch? Small-town life was sure to be slow and boring, but maybe that was what I needed—Dallas sure hadn't done me any good.

"I'll make you a deal," I said. "Let me stay for one month. If I can fit in, make friends, all that, then I get to stay. But if I fail, then I'll leave, and you'll never have to see me again."

Rosalee was quiet a long time. "One week."

"*Two* weeks."

More quiet. "And you'll go back to your aunt?"

I stroked Swan's long, straight neck. "I didn't say that."

"Then say it now or no deal."

She seemed to be blanking on the fact that Aunt Ulla didn't want me anymore—never had, actually—but if Rosalee wanted to listen to me lie, I didn't mind indulging her. "If I can't fit in, I'll go back to Aunt Ulla."

Rosalee sighed, a step-off-the-cliff, no-hope-for-it-now kind of sigh. "Please yourself, then. Just don't say I didn't warn you."

I couldn't believe it. Even knowing what she knew about me, she'd agreed to let me stay. "Yippee!" I waltzed Swan around the room.

Rosalee watched me dance—again as though she'd never seen anything like me—and went to the door, shaking her head.

"Good night, Momma." The name immediately felt weird in my mouth, in my ears.

It must have sounded weird to Rosalee as well. "Don't call me that," she said. "I don't even know you."

I hadn't thought black eyes could look icy, but Rosalee's did. I stopped dancing and squeezed Swan against my chest. "If that's the way you want it."

"It is." She left, and everything felt empty: the room, me.

She hates you, Poppa said. *I told you she would. I told you she was unfeeling.*

I set Swan on the shelf and curtsied to her, thanking her for the dance. "She can feel plenty. She just doesn't want to. I'll make her feel. I'll make her want to keep me."

In a week?

"*Two* weeks." I switched off the overhead light. "That's plenty of time. I'm a likable person, aren't I? And she *is* my mother. Her instincts will kick in."

After sixteen years? I think her instincts died a long time ago.

"Don't be so gloomy, Poppa." I scooched the pallet closer to the shelves so that Swan could better watch over me. I ditched the towel and lay naked on the pallet, pulling the chilly top blanket to my chin. "I can win her over. I know it."

What if you can't?

I yawned. "If I can't, then I'll paint the walls of her house with my blood." A roll of thunder crashed outside and echoed beneath me along the floorboards.

"No matter what happens, one way or another, I'm here to stay."

Chapter Three

Thunder awakened me.

The heavy rain drilling against the window made dark wriggling shadows against the oblique ceiling. The rain echoed in the shadowy attic space and made me feel small and fragile, like a lace glove left behind on moving day—mateless and abandoned.

I shivered on the pile of blankets, waiting for Poppa to whisper to me so I'd know I wasn't alone, but I'd silenced him when I'd taken my pills. Insanity or sanity. Poppa or loneliness. Wretched decisions I had to make every day.

Fucking manic depression.

I shuffled into the bathroom, and by the time I'd showered

the hitchhiking grit from yesterday down the drain, I'd made my choice for the day.

Sanity.

I took my pills and pulled on the lavender eyelet dress I'd made right before Poppa had died, well before I'd gone into my all-purple phase. Like every dress I made, it had princess seams that highlighted my curves, a high bodice, and a knee-length skirt. And because frustrating boys was one of my great passions, this particular dress had a row of tiny, jeweled buttons down the front that had stymied many ham-handed Romeos.

I stood at my window, watching the rain try to drown the world. Rosalee and I could still get to know each other, but we would have to spend the day inside. Surely I could convince her not to go to work today; why would she even want to? She could tell her boss to give her retroactive maternity leave or something.

Surely she wouldn't leave me alone and spend the whole day wondering whether I was destroying her house.

I went downstairs to the kitchen, my rumbling stomach as loud as an engine in the silent house . . . and saw Rosalee. She was hunched over the dining table, scribbling onto a yellow sheet of paper. She raised her head when I came in.

Even in the dull rainlight, even in her tattered red sleep shirt, she was still too beautiful to look at, and so close I could smell the lingering scent of Dove on her skin. Weird knowing such an intimate thing as what soap she used after years of cluelessness.

A glass bowl of mixed fruit, mostly apples and bananas, sat on the counter separating the cooking and dining areas. A whiff of cleanser, something lemony, hung in the air.

As I grabbed a banana, she said, "Go get your pack."

"Why?"

She went back to her scribbling. "Just do it."

I got my empty pack, reluctantly, and went back to the kitchen.

The key on Rosalee's bracelet jingled as she held out the sheet of notebook paper to me. "Take this."

I took it.

Rosalee had written directions to a school called Portero High; she'd even drawn a map. I looked at her in disbelief. "You want me to go to *school*?"

"You only got two weeks to fit in. School's the easiest place to start. Gimme that pack."

I gave it to her as a mild case of first-day-of-school jitters struck me, an absurd sensation this late in September. The rain had seemed so cozy a moment before, but now that I had to go out in it . . .

I eyed the map dubiously, then watched the perilous sweep of water—framed so beautifully in the picture window—rush along the street, and I couldn't help but imagine myself being swept along with it . . . into a drainage ditch.

"You don't expect me to walk, do you? In this storm? I could catch pneumonia."

"I don't mean for you to walk. There's a bike in the garage."

"A bike?"

I went to the back door and peered through the glass panel. Torrents of white water streamed down the driveway from the garage to the street. Waiting to capsize me and Rosalee's alleged bike.

This had to be a test. God tested his followers, didn't he? Cruel tests of faith and devotion? Rosalee wanted to see how far she could push me, see if she could make me snap before I won the bet.

"Here."

Rosalee stood behind me, holding out a shiny black raincoat and a pair of galoshes.

"I don't wear black."

"You're the one don't wanna catch pneumonia." She shoved the rain gear at me. "*Take* 'em."

I took 'em.

"You need lunch money too." She tucked a five-dollar bill into my dress strap—like I was a stripper!—and shoved notebooks, pencils, and pens into my pack. When she was done, she zipped up the pack and turned to me. "Put on the raincoat!"

I did, feeling drunk on the attention.

"Galoshes too."

Even when a mother's child bashed someone on the head, that mother still wanted her child to be protected against the rain. This was what I'd been missing all my life, this motherly concern.

She gave me the pack, then shooed me out the back door. I stepped out into an almost cool breeze. Thunderclouds had hijacked the whole of the sky; heavy rain obscured the morning air like fog.

"Do you want me to be home by a certain time?" I asked as Rosalee peeked her head out the door to watch the sky.

"I don't care if you ever come back," she said, her voice almost lost beneath the thunderous rain. "I hope to God you don't."

Rosalee slammed the door and locked me out in the storm.

Chapter Four

I'd arrived at the school so early, I hadn't expected to see any kids, but they swarmed the pale blue corridors—every single one dressed in black, as though a goth had written the dress code.

Country goths? Whoever heard of such a thing?

The kids at Portero High weren't as diverse as they'd been at my old school but were more diverse than I'd expected. A peppering of brown, black, and even yellow spiced up the sea of white faces. But no matter the color, the expression on each face was the same: watchful.

They silenced as I went squeaking by in Rosalee's horrid galoshes—and didn't I feel ridiculous, like a clown squeezing a stupid, oversize horn at a funeral—so I made a point to smile and wave at everyone I passed.

No one smiled or waved back.

But I refused to let it shake me. I had plenty of time to make friends.

I found the administration office almost right away, but when I stepped inside, I had to resist the urge to step right back out. The feeling that I'd walked into someone's funeral intensified.

Behind the huge counter bisecting the office, a huddle of black-clad people stood weeping around a life-size glass statue. The man's arms were outstretched, his see-through palms flat against a long stretch of window that wasn't nearly as crystal clear as he was. Numerous bloodlike, gelatinous stains pinwheeled hypnotically at either end of the long window, like two giants outside the school had blown their brains out against the glass. But even as I watched, the stains vanished from the window, as though the rain were washing them away.

I decided to ignore the stains—probably all in my head anyway, no thanks to my stupid, useless medication—and concentrate on the statue, which made me feel somewhat at home.

During ski holidays in Finland, Poppa and I had often stayed at a hotel made wholly of snow and full of whimsical ice sculptures similar to the glass statue—a charming absurdity no one here seemed to appreciate.

"How could he have forgotten his earplugs?" said one of the weepers, a short, round woman with mascara trails on her cheeks. "It's such a transy move."

The trio of office workers petted the statue as they sobbed, stroking it as if to console it. The uselessness of the gesture reminded me of how I'd held on to Poppa's hand all night after he'd died, as though my touch had made him less afraid to be dead.

"Whatcha need, gal?"

One of the weepers, an extremely old man in a cowboy hat, wiped his eyes and gave me his full attention at the counter.

"I need to register."

"Needcher birth certificate, medical and dental records, and proof of residency." He patted the countertop, letting me know exactly where I was to set all this information.

"I don't have those things."

"Your folks at work?"

"My father's dead, but my mother is home." Was she?

She'd still been in that sleep shirt when I'd left, and she hadn't acted as though she needed to be anywhere in a hurry. I hoped Cowboy didn't ask me what she did for a living—I had no idea.

"What's the number?" he asked.

That I knew.

"What's your ma's name?" asked Cowboy, punching the numbers I'd recited.

"Rosalee Price."

The weeping ceased abruptly; the mourners around the statue gaped at me, even Cowboy, who exclaimed, "You ain't *never* the daughter of Rosalee Price."

What could I say to that? "Oh, yes I am!" Like a little kid? I just stared at him.

Cowboy punched the final digits, eyeing me warily the whole time like he thought I was playing a tasteless trick on him.

"Is this Miz Rosalee Price? Oh!" He snatched the cowboy hat from his bald head and held it to his chest. "Ma'am, there's a young'un here claiming to belong to you." He looked me over. "Yeah, that's her. Look like somebody drownt her, though."

I wanted to snatch the phone away from Cowboy so I could

hear what Rosalee was saying about me, if she was telling him to lock me in study hall and throw away the key; anything to keep me from coming home. But I restrained myself, marveling at how taking my pills at least made resisting silly impulses so much easier.

"You can go ahead and fax 'em over," Cowboy was saying. "No, thank *you*." He hung up and replaced his hat, tugging it down to just the right angle. "That's one kick in the head, all right."

"Is it?"

He looked me over again in disbelief. "What's your name?"

"Hanna Järvinen."

I spelled it for him and he began to peck at his computer keyboard, searching for each letter like a participant in the world's slowest scavenger hunt. The *ä*, in particular, gave him a run for his money. I gave him my vital statistics, and he had just given me a number of forms to fill out when the door to the office swung open.

A pale, exotic girl strode up to the counter—no, not a girl; she had too much self-confidence to be in high school. She wore skinny green pants and a matching tank top; old scars crisscrossed her bare arms. Her long hair was the bitter black of licorice.

An annoyed-looking boy trailed in her wake, tall and fit like her, but only his T-shirt was green. Aside from me, they were the only two people I'd seen so far wearing color.

"Wyatt!" As he had done while speaking to Rosalee, Cowboy removed his hat. "Ain't we glad to see you! And you brought reinforcements?" He smiled, flashing his big, fake-looking teeth at the green woman. "Sure nice of you to take time out—"

"I'm not here to be nice to you!" The green woman spoke with such force, it drove Cowboy back a few steps. "Neither is Wyatt. *We* need his services for the rest of the morning, so your little project is gone have to wait. *Indefinitely.*"

Cowboy's face fell. "But . . ." He turned to the scowling boy, eyes pleading. "But we was counting on you to—"

"What can I say?" The boy, Wyatt, lowered his head at the green woman in this strange, animalistic way, like a goat before it rams the hell out of something. "Apparently, it's *not my job.*"

"That's right!" The green woman gave Wyatt a heated look that he turned away from in disgust . . .

. . . and then he looked at me.

He was clean-cut: neat clothes, ramrod posture, his dark hair shaved close to his scalp like a Marine. The kind of boy who would happily volunteer his services to a decrepit office worker at his school. One of those high-minded types.

Much too high-minded for a girl like me.

I looked away from his pretty brown eyes and went back to my forms.

"But what're we s'posed to do now?" Cowboy was saying. "I'm about sick of these things." He tossed a set of red earplugs onto the counter; one almost rolled onto my form.

"Put those back in!" the green woman snapped.

"Oh. Sorry." Cowboy did as she said, not caring that the green woman was young enough to be his great-granddaughter.

But as he reinserted the earplugs, I noticed that red jellied blobs plugged everyone's ears—the office workers, the green woman, Wyatt. Everyone.

"Thing is," Cowboy said, "I wouldn't wish this mess on a dog I hated. A body can't even look out the window without—"

"Don't whine to me about it," said the green woman. "The

situation here is isolated; that means it's not a town concern. Besides, Wyatt's already contained the problem. Against all sanction, as usual."

"Contained?" Wyatt said. "Is that why everybody's over there crying over a glass statue?"

But the green woman ignored him. "Wyatt even made you earplugs," she told Cowboy, "but are you people satisfied? No. *Now* you want him to play Sir Galahad and slay dragons for you."

"They ain't anything like dragons, Shoko," Wyatt said, refusing to be ignored. "Besides, I done it before."

"And you see what's happened?" said Shoko, slapping her hand against the counter. "Now they want you to do *everything* for 'em."

"I'm not doing *everything*. Just this one thing. And if I don't do it, who the hell will? The Mortmaine have bigger fish to fry, and these guys can't do what we do."

But Shoko wasn't impressed. "It's not our responsibility."

"What about Ed?" asked one of the women by the statue.

"Do we look like we're in the storage business?" Shoko shrieked.

I sidled away from her.

"Have his people come for him!"

"*Does* he have people?" Wyatt asked in a more reasonable tone.

"I already called his wife," the woman began, but the rest was lost in tears.

"And stop puling!" said Shoko. "The transy's keeping it together better than you are."

The sudden silence again caught my attention, and I looked up from my completed forms to find them watching me.

"She probably don't even know what's going on," said the mascara-streaked woman defensively. "And never mind that she's Rosalee's daughter."

Wyatt's and Shoko's mouths dropped in unison. They drew together, argument forgotten in their astonishment. "*Our* Rosalee?" Shoko flipped her hair out of the way to get a better look at me. "But she's so . . ."

So what? So disgusting that words failed her?

I took the forms Cowboy had printed for me and huffed out of the office.

"Wait!" Cowboy called. "Your earplugs!"

Chapter Five

It didn't matter. None of it mattered.

I let the soothing mantra run a loop in my brain as I entered my first-period geometry class. The teacher, Ms. Harrison, a friendly-looking woman with a tattoo of a dodecahedron inked onto the nape of her neck, was dressed in black like her students.

Like everyone at the school but me.

With the black rain gear stashed in my locker, I stood out in my purple dress like a bird of paradise among crows.

It didn't matter. None of it mattered.

"Hey there," Ms. Harrison greeted me.

"Hello. I'm supposed to give you this." I handed her my schedule.

Ms. Harrison took it and smiled at me, which I appreciated, even though she was just a teacher.

"Class, we have a new student. Hanna Jarva . . ." She looked up from the schedule, turning to me for help.

"Järvinen. The J makes a Y sound."

"What an unusual name!"

"It's Finnish."

"I *wondered* about the accent," Ms. Harrison said, signing the schedule. "I would've guessed Russian. You hear that, class? Hanna's joining us all the way from Finland. How cool is that? Sweetheart, why don't you take the empty seat next to Carmin? Carmin, watch her while I get her a book and some earplugs."

A boy sitting near the back of the room with cobalt blue glasses and hair as red as his name gave Ms. Harrison a thumbs-up before she disappeared into a closet near her desk.

The gaze of thirty pairs of eyes swept over me like a chilly waft of air.

I walked to my desk, feeling as though I'd been thrust into the spotlight and now needed to do something—act, sing, juggle, and quickly—before I got booed offstage. I smiled, looked everyone in the eyes, let them marvel at my prettiness. Everyone wanted to be friends with pretty people.

Everyone except Ms. Harrison's geometry class.

I was smiling so widely my ears hurt, but no one smiled back. I intercepted leers here and there, but mostly the kids had this look of unholy anticipation, like a pack of hyenas sizing up a lone gazelle.

I stopped smiling and sat.

"What's with the purple?" Carmin asked, practically into my ear.

I turned to face him.

He wore a T-shirt with the words DISCO FEVER stamped across it in silver. A carefully knotted silk tie lay against the shirt, and he played with it as he watched me.

"What's with the black?" I said.

"Ain't safe to draw attention to yourself. Ain't safe to stand out."

I stared at the other kids in the class, who weren't even pretending not to listen—they *did* seem to blend into one another.

"This is the only color available to me at the moment," I told Carmin. "I'm in mourning."

He smirked. "We're all in mourning."

"For who?"

He reached forward and snapped one of my dress straps. "Stupid transies who never listen."

But he was wrong.

I heard it clearly:

COMECOMECOMECOMECOMECOMECOME

I stood before one of the windows on the right side of the classroom, straining forward, my fingertips inches from the rain-streaked glass, but I couldn't close the distance.

"Nice save, Carmin," someone said, setting a fallen chair upright.

Carmin had the sash of my dress in a death grip as he reeled me in and half carried me back to my seat.

A path of destruction led from where I'd been sitting to the windows—overturned desks, books and notebooks scattered on the floor along with one or two disgruntled kids, who climbed to their feet and dusted themselves off.

Had I done all that in my inexplicable dash for the window? I didn't even remember leaving my desk. I was afraid to meet anyone's eyes.

"Hey, Carmin?" a girl whispered, as he dumped me back

into my chair. "The transy looks spooked. Why don't you give her a little something to calm her down?"

"Because," said Carmin behind me, "drug dealing is against the law."

For some reason, everyone found this hilarious.

"Let's gamble instead."

"Yeah," someone else whispered, "cuz gambling's totally legal." More laughter.

"Seriously," Carmin continued. "Transies can't handle weird shit, that's known. Who wants to bet *this* transy freaks and runs outta here screaming?"

My classmates cut their eyes at me, waiting for some big meltdown.

Who the hell did they think I was? My life was a continuum of weird shit. I'd just gone on a rampage, for Christ's sake—*they* were the ones who should have been freaking out.

"I say she faints," said a girl to my left.

"This ain't *Gone with the Wind*. Nobody faints anymore."

Money exchanged hands in a flurry of fevered whispers and speculations.

If I had been caught running amok at my old school, I'd

have been sent to the nurse's office, the nurse would have called Aunt Ulla, and then Aunt Ulla would have called my shrink. Here they just laughed and made bets.

Rosalee's words came back to me: *Even if you were Hannibal Lecter himself, around here you're nothing special.*

Ms. Harrison appeared beside me and placed a well-worn book on my desk. "Here you go. And here are your earplugs." She shoved the cold, waxy things into my ears herself, like she didn't trust me. Not that I could blame her after my rampage.

"Okay, class," she said. "Turn to page thirty-two."

That's when I noticed that the book Ms. Harrison had given me wasn't a geometry book. On the cover, a young girl smiled benignly beneath the title, *A Teen's Guide to Living with Bipolar Disorder*.

I opened the book to page thirty-two and squinted at the multiple-choice questions.

12. All work and no play makes Hanna _____.

    a. eat Cheerios   c. go crazy

    b. limp awkwardly   d. very sad

I circled *d* and closed the book just in time to see the cover girl clap her hands over her ears, a pained expression on her face. I bent close to the book, close enough to envy the sparkly red lip gloss coloring the cover girl's mouth.

"What's wrong?" I whispered.

"Can't you *hear* that?" the cover girl asked. Her voice was flylike, wee and buzzy.

"Hear what?"

"Of course you can't hear it." Her little face pinched with bitterness. "You've got those precious earplugs. At least let me borrow *one*. Please?" She held out her hands and showed me the blood staining her doll-like palms, blood that had come from her ears.

Her poor ears.

I removed my right earplug and placed it on the book cover, curious whether the cover girl could reach outside the confines of her two-dimensional world to grab it.

comecomecomecomecomecomecomecomecomecomecome

A bolt of lightning sizzled, and for a second, the windows were full of color. Marvelous color. The voices—!

"Oh no, you don't." Carmin hauled me back into my chair by my dress straps. He couldn't get enough of my dress straps. I reached back and smacked him.

"What's the problem back there?" Ms. Harrison called.

"She took out her earplugs." Carmin withstood my frenzied attack, snatched the earplug from my desk, and shoved it back in my ear.

My struggles ceased immediately, and I stared into Carmin's slap-reddened face. Why had I been fighting him?

"Hanna."

I turned to see Ms. Harrison staring at me from the front of the room. "I only removed one," I explained, "and only because she asked me. . . ."

But the cover girl was gone. The book on my desk *was* a geometry book with a plain blue cover. Page thirty-two was all about coordinates—nary a multiple-choice question to be seen.

"Don't remove either of those earplugs," Ms. Harrison said. "Not inside this school."

If I had ever been more confused in my life, I couldn't remember it. "But—in the window—weren't there—?"

"Ignore the things in the window."

"Things?"

"Things, Hanna," said Ms. Harrison gravely. "*Hungry* things."

Chapter Six

I had been prepared to write off the incident in geometry as a manic episode. Even though I'd never blanked out and gone on a rampage before, the rest of it—the talking book cover, the voices in the windows—was business as usual. I was always hallucinating. Even taking my pills religiously didn't prevent occasional . . . weirdnesses.

Except not all of it had been hallucinatory. Ms. Harrison had acknowledged that something was going on with the windows. *Hungry things,* she'd said.

But I didn't have time to ponder cryptic remarks. Half the day was gone and I still hadn't made any friends. I didn't know what I was doing wrong. I'd never had to make an effort; people had always come to *me*. Maybe people were shyer in small towns, and I needed to be more aggressive.

I spotted Wyatt immediately through the swarming lunch crowd, his green shirt blazing amid the sea of darkly attired kids even more flagrantly than my purple dress. About a million other kids were squooshed in around him, including Carmin from geometry. I squeezed in as close as I could.

"Yeah, we went into the dark park," Wyatt was saying as he demolished what looked like Salisbury steak, "but nothing happened. The Mortmaine just needed help digging a tunnel. I'll probably have to go back before school lets out, though. There're these creatures living underground, and—"

Wyatt stopped, having noticed that his friends were no longer paying attention to him.

They were staring at me, the intruder.

I smiled at Wyatt. He'd been checking me out in the administration office—he still was—so I figured he could be my ticket in. "Do you mind if I sit here?"

"Sit where?" asked Carmin, who sat across from Wyatt, staring at me over the rims of his blue glasses. "You see any other chairs?"

"I can find one."

"Don't bother," said Wyatt, turning away from me. "There's no space, unless you aim to sit in my lap."

Very non-high-minded response. Maybe I was wrong about him. Maybe he only *looked* high-minded.

I gave Wyatt my sweetest smile. "Thank you." I sat in his lap.

"You and transies, man," said Carmin, chuckling. "It never ends."

"What can I say?" asked Wyatt, a *Who, me?* expression on his face. "I'm a polite kinda guy."

"Oh, lovely," I said. "I adore polite men."

"I was being sarcastic."

"Polite and funny? Could I be that lucky?"

"I can't reach my food!"

"I'll share my fruit salad," I consoled him, "if you promise not to take big bites."

He gave me the same look Rosalee had, frowning at me as though I were an alien. A faint scar, almost like a question mark, decorated his chin. All of his face was a question mark. "Who are you?" he asked.

"We sort of met in administration. I'm Hanna Järvinen. And you?" I held out my hand.

He shook it. "Wyatt Ortiga. Pleased to meet you, milady."

"Don't make fun of me," I said. "I'm not half as weird as you lot."

"Weird?" Wyatt said as everyone at the table chuckled. "Us?"

I nodded. "And geometry was even weirder."

"What happened?" asked the girl to Carmin's left. Lecy Gandara. She was in my history class. I remembered her because of the yellow daisies pinned to her blue-black, pig-tailed hair.

Carmin popped the top of his soda. "A lure called her."

"Did she run screaming?" Lecy asked, as though I weren't sitting right across from her.

"Hell, no," said Carmin, glaring at me like *I* was the obnoxious one. "She just sat there taking notes. Cost me ten bucks."

"What's a lure?" I asked, picking at the fruit salad balanced precariously on my lap.

"The things in the window," Carmin said.

"What *things*?"

"Don't scare her," said Lecy. "She's got the whole rest of the day to get through."

"You keep your earplugs in at all times," Wyatt told me, "and geometry will cease to be weird."

While he gazed longingly at his abandoned Salisbury steak, Wyatt squeezed my hip as though testing me for ripeness. Up close, his eyes, though dark, were as clear and lustrous as window glass. I had the craziest idea that if I looked closely enough, maybe tilted his head toward the light, I'd be able to see into his brain.

"Do I get to squeeze back?" I whispered into his ear, and laughed when he seemed honestly startled to find himself groping me.

Then his lap began to vibrate, startling *me*.

"Sorry." Wyatt shifted me a bit to retrieve his cell phone from his pocket, his ears red. He looked at the number and groaned.

"Who is it?" asked Carmin.

"Guess."

Everyone at the table laughed.

"Pet, you got the flu," Wyatt screamed into his phone. "Just lay there and get better, and for Christ's sake, stop calling me!"

"Don't worry," Lecy told me. "Pet's his *ex*-girlfriend."

I can't imagine what she saw in my face that made her think she needed to reassure me. What did I care if Wyatt had a girlfriend, ex or otherwise? He was into *me*, not the other way around.

"Good thing he's not going with Pet anymore." Carmin raised his voice. "Be pretty damn awkward explaining why Wyatt's got a hot-ass girl in his lap!"

"What girl?" The ex-girlfriend's voice was teeny and panicked.

"Nothing," Wyatt said. "I-gotta-go-hope-you-feel-better-bye." He shoved his phone into his pocket, grabbed the empty milk carton off my tray, and bounced it off Carmin's forehead. *"Asshole."*

"Just trying to pave the way for the new transy in your life," Carmin said, pretending to be hurt.

"I already went through that shit with Pet. I'm not gone be stupid twice in a row." Wyatt bucked me off his lap. "No more transies! *Ever!*"

I stood there gripping my tray. Stunned. The journey from being felt up to brushed off had been a dizzying one. Dizzying and irritating.

I dumped my bowl of fruit salad into Wyatt's lap.

"I wish I'd bought something hot." My voice was shaking—*I* was shaking. "Like chili. Something that would have *burned*."

Wyatt, on the other hand, was as steady as a panther moving in on a kill. "They only serve chili on Fridays," he told me, as though imparting great wisdom. "Do yourself a favor, transy, and disappear." He scooped a handful of the fruit salad pooled in his lap and flung it at me.

Everyone else at the table copied him—flinging mashed potatoes, forkfuls of Salisbury steak, handfuls of potato chips, and screaming "Transy!" at me like a curse.

I fled the cafeteria and rushed into the first girls' restroom I came to. At the sink I surveyed the damage, the unfamiliar sting of male rejection creeping over me. Everyone had rejected me, but only because Wyatt had first.

Wyatt.

I cleaned the food off my dress as well as I could, pondering how cocky Wyatt would be if, instead of chili, I dumped *battery acid* in his lap. Where could I get battery acid, anyway? Wal-Mart?

The ever-reddening light in the silent restroom interrupted my scheming. The change of light wasn't coming from the fluorescents overhead, but from the window at the far end of the restroom.

Where another glass statue stood.

The girl's hands were flat against the frosted window. A thick red soup swirled within the glass, reminding me of what I'd seen in the administration office.

Usually my hallucinations made sense: a whispering voice in my ear, a room full of birds only I could see. Nothing like this bloody randomness.

I crept past the statue and reached up to touch the window. The cool red glass sucked ghoulishly at my finger. I wrenched free, finger throbbing as though it had received the mother of all hickeys. But instead of a purple bruise, my right finger, down to the second knuckle, had turned to glass.

I looked from my finger to the statue beside me. Her crystalline strands of bobbed hair. Her translucent dimpled toes peeking from glass sandals.

I wasn't going to become a statue. So what if the other kids didn't like me and had *thrown food* at me; that didn't make me inhuman. I was here. I was real. I could prove it.

I rummaged through my purse for my nail clippers and used the hook on the end of the metal file attachment to cut into my finger. At first the sharp file glanced harmlessly off the glass. I shook my hand vigorously, watched the blood rush down. I cut again, and the glass unfroze into flesh.

"Ha!" I screamed as blood dripped into the sink. *I* was no statue. They wouldn't lick me that easily.

"Oh my God!"

I whirled and saw a bevy of horrified girls crowding the doorway of the restroom.

"It's not that bad," I assured them, running water over my finger, over the growing puddle of blood in the sink. "Just a scratch—"

They pushed past me and circled the statue, crying as the office staff had done.

What was it with these people and statues?

After a trip to the unsympathetic school nurse, who bandaged my finger, I spent the rest of the day being thoroughly and utterly ignored. Maybe Rosalee was right. Maybe in this weird-ass school, I *was* nothing.

Chapter Seven

After school, as I pedaled home, I could feel myself coming undone. My hair, reddish in the sunlight, unraveled from its bun and corkscrewed across my overwarm face, fitfully blocking traffic from sight. My dress straps kept slipping down my shoulders. Even my brain was unspooling: random, unrelated thoughts tangled within my skull, independent of my will.

My control had scattered.

I tried to look on the sunny side, but reality darkened my vision. I had to admit to Rosalee that I'd failed to fit in, just as she'd predicted, and I was damned if I could find the sunny side to that.

I should have been up to my neck in sunshine. Portero was

a *small town*, for God's sake. I should have been beating away nosy neighbors carrying casseroles in Tupperware and eaten up with curiosity about me.

They were all around as I rode, the sidewalks wide and bustling with women in black sundresses and men in black hats gabbing with black-aproned shop owners.

But what destroyed the sepia-toned quaintness was the multitude of missing-person flyers.

The flyers were everywhere, of people of all ages and sizes and varieties, plastered on windshields, tacked into the trunks of the ornamental trees along the medians. The entire exterior wall of an art store was papered top to bottom with the flyers, like a morbid mural.

I wasn't surprised so many people had run away from Portero. Or possibly—considering the way I'd been treated at school—been run off.

I stopped my bike at a red light next to a dark peach juice stand.

Dark peach juice?

A little girl with braided hair flitted up to the drivers of the cars behind me, quick as a hummingbird, exchanging clear plastic cups of what looked like liquid sunlight for cash.

Dark peach juice?

An even littler girl at the stand called out to me, "Dark peach juice. Two dollars a cup."

The oldest girl, who was close to my age, also stood at the juice stand, handling the line of people on foot that had formed down the sidewalk. The oldest girl took time from pouring juice for her customers to box the littlest girl's ear. "Don't offer to transies, nitwit. Might as well pour the juice in the gutter."

"How do you know I'm a transy?" I asked the oldest girl, who didn't know me from Eve.

She took me in at a glance and went back to pouring cups of juice. "Bright, stupid clothes. No visible scars. But especially your eyes. You can always tell by the eyes. Yours ain't never seen anything real."

A horn honked behind me and made me jump. The light was now green. I pedaled on.

Such an unfriendly town. Unfriendly and strange.

I had put the bike away and was closing the carriage doors of the garage when a lemon Jaguar pulled into the driveway, a slick-haired man in a shiny gray suit behind the wheel. As soon as the car rolled to a stop, Rosalee burst out of the passenger-side door wearing stilettos and a tarty black dress.

"Call me tomorrow!" the man yelled at her, and then displayed his tongue the way a snake would, as if to taste the air Rosalee had just vacated.

After the snake man drove away, I went into the kitchen to find Rosalee finishing off a glass of wine. Sparkly red clips held her thick, curling hair away from her face, and she had removed the stilettos. The barrettes and bare feet made her look young, a little girl who'd long since outgrown her clothes.

"It's a bit early for a date, isn't it?" I asked, because we couldn't both be girls—someone had to be the adult.

"I don't date." Rosalee corked the wine and placed it in a rack beneath the counter. "Not that it's any of your business." Her eyes narrowed. "What happened to your finger?"

The school nurse hadn't quite come out and called me a baby, but she had made a point of wrapping a Teletubbies Band-Aid around my "boo-boo" when a plain one would have worked just as well. "It's just a scratch," I told her, in no mood to be sidetracked. "If that guy wasn't a date, what was he?"

Rosalee removed the barrettes and let her hair hide her face. She rubbed the nearly Day-Glo hickey decorating the side of her neck. "Work."

I dropped into the red chair, trying to block the flood of embarrassing images that wanted to fill my brain.

My own mother. A call girl.

Had Poppa known? Had he been a *client*? No wonder Rosalee had never cared about him, about me.

"You want coffee?"

"Ah . . . yes." I had no trouble looking her in the face anymore. She was still beautiful, but the burning, rapturous aura surrounding her had dimmed. "I mean no," I amended. "I can't drink coffee anymore. It interferes with my meds."

Rosalee went to the fridge. "Then I'll get you some milk. Finns love milk. At least that's what Joosef always said. Here." She tossed me a box of Famous Amos cookies.

I gaped at the box in wonder. "Milk and cookies, Mom? Really?"

She set the milk before me. "Eat 'em and shut up."

"But it's just like TV!"

"How? It's fake and unhealthy?"

Let her be sarcastic. I was over the moon. The horrible day I'd had was almost worth it, as I sat with my mythical milk and cookies and felt at ease with Rosalee for the first time.

"What's a transy?" I asked.

"A transient." She grabbed an apple for herself and leaned against the picture window, since she couldn't sit with me at the table. "Anything transient. Like a mayfly."

I knew about mayflies, had seen them in action during the slow summers at our lake house in Finland. Huge swarms of them rising like dark mist from the lakes, mating in the air in winged orgiastic abandon, only to flutter back down into the water, drained. Dead. An entire lifetime played out in the space of a few hours.

But what the hell was mayflylike about *me*?

Rosalee polished the apple on the scant bit of fabric covering her chest. "How well did you fit in today?"

"Not too well, actually."

"I knew you wouldn't." She took a triumphant bite of her apple. "That's why I sent you to school. I figured it'd be better if you tried and failed on your own. Better if you could see for yourself."

"See what?"

"That you don't belong here."

"*Yet*. I have a few prospects." Just one, and a lousy one at that, but she didn't need to know everything. "I hung out with this popular boy and his friends at lunch. I could tell he was really into me." And he was. Too bad he was rude and not at all a nice person, despite what he'd looked like.

After a lengthy silence, Rosalee took another bite of her apple, chewed carefully. Swallowed. "Just so you know, sleeping around doesn't count as fitting in."

If anyone else had said such a thing to me, I would have slapped her, but this wasn't just anyone.

The milk and cookies lost their sweetness. "Sex isn't the only thing I have to offer," I said, the words so low I could barely hear them.

"But it's the only thing they want." Rosalee frowned out the window at all the sex-hungry men in the world. "Besides, what else *is* there to offer?"

"Trust. Affection. Respect." I shoved her tainted after-school snack across the table. "It must be hard to think of qualities you don't possess."

Rosalee's hand tightened on her apple—for a second I thought she was going to hurl it at me. "Go take your pills," she said, her voice as empty as her expression.

I took my pills all right, but not the ones she wanted me to take. I went upstairs and downed four sleeping pills before crashing on my pallet. I watched the light grow dim as the sun traveled low in the sky, but mostly I watched the box of sleeping pills I'd replaced on the shelf. Right above my head. So easy to reach up. Never mind how heavy my arm, how tired my heart, how bleary the box. So easy to swallow the remaining four. Or more. If I could just reach—

A sharp pain stabbed my hand as Swan landed between me and the box, wings outstretched, feathers bristling. She eyed me balefully, a spot of blood on the end of her hard yellow beak, the same blood that now dotted the back of my sore hand. She whooped angrily.

"Not the boss of me," I muttered, barely able to get the words out as the pills I'd already taken worked their magic.

Swan scooped the box of pills into her beak and swallowed it whole, as though it were a particularly good piece of fish, the last thing I saw before sleep took me. I was glad to be taken.

Outsmarted by a bird.

How humiliating.

Chapter Eight

"Hanna!"

I awoke with a start, Rosalee shaking my foot like a castanet. I jerked free and kicked at her, but she had excellent reflexes and easily dodged me.

"You awake now?"

"What do you think?" I would have thrown my pillow at her, but I had none. I had nothing.

I turned over on the sweaty, twisted blankets, willing my heart to slow down and my hand to stop burning. Yellow light from the open doorway behind Rosalee spilled into the dark room. I looked at Swan up on the shelf in all her wooden majesty, her long neck ruler-straight, her wings folded close to her body, aglow in the half dark. "You didn't have to bite so hard," I muttered.

"What?" Rosalee watched me closely.

"Nothing." I drew my knees to my chest; my dress was damp and sticky-feeling, giving me chills. "What time is it?"

"Almost six."

"In the morning?"

"I figured you didn't have an alarm clock, so I brought one up. I *should've* brought you a nightgown." She pulled one of the blankets free, untwisted it, and draped it over me. Then she set the ticking wind-up clock on my shelf.

And then, instead of leaving, she knelt beside me again. The tarty black dress was gone, replaced with fuzzy red pj's.

"I was gone sneak in and out with that clock," she said, "but you were making that noise."

"What noise?"

"That nightmare noise. What were you dreaming about?"

I hadn't remembered my dream until she mentioned it. And then I relived it.

"I dreamed I was at Poppa's grave," I said. "And he asked if I would lie with him beneath the earth because he was lonely. He said . . . being dead was lonely." I rolled onto my back, and tears pooled into my ears. "So I lay with him in his grave, and worms squiggled between my toes and bones poked the backs of my thighs. He missed me so much and was so happy to be with me, but all I wanted was to get away from him. The only person who ever cared about me." I looked at Rosalee, a shadow-woman in the half-light. "How stupid is that?"

Rosalee listened to me cry for a while, staring out the open door as though wishing she'd fled when she had the chance. "You should do us both a favor," she said, "and give me back the spare key you swiped. Because you won't be happy here, either. Not with me."

"But that's just it," I said, brushing my tear-wet hair from my face. "I'd rather be miserable and free than happy and caged."

To my surprise, Rosalee nodded. "Love is a trap," she said. "The ultimate cage."

The trill of the alarm clock startled us both. Rosalee reached over and slapped at it—like it had cursed at her—until it shut off. We looked into each other's wide, startled eyes. I laughed. I think Rosalee might have laughed too if she'd been capable of something so human. I wasn't happy, but at least I wasn't as unhappy as Rosalee. At least I was still able to laugh.

Maybe it was the laughter or the fact that Rosalee cared enough about me in her own weird way to drag herself out of bed at six in the morning just to bring me an alarm clock, but I didn't feel hopeless anymore. What I felt was that I might be able to face another day.

This time when Rosalee insisted I take my pills, I took them.

The next two days were lonely, to say the least.

I'd meant to give Wyatt a piece of my mind for kicking me out of his lap, but I didn't see him anywhere, not even at lunch. I saw his friends, Carmin and Lecy, and they saw me, but they ignored me, cold-shouldering me because Wyatt had.

Fucking herd mentality.

But before I could dissolve into a puddle of misery, Aunt Ulla made good on her threat to ship all my earthly possessions to Rosalee, who, screaming at my aunt over the phone, threatened to ship it all right back. I ignored them both and set to work building a nest for myself, glad to be able to make the empty attic my own.

That Thursday evening I opened the door to Rosalee's room and found her sitting in the dark, her curly hair falling into the open red box in her lap. The hall light touched the box's smooth, lacquered finish, imbuing it with a ghostly aura. Rosalee stared into the box, entranced, as if the box were whispering secrets only she could hear.

"Hey."

Rosalee started and slammed the box shut, the look she gave me more outraged than entranced. "*Knock* next time!"

I backed up. "Sorry."

She put the box in her nightstand drawer and locked it with the key dangling from her red bracelet.

"What was in the box?"

"None of your business." Rosalee snapped on her bedside lamp so that I could clearly see how angry she was. "What do you want?"

"I made dinner. Are you hungry?"

She looked like she wanted to say no, but she didn't. Instead she followed me to the dining table, her stomach rumbling, and sat in the red chair. I sat in the desk chair, which I'd pilfered from her office so we could finally sit at the table at the same time.

Rosalee stared warily at the bowl I set before her, prodding the contents with a spoon. "What is this?"

"Stew," I said, in front of my own steaming bowl.

She swallowed a hesitant mouthful, then relaxed. "Your father fixed me a bear meat sandwich once. Been kinda leery of Finnish cuisine ever since."

"What's wrong with bear meat sandwiches?" I asked, curious.

She gave me a long look. "From now on, *I* do the cooking."

If she wanted an argument, she wouldn't get one from me. I couldn't believe she'd volunteered to do something so domestic in the first place. After giving me milk and cookies that first day, she'd left me to fend for myself.

"What was all that racket you were making?" she asked.

"I just finished putting my room together," I said, bouncing in the chair. "I had to borrow the armoire from your office since I don't have a closet, but even still, all my furniture fits perfectly, even the sewing machine, like the room was made for me."

"It *wasn't* made for you. Don't you dare get attached to that room."

"You said I could stay."

"For two weeks and that's—" Her spoon clattered to the floor. "You took my armoire?"

"I needed a place to store my clothes."

"I had all my books in that armoire!"

"I saw." Hundreds of books, several in German and Dutch, and endless stacks of bound manuscripts had crammed the armoire; I'd sweated through my chemise removing them all.

"I stacked them neatly on the floor," I said, so she wouldn't think I was a slob.

Rosalee pushed away from the table, chair legs squealing angrily against the tile. I thought she was going to go into her office to see what I'd done with her books, but she went up to my room instead and did a slow 360-degree turn.

"Why is everything *purple*?"

"It was Poppa's favorite color."

"You painted my armoire *purple*!"

"It would have clashed otherwise." She was making me feel like I'd murdered her best friend. "Why don't we go finish that stew, hmm? Before it congeals?" Anything to get her out of my room before she decided to take back her armoire, and to hell with that. It had taken me forty minutes to wrestle it up the stairs—I'd *earned* that armoire.

Rosalee, looking like the only survivor of a train wreck, followed me downstairs. I tried to lead her by the hand, but she wouldn't let me touch her. She was almost shy about it, the way she tucked her hands into her armpits, hiding them from sight. She was like the moon—part of her was always hidden away.

She sat at the table and stared at her spoonless stew.

"Take mine." I handed her my spoon and stood to get another for myself. A thrill shivered up my spine as I watched her take my spoon into her mouth, watched her swallow my germs as though they were old friends.

"Did you like it, at least?" I asked when I took my seat.

"Like what?"

"My room. The layout. The design."

"It's fabulous!"

"Thanks," I said, ignoring the sarcasm. I waved my hand at her kitchen decor. "I noticed you like the Scandinavian style. So do I."

"You *are* Scandinavian."

"Then you must like me, too."

I immediately regretted having set myself up so perfectly for what was sure to be a devastating put-down. But Rosalee didn't say anything mean. She didn't say *anything*. Just chewed and didn't say no. She didn't say yes . . . but she didn't say no.

Chapter Nine

I met Petra on Friday. She cornered me at my locker before first bell. Petra van den Berg, dressed in all black, of course, with a silver key exactly like Rosalee's dangling from a long, thin necklace. Blond, pretty, and bone thin. I wasn't sure if her recent illness had wasted her flesh or if fashion had.

I figured she wanted to get into it with me, some he's-my-man-so-step-off song and dance. If so, she would have to dance solo.

I don't do drama.

"It's not gone work with you and Wyatt," she said, sounding congested.

"It isn't?"

She cleared her throat and then leaned against me—like I was a wall!—resting her bent arm on my shoulder. "I get where you're coming from, okay? You're just a candy-ass transy; believe me, I've been there."

Been there? She was still there. The slightest breeze would blow her down to Mexico.

"So you think, 'Wow!'" she continued, her greenish waif's eyes bright with sincerity. "'Look at this strong, fearless, yummy-looking boy. He's the answer to my prayers.' Right? Well, wrong." The sincerity darkened. "Wyatt's Mortmaine duties always come first, so you'll always come second. Or third. Or *tenth*."

Petra took a break from her speech to cough into the back of her hand. She was *very* congested and still leaning against me, so I patted her on the back, wishing I had a jar of Vicks so I could offer it to her.

She needed a keeper.

"I don't care about Wyatt's priorities," I told her. "I don't care about Wyatt."

Shock cleared away Petra's congestion. "You don't?"

"No."

"So you're not gone go for him? At all?"

"I wouldn't cross the street with that boy." I hadn't forgotten or forgiven the lap incident.

"Well . . ." Petra seemed surprised I hadn't put up more of a fight. Surprised and relieved. "Good. Great! You're too strong for him anyway."

"You say that like it's a bad thing." As an experiment I sidled away from her oppressive leaning, just to see if she'd stand on her own. She didn't. She backed up against the dark blue lockers and leaned against them.

"It's not bad. Must be nice to be strong." Petra ducked her head, examining the delicate framework of papery skin and spidery bones that was her body. She sighed. "But if I was, I wouldn't need Wyatt. And he's the kind of boy who needs to be needed."

"You need air. You need food. You don't need some beastly boy."

A spark lit within her waif's eyes, like the gleam of a razor blade in a bowl of pudding. "Wyatt's not just some boy, and he's *not* beastly. He's Mortmaine. An initiate, but a survivor. A real badass."

"Mortmaine?"

"They're a family. Not a blood family, but they all take the name Mortmaine when they pass initiation. You have to be real special to join." She took note of my blank face. "You must've seen 'em around. They dress all in green, drive green trucks, keep us all safe? Duh."

I remembered the bossy woman all in green from the administration office my first day. "Safe from what?"

Petra's eyes lost their spark. For the first time I understood what the dark peach girl had meant when she said you could always tell by the eyes who had seen something real and who hadn't. Petra had seen something real—some *thing* that had burned itself into her retinas.

"I can't even remember what it's like to be that clueless," she said, her voice low and awful. "I almost envy you."

"Pet!"

Lecy stood near the stairwell, waving Petra over.

Petra grabbed my shoulders, leaning on me again, but this time so she could whisper in my ear. "Do yourself a favor and find someone tough, someone like Wyatt, who'll look after you. You'll thank me." She let me go and rushed off to join Lecy.

Someone tough to look after me?

Petra seemed like a nice girl, not quite the bitch I'd been

expecting, but even if I'd wanted to be her friend, her attitude would drive me insane. Did she think this was the *fifties*? I didn't need some guy to look after me. I could look after myself.

I hurried to administration to give Cowboy my medical records before the bell rang, but the office was empty. Even the statue had gone. I'd turned to leave, assuming the staff were in a meeting or something, when the long stretch of window on the other side of the counter began to rattle.

My first thought was that the wind must be high and hard, but the scene outside the window was placid; the trees across the street could have been sculpted, their pale yellow leaves motionless. The perennial East Texas cloud cover eased momentarily and allowed a shaft of sunlight to blaze forth. The light struck the windows. . . .

It was as though I were standing before a row of stained glass.

Reds and blues and yellows pinwheeled across the window. Colored light lasered into the office, falling across my dress, my skin.

A lone swirl of green flowed down the glass in a long, snaky line, dragging one of the pinwheels in its wake. At the bottom of the window the line of green spilled out and thickened, hitting the tile floor with a sound like wet clay before it lengthened and darkened, stretching upward, shape-shifting into black boots. Blue jeans. Green shirt. Smooth brown neck. Dark, closely shaved hair.

It was Wyatt before me, his back to me. Wyatt had poured from the glass.

The clouds regrouped once more and swallowed the sun, and the pinwheels of color in the glass disappeared, except for the one Wyatt, arms straining, had pulled halfway from the window, forcing it to lose its flat, pinwheel shape and all its color so that he seemed to have hold of a trickling stream of water.

I must have made a noise, because Wyatt whipped his head around. Saw me. Gaped. "What're you—?"

He lost his grip on the sparkling mass, which, like a rubber band, immediately snapped back to the window. Wyatt, catlike, grabbed it before it could be fully reabsorbed into the glass.

"Is that a lure?"

"Get outta here!" Wyatt yelled, pulling that long, sparkling strand—of light? of glass?—farther from the window.

I didn't get out. My body didn't seem inclined to take orders from either Wyatt or me. I was in the presence of the one person on Earth who was more of a freak than I was; I wouldn't have left even if I'd been able to.

He tried to reach into his pocket, but the struggling lure—was it a lure?—whipped forward and pulled him off balance. Before Wyatt's face could smack into the window, he got his booted foot up between him and the wall and used the leverage to push himself and the lure he'd captured away from the glass.

My head felt stuffed with cotton, not because of the earplugs I had taken to wearing in school like everyone else, but because I couldn't take it all in, couldn't focus on the existence of lure *and* a boy who could flow in and out of window glass at will. Not at the same time.

"Hanna!"

"I don't have to go if I don't want to." Extremity had turned me into a five-year-old.

"I don't want you to go," said Wyatt, sweating and fighting to keep hold of the lure. "I want you to reach into my pocket and—Hanna! Are you listening?"

"Okay."

"Get the red card from my right front pocket."

I moved forward past the counter, super-slow, as though I were in a dream where the air was thick and spongy and hard to move through. Up close, a thin reflection of my face drifted across the glassine surface of the lure in Wyatt's hands; I looked like a ghost.

"Hanna! The card!"

I stood within kissing distance of Wyatt, close enough to smell his sweat and the minty gum on his breath. Rummaging in the pants of a boy you intensely disliked had to be the most obnoxious chore in the world.

The pocket of Wyatt's dark jeans was warm, but the cards I encountered were chill enough to numb the tips of my fingers. I pulled out the small deck, half the size of regular playing cards, and shuffled through them quickly, hating the feel of them, until I found a red card. It had a tissue-thin paper backing on one side; the other side was silky-slick and etched with curious black markings. I shoved the rest of the cards back into Wyatt's pocket.

"Okay," he said. "Pull the paper off the back of the card, and— Where're you going?" He looked frantic, as though I were abandoning him.

I held up the tissue backing I'd removed. "I'm going to put this paper in the trash."

"Never mind the goddamn trash! Put the sticky side of the card on the lure, but *don't touch the lure!*"

I noticed then that Wyatt was wearing black rubber gloves, from which the color was fading even as I watched, fading only to reappear in thick black swirls within the struggling lure in his grip.

"Do it!"

I did it, and after I settled the card on the lure, Wyatt released it, and it immediately snapped back into the window, invisible except for the card stuck to it. But the lure didn't remain invisible for long. The red rectangle quickly lost its shape, growing and altering, until it filled in the pinwheel shape of the lure, exposing it.

And the others.

The red color infesting Wyatt's lure spread like licks of flame until the entire stretch of rattling glass was full of bloody-colored pinwheels throbbing like sick, misshapen hearts. The same inexplicable hallucination I'd seen before . . . but Wyatt could see it too.

He hustled me to the other side of the counter, and as soon

as he pulled me to the floor, a loud, jangling explosion blitzed the office.

Red shards of glass fell all around us like hellish rain.

I ignored the glass and watched Wyatt instead, panting and warm beside me; a trickle of sweat rolled past his ear, such a fantastically normal sight after what I'd just seen.

Normal until Wyatt turned and smashed his hands against the counter at our backs. The gloves encasing his hands had turned to glass and shattered easily against the wood, freeing his fingers.

He hopped to his feet and hurried to the other end of the room, where he banged on the frosted glass door of the principal's office and let the staff hiding within know the coast was clear.

They all came out, Ms. Eldridge the principal in the lead, with Cowboy right behind her. They took in the destroyed windows, the glass glittering on every surface.

"You got them all?" Ms. Eldridge asked, the girlish hope sparkling in her eyes at odds with her black power suit.

"Every single one."

Who knew that five grown-ups could make such a racket? Cowboy even danced a jig.

"I'm going to make an announcement right away," Ms. Eldridge began happily.

"*No,*" Wyatt snapped, as bossy as that green woman had been. "You know how the Mortmaine feel about me doing favors. The last thing I need is you crowing about what happened here. Like I'm dancing all over their rules."

"Of course not," said Ms. Eldridge, abashed. "Tell me what you want me to say."

"Tell the kids they don't need earplugs anymore; just don't tell 'em why."

I peered over the counter to see for myself that the pinwheeling lure were really gone. The only view that greeted my shell-shocked eyes was broken window and cloudy sky, so I stood and retrieved my records from the counter where I'd left them. Shook the red glass off. Handed them to Cowboy.

It was like my first day of school all over again, with everyone gawking at me.

"*She* was here?" Ms. Eldridge asked.

"The whole time?" Cowboy added.

"Unfortunately," said Wyatt.

Obnoxious beast of a boy.

I kicked some red glass aside so I could close in on him.

"Unfortunately? Really? Because you'd never have defeated those lure without me, and you know it."

Everyone turned to Wyatt for confirmation.

He swiped his hand over his face as though he had to manually wipe away his peevish expression. He looked much better for the effort, more like the high-minded person I'd initially taken him for.

"Don't mind me," he said. "My blood's still up. Maybe it didn't *totally* suck that you came barging in here."

Worst apology ever, but it was enough validation for the grown-ups. This time when they cheered, they cheered for me.

Chapter Ten

By lunchtime news of my administration adventure had spread all over school like mono. I couldn't breathe for all the kids pressed around me—Pet, Lecy, Carmin, and numerous others I mostly didn't know—firing questions at me like nosy machine guns.

"So what was it like coming face-to-face with lure?"

"What kinda weapon did you use?"

"Weren't you scared?"

"Where'd *you* learn to hunt?"

So much for Wyatt's desire to fly under the radar. But I, unlike the principal, knew how to keep my mouth shut.

"I don't know what you're talking about," I told them.

"Oh, come on," said Lecy. She sat on my left, her black pigtails threaded with small pink hydrangea petals. "It's the *Mortmaine* who aren't supposed to know. Not *us*."

"So did you really help kill the lure?"

"Yeah, tell us what happened."

Eventually I caved under the pressure and told them everything . . . except for how Wyatt had come out of the window. I didn't know how to *think* about that, let alone talk about it.

"Bad*ass*, new girl," Carmin said when I'd finished talking. I'd progressed from transy to new girl—that was gold by itself.

"I just followed instructions," I said, trying for modesty. "Wyatt did all the work."

"But Wyatt trains with the Mortmaine," said Lecy. "Going on dangerous hunts into the dark park, all that crazy stuff."

"The dark park?" I said, but someone else was already talking over me.

"Yeah, Wyatt's used to it. You're not."

"I hope you got the one that got me," said a boy with orange braces named Casey.

"Got you?"

Petra said, "Duh, transy. Haven't you noticed the glass people all over school?"

The statue in administration, the statue in the restroom. "Those were *people*?"

"Yeah," Lecy said. "The lure call you to the window and suck out all your juices and organs, all the good stuff, and leave this glass shell behind."

"Like me almost," said Casey. "I fell asleep with my head against the window during study hall." He brushed his hair away from his forehead and showed off the blood swishing through his capillaries, the blue veins at his temples. The odd, skinny cracks in his skull.

"Jesus."

"I know, right?" Casey said, letting his hair flop forward. "It's a lot better now, though. Mr. Fisher woke me up before the lure could really go to town. The feeling's coming back. My eyesight. And you can hardly see through my head anymore. Pop took one look at me after it first happened and went straight to the Mortmaine for permission to hunt down the lure. Thank God he doesn't have to worry about that shit anymore. I don't know what he thought he could've done anyway since the lure live *inside* the windows."

"*Lived* inside the windows," Carmin said. "Past fucking tense." Everyone laughed as Carmin pulled his earplugs from his ears. "You believe we don't have to wear these anymore?"

Suddenly the whole table was full of laughing kids tossing earplugs at one another.

"Hey!" Lecy shouted over the tumult. "Casey brought up a good point." She peered at me. "Since the lure live—"

"Lived!" shouted the whole table.

She laughed. "Since the lure *lived* in the windows, how did Wyatt get to them?"

I tried to think of what to say to the curious faces trained on me. Wyatt's *own friends* didn't know what he could do?

Oh my God, what he could do.

"Was it something bad?" Lecy asked, responding to whatever she saw in my face.

"Not bad," I hurriedly assured her and everyone else. "Just . . . secret."

Collective groaning protest.

"Bogus!"

"Why should you know when we don't?" Petra whined. "You're not even from here!"

"Come on, you can tell *us*."

"I can't," I said over the ruckus. "You know how the Mortmaine are." I was grasping at straws, but apparently, they knew exactly how the Mortmaine were, because they stopped pressing me.

"I'm so jealous," Lecy said, butting shoulders with me. "You have no idea."

"Me too," said Petra, butting me on the opposite side hard enough to hurt.

But I was a zillion miles from hurt. Just wait until I told Rosalee.

She'd have to admit I was fitting in now.

After school, Wyatt was waiting for me at the bike rail.

The clouds from that morning had burned off, and he stood crystal clear in the steamy sunlight, tall and straight as a young tree in his green shirt. Solid. Nothing about him suggested I'd seen him liquefied. He looked so normal. So . . . Boy Scout.

His gaze was forthright. "We need to talk about what you saw in there."

I unchained my bike. "I don't know what I saw."

"You know exactly what the hell you saw!"

I shook my head, an involuntary twitch of negation as everything I'd witnessed crashed down on me. I hopped on my bike and pedaled away.

But Wyatt didn't let me escape that easily.

He caught up with me, jogging alongside me as I rode off campus down a shady street lined with dogwood trees. "Why won't you talk to me?"

"I want to talk to Rosalee first." I hadn't known it was true until I said it aloud.

"I could come over later."

"You know where I live?" I asked, startled.

"Rosalee's house." He said it as though it were the Statue of Liberty or Mount Rushmore. "Hanna." He grabbed my handlebars and brought my bike to a stop, jarring me. "Don't tell Rosalee about me. Okay?"

He looked so worried, I couldn't help feeling offended. "I want to tell her about the lure, not about *you*."

A look of relief brightened his face as he stepped aside and let me pedal away. I was all the way down the street when he called out, "Around five, okay?"

But I didn't look back.

Now that I had recovered from the shock of what I'd witnessed in administration, I'd relaxed enough to remember that I was still pissed at Wyatt. When you had no one to vent to, everything stayed inside and festered like old meat in a hot fridge. But now that I had finally made some progress at school, maybe Rosalee would let me vent to her.

When I finally got home, however, bursting with news, Rosalee wasn't even there. No reason she should have been—she hadn't been home in the afternoon since I'd moved in. I'd decided she reserved afternoons for her clients, but I'd still been hoping that my need for her would be enough to make her spontaneously materialize.

I went into her room. Since I couldn't have her, I wanted at least to be surrounded by her essence, and Rosalee's room was so uncomfortable and unwelcoming that it was exactly like being with her.

Hard, skinny furniture rested atop a cold wooden floor, furniture fitted with cabinets and innumerable drawers, all shut tight or locked. Black clothes choked her closet: loungy sweats and yoga pants on the right; tight, skimpy work clothes on the left. I should make her a dress—something non-sluttish. Something bright and pretty. Would she wear anything that wasn't black? I bet she would if I made her something red.

I went to her nightstand, having saved it for last, curious as hell about what was in that red box.

But that drawer was locked. And the key was on her bracelet.

I went up to my room briefly, then came down and stripped the covers from Rosalee's bed. With the needle and red silk thread I'd brought down, I stitched "I Love You" into her mattress.

As I remade the bed and stretched myself across it, I imagined the words beneath my body seeping into her as she slept, weakening her resistance to me.

Chapter Eleven

Wyatt beat on the door at five o'clock sharp, fresh and pristine in his green overshirt; I bet he knew where *his* mother was. Before I could close the door in his face, he stretched out his hand.

"Hey," he said, perplexed. "You said I could come over."

"No, I didn't, but since you're here"—I gave him a bright smile—"hi!" I sent the smile to a dark place. "Now piss off." I tried to shut the door, but his arm didn't budge, even with all my weight behind the door.

Beast.

"I thought we were gone talk."

"I don't want to talk to you," I said, hating his stupid accent. "We don't even speak the same language."

"You think I'm some freak?" he said, indignant. "Some monster? You scared of me?"

"Scared of what?"

"You know." He hesitated. "What you saw."

"Oh. Ohh yeah." How could I have forgotten that, Wyatt swirling greenly in the window? My smile came out of hiding all by itself. "Are you hungry?"

"Maybe," he said in this cautious tone, as though he didn't know what to expect from me.

"Wait here."

I left him on the porch and went into the kitchen to prepare refreshments: bottles of iced tea and open-faced roast beef sandwiches. I was shocked by how anxious I was to get back to him. He was so normal-looking. But then, so was I. No one could tell just by *looking* at me how scrambled my brains were.

On the front porch the white garden chair sat next to a long shelf of potted red chrysanthemums. I removed a few of the pots and set the tray of food on the shelf.

"Good," Wyatt said, eyeing the tray. "I thought you was gone dump that one all over me too."

"You deserved it," I said, unrepentant.

He sat on the floor next to the chair. "I guess I did."

"You can sit in the chair," I told him. "I'll bring the chair from the kitchen out here for myself."

"What for?" Wyatt kneeled up and grabbed a sandwich from the tray. He exhibited none of the cockiness from before, none of the bossiness. Or maybe it was harder to see those qualities with him crouched at my feet like a dog.

I sat in the garden chair and we ate in silence a minute, until I couldn't resist. "Do what you did before, what you did in the window. I want to see it."

He looked as shocked as if I'd asked him to masturbate in front of me.

"Come on. I won't laugh." But I was already laughing. He had such an old-lady look on his face. "I've already seen you do it."

He had to think about it for a long time. "Hand me a drink," he said.

I poured the bottled tea into a glass of ice cubes that had half melted in the heat and gave it to him.

"Not the glass, the bottle."

I handed it over and watched him press his hand to the opening. And like the ice, his hand melted and slipped wetly into the bottle, a wet, brown blob dancing just over the remains of the tea.

After a few moments, he pulled his hand free, and once it resumed its proper shape, he drained the last of the tea from the bottle. He watched me warily the whole time.

What a freak! What an amazing and marvelous freak!

Hope brightened his face as he studied my expression. "You don't think it's weird?"

"It's beyond weird," I assured him breathlessly. "Beyond cool, even."

"Only another weirdo would think that was cool."

"Busted."

"Bullshit. What's weird about you?" He looked me over. "Besides your fixation with purple."

"It doesn't matter. Compared to what you can do, I'm boringly normal. So what are you?"

He put his half-finished sandwich on the tray as though he'd lost his appetite. I thought about what I'd said and immediately felt bad.

"I'm sorry. I can't believe I asked you that. I hate it when people ask me that."

He lifted his eyebrows, bemused. "Why would they ask you?"

"Because I'm biracial. People look at me and can't figure me out, so they ask, 'What are you?' Like I'm a whole other species. But you . . . *are* you another species?"

He did some more thinking. "You had to accept a lot today. I don't wanna blow your mind."

"It's already blown."

"You *think* it is. I could vaporize it if I wanted to. But I don't. Especially now that you know about me. And it doesn't bother you."

He crossed his legs in front of my feet, leaned forward, and rested his chin on my bare knee. The underside of his chin was sweaty, but I didn't push him away; he was so cute, like a little boy, looking up at me. The late afternoon sun burned in his eyes, letting me see all the way inside him, but not in a spooky lure way. This was something else.

I folded my hands in my lap; his breath tickled my fingers. "Does it bother other people? What you can do?"

"It might if they knew about it." His expression turned grim. "Only the Mortmaine know."

"Don't you like them?" I asked, noting how straight he kept his back even while he leaned against me. "The Mortmaine? I mean, you are one of them."

Long silence. Someone was playing "Stoptime Rag" halt-ingly on the piano next door.

"They're okay," Wyatt said. "But they're so *rigid*. There's all these nitpicky rules and stupid channels to go through. Like they'll help people, but not individuals. If you and a bunch of people are at the park and y'all are about to get eaten by a monster, they'll come to the rescue; if you're at home about to get eaten by the same monster, they won't do shit.

"Or like at school. They knew about the lure, but since the lure only attacked people who touched the windows, they were just like, well, then don't touch the windows, dumb-asses.

"And the Mortmaine have this thing about how they only want people to use standard weapons on hunts. Like, the card I used on the lure? I'd have got my ass handed back to me for using that. They *hate* when I use my cards."

"Why? It worked. I don't know how, but—"

"They don't care if stuff works. 'We can't take the risk of your experiments blowing up in our face,'" he said, mimicking some hardass he knew. "If the goal is to fight evil, what does it matter what weapon you use? I wish they'd leave me the hell alone and let me do my own thing."

I brushed my palm over his head, to see if his buzz cut was

as prickly as it looked. It was. "If you were left alone, you'd hate it. Loneliness gets old in a hurry."

He leaned his head into my hand. "Hanna? Do you believe in redemption?"

"Of course."

"Then will you sit in my lap again?"

I laughed in his face.

"Seriously," he said, pretending to be hurt. "If you really believe in redemption, you'll let me try to replace a bad memory with a good one."

Almost before he finished speaking, I slid out of the garden chair and sat sideways in his lap, settling my hips into the cradle of his crossed legs and slipping my arm around his strong shoulders.

Much better than our time in the cafeteria—no trays, no cell phones, no friends in the way.

A ghostly breeze filtered through the porch screen and cooled the wet spot Wyatt's chin had left on my knee. The skirt of my dress had bunched around my hips, exposing a good portion of my legs. Wyatt got an eyeful, but he didn't try to feel me up. He really was a good boy. It made me glad to know I'd been right about him.

"Nice?" he said, squeezing my waist.

"Um-hm."

"It'd be nicer if you let me take you out."

I laughed again. "What happened to all that no-more-transies-ever crap?"

"That was before I knew you were cool."

I rested my forehead against his and watched his lips pull up into a smile. "Your girlfriend will come after me with a rock if I go out with you."

"*Ex*-girlfriend. And Pet ain't the violent type. She's . . . kind of a wuss." He said it as though he were disclosing a shameful secret, like that she had a tail or a third nipple. "There's a movie theater just down your street—the Standard. They're showing French movies all week, but—"

"I love foreign films!"

"You would." He tugged a wayward strand of my hair that gleamed blondly in the sun. "You're Swedish, right?"

"I'm *Finnish*. And American. And white and black. And neither thing excludes the other, regardless of what you've been taught to believe."

He smirked at me like I was being naive, like he was humoring me. "Say something in Finnish."

I told him to get bent.

"What's that mean?"

"I said you're very charming."

He ducked his head in this cute way that made me feel guilty for teasing him. "If you come tomorrow at six," I told him, "I'll cook dinner before we go."

"Sweet."

I gave him my number and he stored it in his cell phone, slim and green as a dragon's scale.

The sound of squealing tires broke the mood. Far beyond the porch screen, a familiar lemon Jag screeched into the driveway.

Wyatt helped me to my feet. "Is that Rosalee?" He pressed his face to the screen, trying to peer around the side of the house.

"Do you want to meet her?"

He looked shaky-excited, like a girl at her first boy band concert. "Hell, yeah," he said, following me into the kitchen.

We stepped through the back door in time to see Rosalee slam the car door shut. The man with the snakelike tongue got out as well, scowling.

As Rosalee stormed our way, the snake yelled her name. "Don't walk away from me! Who the hell do you think you are?" He grabbed her arm, and before I could move, Rosalee turned and kneed him in the groin.

"What part of 'it's over' don't you understand?" she shouted.

The pained look in his face mixed with incredulity, as though his favorite teacup Chihuahua had somehow sprouted fangs and chomped his ass. He slithered to the ground like an oil spill in his expensively slick suit.

Rosalee hauled him up and shoved him back in his car. "Get out of here!" She kicked out his right taillight with her stiletto heel, but he peeled away in reverse before she could get the left one.

She pulled down the miniscule skirt of her dress and fluffed her hair, ignoring Wyatt and me as she walked past us into the house.

I was worried about what Wyatt would think of that little show, but he was beaming, staring through the glass of the door after Rosalee. "She's such a badass."

Envy swamped me in a surprising flood. "Maybe it's not such a good time for introductions, after all."

"Yeah," he agreed, disappointed, and trudged down the back steps.

"But I'll see you tomorrow, right?"

"At six," he said, heading toward his dusty green Ford parked at the curb.

I wrapped my arm around the porch post and admired his no-nonsense stride. "Wyatt!"

"What?"

"I'm glad you're a freak."

"Thanks," he said, and then frowned as if wondering what he'd just thanked me for.

I stayed on the back porch until he disappeared down the street in his truck.

Rosalee was in the kitchen in a frilly red apron, cutting potatoes while a big pot of water came to a boil on the stove. A pornographic Betty Crocker.

"Rosalee?"

She glanced at me, frowning and silent.

"Are you all right?"

"Obviously." Her cheek was bruised wine-dark, as though that lowlife had smacked her. I felt bad then, mooning over Wyatt while Rosalee suffered alone, battered and bruised.

"Maybe we should call the police?"

She shrugged off the suggestion. "I know how to handle men. Who was that boy?"

"Wyatt Ortiga. He trains with the Mortmaine."

"I noticed the green," she said, not even slightly impressed.

I leaned my elbows against the counter beside her. "Did you know that there are monsters in this town?" I said it to hear what it would sound like aloud.

"Of course I know." Since this was usually the point where I got shipped off to the psych ward, her agreement was more than a little deflating.

"I helped kill one—this weird thing that was living in the school windows." I told her the whole story, minus the part about Wyatt pouring from the glass.

"Always something going on at that school," she muttered, tossing her knife on the counter. "Turn around."

I did as she said, stunned as she looked me over. She seemed almost . . . concerned. "You're all right," she decided before going back to her potatoes.

"I am," I agreed. "You know why? Because I won the bet."

The sound of chopping ceased momentarily, the knife trembling in Rosalee's hand. "Is that right?"

"Yes. I have a friend now. Kids like me at school. They think I'm a *hero* at school. I win. I get to stay."

"You got half-hypnotized by a lure," she said, popping a

raw potato slice into her mouth. "You admitted yourself that that boy of yours had to keep telling you what to do. If that's your definition of a hero, it's pretty lame."

"But I get to stay, right?"

"You're dead if you stay here. A ghost."

"Is that why you want me to leave?" I said, the truth dawning on me like flowers unfurling. "Because you're worried about me?"

She said nothing.

"I can take care of myself. I'll prove it. Tell me how to prove it. Momma?"

Silence.

The flowers wilted. "So you're going to ignore me?"

"Why not?" said Rosalee, dumping the potatoes into the pot. "What's the point of talking to a ghost?"

Chapter Twelve

Wyatt came over the following evening in a green button-down shirt and black jeans, but from the way he carried himself, he might as well have been in full dress uniform. His every movement, every gesture, had an air of formality. Like the way he handed me the angel food cake he'd bought on the way over, half bowing as he held it out to me.

"It was Pop's idea," he said as I led him into the kitchen and sat him in the red chair. "He said it'd be classy to come bearing gifts."

"He was right. Thank you." I found a dish for the cake and poured Wyatt a cup of coffee.

"Is Rosalee here?" he asked, hopeful, as I handed him the cup.

"She's in her office, working." Actually, I had no idea what she was doing in her office. I'd knocked on the door earlier and told her that company was coming, but as far as Rosalee was concerned, I was still a ghost.

Wyatt was grinning.

"What?"

"It must be cool having her as a mom."

I tried not to be mad that his smile hadn't been for me. "Must it?" I brought the food to the table. "Why is everyone so in awe of my mother?"

"The whole Mayor thing. I mean, forget about it. Rosalee's the badass of the universe."

"The Mayor?"

"You don't know?" Shocked. "Damn. Her own daughter, and you don't even know. What's all this?"

"Veriohukaiset," I said, sitting in the garden chair. "It's a type of pancake."

"All that gibberish means pancakes?"

"It's not gibberish just because you don't understand it."

"You burn 'em?"

"Of course not."

"Why are they *black*?"

"The blood darkens them."

"What blood?"

"Pig's blood. Eat, eat," I said. "A person would think you'd never had blood pancakes before. And there's more coffee. I can't indulge anymore, so have as much as you like."

"Why can't you indulge?" he asked, staring at his forkful of *veriohukaiset* as though it might bite him.

"Caffeine no longer agrees with me." I poured myself a glass of milk. "So tell me about Rosalee."

He made the sign of the cross and then finally took a bite of my cooking; he seemed amazed that he didn't fall over dead.

"It starts with Runyon Grist, this guy who used to be Mortmaine. Maybe the greatest one ever. Killed more monsters, saved more people. But then he lost his daughter and everything changed.

"The reason we have to deal with shit like lure is because of all the doors. Portero's full of 'em, doors to everywhere and nowhere. Porterenes, the Mortmaine especially, keep an eye on the doors because things come through all the time. And sometimes, people go out. The way Runyon's daughter did.

"She was walking home from school with some friends, just walking, and suddenly she wasn't there anymore—disappeared right off the sidewalk.

"When she vanished, Runyon became obsessed with finding where she'd gone. So while he was trying to figure out where his daughter was, he ran across this woman who wasn't all the way human and had a tongue-breaking name he couldn't pronounce, so he called her Anna. Well, Anna could travel from one street, one city, one *world* to another anytime she wanted, and she didn't even need to use any doors. She said the ability was innate. In her bones. So Runyon took 'em."

"Took what?" I asked, when he paused to drink.

"Her bones. He made a Key out of them."

"Out of her *bones*?"

"Not all of them. When I say Key, I don't mean a house key. This is bigger than that—capital *K*. There's five Keys spread out across Portero, including the one Runyon made—they're the reason the doors exist. But the other four ain't user-friendly, and they sure as hell ain't man-made. What Runyon did, making his own Key, had never been done before.

"After he made the Key, he figured out which world his daughter had disappeared into and was gone see if he could get her back."

"He was going to search an entire world?" I said. "That's ridiculous. How would he even know where to start looking?"

"He stole a woman's bones and made a Key out of 'em. I don't think he was thinking too clearly by that point. It didn't matter anyway. When the Mayor found out Runyon had tortured Anna and stole her bones, she put a stop to his travel plans. She forbade him to ever leave his house again, even after he died. He ain't left that house in something like eighty years."

"Wait. The Mayor forbade him to leave even *after* he was dead?"

Wyatt gave me a hard grin. "The Mayor can be pretty tough when she wants to be."

"But what does this have to do with Rosalee?"

"I'm getting there. Thing is, when people found out Runyon Grist was haunting his own house, they started daring each other to run up and knock on the door, shit like that. The thing you gotta understand about Porterenes is we'll do anything to prove how brave we are. Well, when the Mayor found out about people going over to Runyon's house, she got pissed. She didn't want Runyon to have any contact with people, not even pesky little kids playing ding-dong ditch. So she ordered the Mortmaine to ward off Runyon's house."

I put away the empty plates and served the soup.

Wyatt lowered his voice, his eyes shining. "The day before they put down the wards, Rosalee walked up to Runyon's front door, and she didn't just knock and run. Rosalee went inside the house. Just walked right in, *even after the Mayor forbade it.*" He blinked at the bowl I set before him. "What's this?"

"Blueberry soup."

"What *is* it with you and purple?"

"Wyatt, focus," I said, taking my seat. "Rosalee went into the house and then?"

"And then she came out."

"And? What was inside the house? Did she see Runyon?"

"Who knows?" He looked as frustrated as I felt. "She would never talk about it! She wouldn't even tell the Mayor. After Rosalee left Runyon's house, she was hit by a car, and she claims that she got amnesia, but I think Rosalee was just like"—he paused and looked over his shoulders before whispering—"fuck the Mayor. I can go where I want when I want and see who I want. *Fuck* her rules.'"

I could believe that of Rosalee, that she had no regard for other people's rules, approval, or feelings, but why a boy as high-minded as Wyatt—why an entire town, for that matter—could revere such qualities was beyond me.

"That's why Rosalee is held in awe? Because she disobeyed the Mayor?"

"The Mayor who can control you even after you're dead," he reminded me.

I kept silent a long while, thinking about everything Wyatt had told me: doorways to other worlds, a mayor with power over the dead, a Key made of bone. I let it all sink in and found myself smiling. I was right to have come to Portero, a town more insane than I could ever hope to be.

"So my mother is the supreme badass of Portero," I said, embracing the strangeness and letting it embrace me in return.

The look Wyatt gave me brought me back to earth, that mocking transies-are-so-lame look that I had come to hate. He shook the soup spoon at me. "You can't ride on Rosalee's back. You want respect, you gotta earn it."

"True," I said thoughtfully. "Very true."

"I thought the movie was good," Wyatt said as we left the Standard. It was full dark and humid, the street crowded with people walking home from the theater. "I just don't get why it was called *Breathless*. It sure as hell wasn't fast-paced. But that Jean Seberg was something else."

I took his arm. "A scumbag. She turned her own boyfriend over to the police. I'd never do that."

"She was doing her duty."

"Duty schmuty. Plus, she was an idiot. Letting herself get pregnant."

"She was in love!"

"She was bored. Don't be such a romantic."

"What's wrong with romance? I don't go to the movies for realism. I get plenty of that every day. And you got some nerve telling me not to be romantic. Look at you."

Wyatt pulled me beneath an ornate streetlamp and spun me around by the hand like he was a cowboy and I the lasso. I laughed and laughed, my skirt whirling out in shameless ripples, dusty-winged moths dancing over our heads.

"Look at that petticoat," he said. "You gotta be sorta romantic to even *want* a petticoat."

"That's not romance; that's style." When he stopped spinning me, I slid my arms around his neck, and in my heels, we were eye to eye.

People shuffled past us in the dark, beyond the lamplight, but I couldn't see them; as long as Wyatt hid with me in the light, who else did I need to see?

I pushed his collar aside and bit his neck.

"Hey!" He shied away, clapping his hand over the bite

mark. He laughed. Nervously. "Why'd you bite me?"

"Because I wanted to." I pulled his hand away so I could see the mark I'd left on his skin. The tiny grooves of my teeth decorating his neck thrilled me. "Do you mind?"

He had to think about it a long time. "You a vampire or something?"

I laughed at him, not because he was leery of vampires—for all I knew this freaky-ass town was crawling with them—but because he was so uptight. I pressed my hips against his, earning another nervous chuckle.

"Vampires are lame." I unbuttoned the top two buttons of his shirt. "Do you think I'm lame?"

"No," he said quickly, rebuttoning his shirt. "But what're you doing? Don't undress me out *here*."

Such an old lady. I re-unbuttoned his shirt. "I'm not undressing you. I just want to bite you where no one can see it."

"Under a lamppost?" He cast a half-annoyed, half-excited glance about the street.

"Under your *clothes*, doofus."

"People're looking at us."

Wyatt's disapproving tone was at such odds with his erection that I decided he secretly wanted to give "the people" something to look at. I would have obliged him, but the gold, heart-shaped locket gleaming warmly against his skin distracted me.

"How sweet!" I said, lifting it from his chest. "This looks like the one I had when I was a little girl."

"It belonged to a girl," he said, so reluctantly it put me on guard.

"Was it Petra's?"

He shook his head, a dark look on his face, his erection lost. He pulled away from me. "It was my nana's. I don't wanna talk about it."

I was sure he was lying, sure that if I opened the locket, I'd see Petra's bony face smirking at me. But before I could call him on it, his phone rang, and I could tell he was glad for the reprieve.

"You found her house?" he said into the phone. "I know where that is. Well, I'm on a date, and you said I could—" He sighed. "Fine. I'm on my way."

"What is it?" I asked when he put the phone in his pocket.

"Mortmaine stuff." He left the circle of light beneath the lamppost and plunged into darkness, pulling me after him, and before I knew it, we were at my house, where Wyatt's truck was parked at the curb.

Lights blazed in every window down Lamartine, except at

my house, which was dark. Uninviting. Cold. I was not in a hurry to go inside.

"Where do you have to rush to?" I asked, trying to prolong my last moments with someone who actually liked having me around. "A hunt?"

"What do you know about hunts?" He sounded surprised.

"Lecy said something about dangerous hunts in the park."

"The dark park," he corrected.

An idea occurred to me. A marvelous idea. "Would a dark park hunt be considered badass?"

"Oh, yeah."

"And a *person* who went on a hunt would be considered badass—totally capable of handling herself?"

He gave me a long look. "Yeah, but Hanna, you need permission. And the Mortmaine don't give it to people just trying to show off."

"Well then, let's not tell them," I said archly. "The way we didn't tell them about how you used nonstandard weapons to defeat the lure. Actually, let's not mention lure at all, since you were expressly forbidden to involve yourself in the first place."

"So you just gone blackmail me?"

"Yes."

Wyatt unlocked his truck and climbed inside, his face conflicted in the overhead light. "I'm never gone get outta the initiate if I don't stop breaking the rules."

"You can follow all the rules you like," I told him sweetly, "*after* you take me hunting."

"I'm not even going to the dark park; this is just some shit detail my elder wants me to take care of."

"But you'll go on a hunt in the dark park soon, won't you? Listen to me, Wyatt. I'm sick of hearing transy this and transy that. I mean to make a name for myself in this town, and you said it yourself—if I want respect, I have to earn it."

"Yeah, throw that in my face," he said glumly.

"If you don't help me, I'll go into the dark park alone and find something to hunt by myself."

He looked into my eyes long enough to see that I was dead serious.

"Tell you what," he said. "Come with me to Melissa's right now. All you have to do is stay put and not bolt, and if you still want to hunt after that, I'll set it up."

I was buckled into the passenger seat before he'd even finished speaking. "So come on," I said, bouncing like a little kid on the way to the fair. "Let's get this show on the road!"

Chapter Thirteen

The crooked rows of cramped houses rolling past the truck's window were unfamiliar. "Where are we?" I asked.

"Downsquare." Wyatt braked for a reckless group of tweens sullenly crossing the road. "Portero was built around Fountain Square. So you can live upsquare or way upsquare, downsquare or way downsquare."

I thought about this. "Where do I live?"

"You and me live in the square. In the middle of everything."

"What about sidesquare? Can a person live sidesquare?"

"Maybe *you* could, transy."

I didn't even mind that he called me transy, now that I

was getting what I wanted. I rolled down the window and let the warm, sticky air blow over me, and smelled the electricity as blue lightning flashed above the tree line in the distance. Such a stormy part of the state I'd moved to. Stormy and dangerous.

"Will there be monsters where we're going?" I couldn't believe I was asking such a question aloud in the real world.

"Just one," Wyatt said, punching through programmed radio stations. "A stealthy one we been tracking for two years." When "Welcome to the Jungle" blasted from the speakers, he cranked it. He could have been driving me to the mall.

"Shouldn't we have weapons?"

"I got my push dagger." He grinned. "Handy little sucker."

"Shouldn't *I* have weapons?"

"You're not gone do anything," he said. "Except watch."

Wyatt parked the truck in front of a tiny, boxlike house behind a chain-link fence. He took something from the glove compartment—a photo, I think—and then we got out of the truck.

Weeds overran the sidewalk and caressed my ankles. I hoped they were weeds. The only light on the whole inky street came from the anemic porch light gleaming ahead of us. We walked to the front door, and I twitched the wrinkles from my dress as Wyatt rang the bell.

A strange design had been branded into the white door, a square with three squiggles inside it. "What's that?"

"A glyph," he said tersely, eyes focused on the door and whatever was on the other side of it. "My elder, the guy who called me, marked the door to keep the smell from escaping."

"What smell?"

A middle-aged man with a huge belly opened the door, and a stench barreled from his house like a rampaging army.

"*That* smell," said Wyatt.

"Mortmaine!" The fat man's womanly voice should have been comical, but somehow wasn't. "What's the special occasion?" He peeked out the door in mock terror. "Is a hell beast lurking in the azaleas?"

"Good evening, Melissa," said Wyatt politely.

Melissa?

"This is my friend Hanna."

Wyatt had to elbow me in the ribs. "Ah. Hi. Melissa." I spoke through my teeth, not wanting the smell to get in my mouth.

"May we come in?" Wyatt asked.

The fat man waved us inside, and I was unsure how I was able to trick my legs into following Wyatt into that house when my brain was screaming at me to run away. Inside, with the door closed, the smell was corrosive enough to rot the delicate fabric of my dress clean off me. I pulled out the hanky I usually kept tucked into my bra and held it over my nose, and if the fat man took offense, so be it.

Almost as bad as the smell was the condition of the house. Plagues of flies swarmed in the rafters and beetles trundled along the warped floorboards. Everything was gummy-looking—the big cushy furniture, the mounted fish on the walls. Even the light seemed diseased, flickering and failing.

"Have a seat."

Wyatt pulled me down onto a dark couch that had probably been white once upon a time. I sat on the edge. I was *on* edge. Melissa, however—was his name really Melissa???—was as carefree as summer.

"You kids like a cool drink?" he asked.

"No, tha—"

"Yeah, that'd be good," Wyatt said. "Thanks."

When the fat man disappeared into the kitchen, I turned

to Wyatt, who was sifting through his cards, singing "Welcome to the Jungle" under his breath.

"Are you crazy? I am not drinking anything from this house! That *smell*! It's like . . ." Words failed me.

Wyatt gave me an incredulous look. "You really never smelled a dead body before?"

I looked around the living room, where even the light seemed to be rotting. "A dead body in here?" I whispered. "With us?"

"Bodies." He removed two black cards from his deck. "In the back rooms. And in the kitchen. Wanna see?"

"No!" The horror in my voice made him chuckle.

Chuckle!

"Why are we even sitting here with a serial killer?"

"Because you have to prove your worth," he reminded me, pulling the backing off one of the cards.

I thought of the hunt and why I had to go on one. Why I had to succeed. The urge to flee slowly dissolved.

Wyatt seemed impressed by my ability to suck it up, smiling encouragingly as he stuck his hand down the front of my dress.

He did it so quickly, pressing one of the black cards to the skin beneath my left breast, that I barely had time to gasp. I didn't want to get felt up in that horror house, not even unintentionally, but before I could shove him away, he was done. He did the same thing to himself, reaching into his shirt to press the other card over his heart.

"Here's those drinks!" The fat man, cheery and chubby cheeked, waddled forward and set two tumblers before us on the coffee table, *smiling* as if he didn't know he had a house full of corpses.

The icy drinks were grisly-colored, full of shifty, floaty bits. I didn't even try to touch mine, not even to pretend, and neither did Wyatt.

"So, what's the problem?" asked the fat man with his woman's voice, settling his girth into the love seat opposite ours. "Why would the mighty Mortmaine pay little ole me a visit?"

Wyatt sat forward, waving a fly from his ear as he slid a picture across the coffee table. "Let's talk about John, Melissa."

The fat man pinched the picture delicately between his thumb and forefinger. His expression changed, became sad and wistful as he tucked the photo into his mouth and slowly ate it, relishing it, as though it were Swiss steak. "Even in a photograph, he tastes good."

"Is that what happened to John?" Wyatt asked, his voice low and curious. "You ate him?"

The fat man's cheeks reddened. "I had to. John wasn't a good provider, and I'm eating for two. A mother has needs."

As I watched this hellish ventriloquist act, it clicked into place for me: I wasn't staring at a man with a woman's voice, but at a woman with a man's body.

I would normally have been excited to see a person so strange as Melissa, but the excitement was lost in a sea of revulsion as she chased the photograph with a deep swallow from her tumbler of gore.

"Where's John now?" asked Wyatt.

"In the bedroom," said Melissa. "I don't know why I keep lugging him from house to house. Hardly anything left of him *worth* lugging."

"Hardly anything left of you, either, Melissa. Or your baby."

The man rubbed his fat belly gently. "The baby is fine. I just fed her."

"You been feeding her for two years. Ever stop to wonder why you haven't borne her yet?"

When Melissa lifted her tender gaze from the fat man's belly and locked eyes with Wyatt, the tenderness morphed into a disturbing regard. Wyatt didn't seem bothered, just raised his chin and let her look her fill.

"What're you thinking about, Melissa?"

"About you." The hunger in Melissa's voice prickled along my skin like needles. "About how good you'd taste. How good for the baby."

In reply, a dagger shaped like an upside-down T appeared in Wyatt's hand, his fist wrapped around the bone handle so that the blade rose between his middle and ring fingers like a wicked metal thorn.

Wyatt lunged over the coffee table and stabbed his handy little push dagger up the fat man's nose.

The fat man went rigid, and then kicked his legs convulsively in a horrible tap routine. Wyatt freed his dagger and flopped back beside me as the fat man finally stilled and slumped over the arm of the love seat.

In the space where he'd been sitting gleamed a hazy outline, almost a blur, of a woman who, aside from her huge stomach, was so gaunt that she looked more like a fat-bellied third-world child than a mother-to-be.

Melissa gazed down at herself. Her exposure seemed to confuse her, but the confusion didn't last long. When she noticed her host lying dead on the couch, she screamed, and without the limitation of flesh, her mere suggestion of a face contorted unnaturally. She literally flew at us. I cringed backward into the disgusting cushions.

"Shh," said Wyatt, pausing from cleaning the blade of his dagger to squeeze my knee. "We're cool."

He was right. Melissa could only get within a foot or so of us, no matter how hard she strained. The reason was the card smoldering beneath my breast.

A black filigree spread from the card below my bosom, racing along my skin like a fancy, curlicued cage. Wyatt was protected by the same filigree.

"I can't let her die," Melissa was screaming. "I have to feed her! Please!"

Beside me, Wyatt counted under his breath. "Eleven, twelve, thirteen." On thirteen, Melissa began to break apart. She wrapped her arms around her belly, protective to the last, but useless as pieces of her broke off and floated into the air like a dandelion dispersing.

When Melissa's pieces had vanished completely, when the

filigree erased itself from our skin, Wyatt bounced up and went through the fat man's pockets. Found his wallet. Rifled through it.

"Bob Gardineau," he said. "From upsquare. There's one flyer that can come down. Gone have to get a crew in here to clean up. You wanna help?" He said it like he was offering me a treat, and then he saw the look on my face. "What?" He came to me, put his hand on my shoulder. "You need to hurl?"

"Did you have to kill him?"

"Yeah."

No hesitation. *Whatsoever.*

I brushed away his hand. "I mean . . . it wasn't *his* fault he was possessed. Couldn't you have given him an exorcism?"

Wyatt's expression was both amused and exasperated. "I'm not a priest."

"Couldn't you have asked Melissa to leave?"

"Spirits don't just leave."

"But you didn't even *ask*." His apathy was beginning to piss me off. "Maybe you could have made a deal with her."

"I don't negotiate with evil," he said, all pompous.

"She was worried about her baby."

"She killed eight people trying to feed a baby that's been

dead for two years. Not exactly mother of the year."

"Even still . . . *Bob* didn't kill anyone."

"Maybe you're right," he said, relaxing his self-righteous pose. I didn't know how important it was for me that he get off his high horse until I saw him sink to my level. And Bob Gardineau's level.

I knew what it was like to have no control over your own actions. I'd done many things while manic that I regret to this day; smacking Aunt Ulla with that rolling pin was at the bottom of a very long list.

Wyatt sat next to me and took my hand. Plucked a beetle from my hair. His expression was as gentle as baby's breath. "Maybe Bob didn't *deserve* to die, but he still had to. You have to kill the host to force the spirit out into the open—there's no other way to do it."

"But it's so . . . merciless."

"I'm Mortmaine," he said, somewhat defensively. "Mercilessness is part of the job." It disturbed me that he saw things in such black-and-white tones. I sure didn't. For me, the world was a confusion of color.

"If you're gone get all caught up in moral ambiguities," he said, reading my mind, "maybe you shouldn't hunt."

"Oh, no," I said quickly. "I'm not ambiguous about hunting. I *have* to hunt."

"Why? You trying to impress me?"

"Of course not."

"Then who?" he said, taken aback.

"Rosalee."

A look of understanding came into his face. "My ma's a badass too. Kinda sucks having that to live up to. But at least your ma is cool. Totally worth dying over."

"Dying," I repeated, looking at Bob's body on the love seat. His ruined nose. *Wyatt* had ruined it.

He smiled at me like he knew what I was thinking. "Death so close you can smell it, right?"

I nodded. I'd never thought about my own death in such real terms. Would *I* smell this bad when I died?

Wyatt texted a message to the other Mortmaine about what he called the Melissa Situation, and how he'd dealt with it.

"Are you going to call the police, too?"

"Sheriff Baker?" The contempt in his voice was deep. "Baker handles speeding tickets and helping old ladies cross the street. *We* handle the weird stuff. And sometimes it gets really weird, Hanna."

He pulled me up by the hand and, thank God, led me out of the horror house. "Part of my job is dealing with death, dishing it out, avoiding it. There's no reason for you to put yourself in that position. Not even for Rosalee."

I took a moment to breathe in fresh air, to let the Gulf breeze clean the crawling sensation from my skin.

We walked to his truck and leaned against it, facing each other in the faint light of the porch as the trees creaked in the wind.

"There is a reason," I told him. "Rosalee thinks I'm so weak I'll drop dead any second. So weak it's easier for her to pretend I don't exist. I can't live like that." Crazy how easy it was to admit things in the dark. "I have to prove her wrong."

"You ever stop to think she might prove you wrong?" he said, and then reached his warm hand down my bodice again.

"You know, most boys settle for a good-night kiss after a first date."

He laughed and shook the black card he'd removed from my chest like a Polaroid picture. But unlike a Polaroid, the card disintegrated and wafted away on the breeze, much as Melissa had. "You just watched me stab a guy in the face. Don't you think we're beyond the usual dating formalities?"

He'd get no argument from me on that point.

"You did good in there, by the way. Didn't run. Didn't even puke." He seemed amazed by this. "I'll set something up for you."

"A hunt? With the Mortmaine?"

Wyatt opened the truck door, smiling in the light. "It's so weird to see a transy amped up about hunting."

After everything I'd seen him do, after watching him *kill* a guy right in front of me, he thought *I* was weird.

Unbelievable.

Chapter Fourteen

The following Monday, after school, I rode my bike to Fountain Square. Anything to avoid going home to Rosalee's unrelenting cold shoulder, at least until I could melt it by regaling her with my fabulous exploits in the dark park.

Fountain Square was much more impressive than it had seemed on the postcard Rosalee had sent all those years ago, a wide space surrounded by buildings that gave it a closed, protected feeling: the courthouse to the north, St. Teresa Cathedral to the south, the library to the west, and the Pinkerton Hotel to the east.

The square was European-like, with old gray flagstones and colonnades and throngs of darkly attired Porterenes ghosting about in tight little cliques. I understood their herd mentality better now, their need to always travel in packs, their black clothes that made them easily identifiable to one another, their wariness of outsiders—this was what living with monsters had made of them.

I parked my bike at the rail near the courthouse and weaved through the crowd. Various carts were stationed around the square, mostly selling ices and ice cream due to the stifling heat. One cart, however, was selling barbecue, and the sweet, meaty smell hung heavy in the air.

The fountain itself sat in the center of the square, at the bottom of a sunken amphitheater made of a paler shade of gray stone. Shallow, descending tiers, on which at least a hundred people sat basking in the sunlight, led down to a huge spout of water.

Wyatt and I spotted each other at almost the same time, my purple dress drawing his eye as effectively as his green shirt had drawn mine. He sat on the top tier above the fountain, huddled together with his friends.

I made my way down to him but had to sit next to Carmin, since Wyatt was sandwiched between Lecy and Petra. The stone was hot beneath me; I had to sit carefully to protect my bare legs.

Carmin and Lecy were discussing the list of names on the notebook in Carmin's lap. I leaned forward to catch Wyatt's eye.

He looked glad to see me, and as I beheld his smiling face, it seemed impossible that he could have carried out the pitiless slaying I'd witnessed Saturday, impossible that he could be both a hero and a killer.

People were surprisingly complex.

"I missed you at school today," I told him.

"I'll be there tomorrow," he said. "The Mortmaine won't need me till afternoon."

"How are you able to skip school like that?"

He didn't shrug exactly, just shifted his shoulders as if he wanted me to see how broad they were. "It's not skipping. I don't even have to go to school. It's a pain in the ass trying to do schoolwork *and* fight the forces of evil. I'm the only initiate who bothers."

"Why *do* you bother?"

"I hate being stupid more than I hate school." He smiled at me. His lips looked bitable. I hated that he hadn't kissed me good night when he'd dropped me home Saturday, but after getting to second base with me twice in one night, maybe he hadn't seen the point.

"I was gone call you," he said. Something in his voice brought me over in goose bumps.

"Good. Saturday was . . . fun?" The pre-Melissa parts had been.

"I thought you wasn't into him." Petra's interruption disoriented me; I'd forgotten other people were crowding around.

"I thought he was too *beastly* for you," Petra said, wilting against Wyatt's side in a way that grated, as though she didn't have enough backbone to sit up on her own.

"He is beastly," I said, flashing back to Wyatt's dagger jabbing into Bob's nose. "In part. I was just thinking about how complex people can be. How the good and the bad can mix up and make these intricate layers."

"*Qué una* egghead," said Petra, her broad accent doing weird things to the Spanish words.

"Really," said Lecy, agreeing with Pet. She gave me an assessing look, a wreath of orange tiger lilies decorating her dark hair. "You're too blond to be that smart."

"Sunlight alters my hair." I pulled the length of my spiraling ponytail over my shoulder so they could study it. "Some days it looks blond, other days it looks red, but it's actually brown." I frowned at the sun. "It's a very confusing phenomenon."

"*Such* an egghead."

Wyatt poked Petra in the side. "You're as much of an egghead as she is, Miss Honor Roll. How is that an insult?"

"I wouldn't insult Hanna," said Petra, as though wounded to the quick. "I barely know her."

I had to focus on something else, anything but the two of them bantering like an old married couple, so I peeked at Carmin's list. "What's that for?"

Carmin was stressing big-time, tugging the tie at his neck as if he meant to strangle himself. "I'm trying to figure out who to invite to my birthday party, but it's impossible. How the hell do I know so many people?" he asked me, as if I had the answer.

Since I had no answer for him, I asked a question of my own. "Why isn't my name on your list?"

He gave me a considering look, his eyes almost the same shade of blue as the cobalt frames of his glasses. "Well, you did fight off that lure. . . ."

"*Who* fought off the lure?" Wyatt asked.

"Don't be a glory hog, Wyatt," said Lecy. "The Mortmaine don't hold the patent for bravery. Go ahead and add Hanna's name, Carmin."

With an almost unholy amount of satisfaction, I watched

Carmin scratch my name into his already overcrowded list.

I was joining the herd.

"What's with the guest list, anyway?" Wyatt asked. "You gone hold the party at the country club?"

"Don't be like that," said Petra. "This is a big deal. Carmin's *sweet sixteen* party. He's gone have a little tiara and everything."

Carmin flipped Petra the bird, and someone screamed.

The screamer was on the other side of the amphitheater, but I could barely see past the fount of water, let alone the growing crowd of people standing above on the square.

"Did you hear that?" I asked carefully, unsure whether the sound had been hallucinatory.

"What?" said Carmin. "The scream?" He waved his hand dismissively. "It's just a suicide door. Tweener-wieners always go apeshit over 'em."

"It's so junior high," said Lecy derisively.

"Suicide door?"

"I told you about all the doors," Wyatt said. "But suicide doors are special. Only the Mayor can open one, and she *only* opens 'em for cowards." He laughed. "She's gone open one for Pet any day now."

Petra slapped Wyatt hard across the face.

In the silence that followed, Petra looked more shocked by the slap than we did. Certainly more than Wyatt did.

He smiled at her. *Smiled.* "I wish you'd do that more often."

Petra flushed all over, blinked her waif's eyes at him. "Really?"

"It's good to see you show some spirit," he said, in the same tone that had given *me* goose bumps. But he wasn't talking to me.

Ex-girlfriend my ass.

I hopped up and followed the crowd in the direction of the scream.

I doubted anyone noticed my absence.

At the colonnade between the hotel and the courthouse, a deep mahogany door with a silver handle stood a foot off the ground, attached to nothing. I shoved through the crowd, wanting to see this oddity from every angle, but no matter how I looked at it, it remained a door hovering freely in the air.

A group of eleven- or twelve-year-old boys were goading and shoving one another before it. "You open it."

"You first."

"No, you."

"I'll open it," I said.

The crowd immediately silenced and parted until I stood alone before the floating door, like a girl in a surreal painting. The silver handle was icy, despite the heat, and I had to strain to swing the door open on its invisible hinges.

A man hung by his neck inside a gray space the size of a coffin, his face blue, his tongue out as though he was making an ugly face at me, as though *I'd* put the noose around his neck. The rope wasn't attached to anything; it disappeared beyond the outline of the door.

I wasn't attached either. I could have floated away on the slightest breeze.

The kids behind me were squealing. I slammed the door, thinking I'd traumatized them, but the squeals were happy squeals. Horror movie squeals. Many of the tweens waited impatiently behind me for their turn to open the door, like it was all a game.

I walked back to the amphitheater as the cathedral bells struck. It was four o'clock. Broad daylight, yet it felt like three a.m. I gazed at the little kids splashing barelegged in the fountain below, mere yards from a dead body shoved in a door. Not a care in the world.

I sat well away from Wyatt and his friends, but suddenly they were all around me. "Have some of my smoothie," said Lecy, offering me a cold plastic cup full of orange slush. "It'll calm your nerves."

"Why?" Carmin asked, curious. "Did you put gin in it or something?"

"Yeah, Carmin." Lecy rolled her eyes. "Tons."

"Can I have some?"

"She's kidding, you retard," said Petra, putting her arm around me. Petra's embrace would have shocked the hell out of me, but my shock had been used up for the day. "She's shaking," she told the others. Then she said to me, "Maybe one day I'll take you to Evangeline Park. That's where I always go when I get scared."

"Whenever *you* get scared?" said Carmin. "They must make you pay rent up there."

"Ha, ha, asshole." Petra poked her tongue out at him.

"Hanna don't need to go anywhere," Wyatt said. "She's tough."

"You really are," Petra assured me, as though I'd denied it.

"I thought for sure you'd run back to Finland after seeing that corpse."

"Finland has corpses too," I said. My voice didn't sound like it belonged to me. "My poppa's buried there. He died in our summerhouse in Turku. From bone cancer. I took him his breakfast one day and saw him just lying there. And it wasn't like what the doctors said. He wasn't at peace. He didn't look peaceful; he looked weird and shrunken and *empty*. Like snake-shed skin."

"Exactly," Wyatt said, sounding worried about me. "A dead body's just meat. No reason to get upset over meat."

"Meat?" I scanned the square, tried to encompass the breadth of it. "Jesus Christ, where did I move to?"

"So your mind's finally blown?" asked Wyatt. I thought he'd be disgusted by such a transy reaction, but he only seemed amused.

Amused!

"Maybe a little, Wyatt. Maybe the idea of living in a town full of magic and monsters is worthy of at least a *small* blowout!"

"There's no such thing as magic," Carmin said, as though it were the most ridiculous thing he'd ever heard of.

"That door was standing in the middle of nothing—"

"Nothing that you could see."

"—and a man was inside it, but that wasn't magic?"

"No." Carmin was adamant.

"So what was it? Advanced physics?"

I watched the four of them exchange a helpless look, the kind of look you reserve for a kid who wants you to tell her *why* she can't see the wind.

"We're Porterenes, Hanna," said Wyatt. "Doorkeepers. Death is just another kind of door."

Chapter Fifteen

Early Wednesday evening found me again in Rosalee's room, but I wasn't being nosy this time. True, I was rifling through her tiny wooden dresser drawers, but I was looking for something specific. It wasn't my fault her belongings kept distracting me: her bottle of Chanel No. 22—I hadn't even known there were other numbers!—her bottle of lavender nail polish that was the same shade as my gauzy, sleeveless dress, which cinched so tightly at my waist that if I wanted to take a deep breath, I had to breathe from my chest. A pain to wear, but Wyatt would like it—what else mattered?

As I tried on a pair of Rosalee's silver drop earrings, I spied the red box on her nightstand. Also not what I was looking for, but maybe what I was looking for was inside the box. That's what I told myself as I lifted it, noting the almost invisible golden inlay, the puzzlelike design. By the time I figured out how to open the box—

"Hanna!" Rosalee, in black yoga pants and ladybug slippers, stood in the doorway holding a glass of water.

I almost dropped the box, more startled that she had spoken at all, even to yell. It had been ages since I'd heard her voice.

"Put it down." She snatched the box from me before I had a chance to obey. "You ever go near this box again, you die."

"Literally?" I asked, staring at my hands. Portero was so strange, I couldn't take anything for granted.

"Don't be a smart-ass." Rosalee locked the box away in the nightstand drawer. "What're you doing in here?"

"I've decided to have sex with Wyatt," I told her. "I was looking for condoms."

Rosalee drank her entire glass of water in two gulps and didn't say anything for a long time. Just when I'd decided she'd gone back into silent mode, she said, "That might not be a bad idea. If you put out for him, maybe he'll look out for you. Tit for tat, so to speak."

"That's such a call girl rationale," I snapped. "Not everyone uses sex for barter."

She smiled down at her empty glass, a secret, bitter smile. "Unlike me?"

"*Very* unlike you."

"I'm not a call girl."

Now I was the one in silent mode.

"If I charged for sex," Rosalee said, the bitter smile lingering like a canker sore, "I'd live in a mansion." She unearthed a box of condoms from her nightstand and handed the whole thing over to me. "I translate manuscripts. German to English."

As I stood waiting for her to disclose more precious information about herself, she said, "You need anything else? Lube? Instructions? Handcuffs?"

"No."

"Then get out."

I thought about what Rosalee had assumed about Wyatt and me, how she thought I was trying to use him for protection the way Petra had suggested I should. I guess I *was* using him, not for protection, but as a way to connect. Even a simple physical connection would be more than I had now.

I was tired of feeling cut off from everyone.

Wyatt had bought me a snow cone at Fountain Square, where we'd agreed to meet, and we now wandered the streets sucking raspberry ice in the warm, muggy twilight.

"I think we should have our sex talk," I said, bumping against his shoulder. "I think it's time."

He fell over laughing. Not quite the reaction I was expecting.

"That's almost word for word what Ma said to me when I turned thirteen," he explained, wiping the tears from his eyes.

"You got the sex talk from your mother?"

"Yeah. I guess she didn't think Pop was up to the task." He grimaced. "So to speak."

"I didn't mean it like that. I don't feel like *that* toward you." I looked him over. "Not motherly."

He pulled a purple flower off a crepe myrtle tree and tucked it behind my left ear. "So let's talk."

We trashed the cones and left the busy street for a quieter one, the only street in town that fall had managed to infiltrate.

"You mean talk about all our diseases and partners and all that?" he asked as we kicked through the drifts of decaying leaves littering the sidewalk.

"You've had diseases?"

"Hell, no! You?"

"Of course not. STDs are for losers. But I have had lots of practice. So much that it's not really practice at this point. It's more like art."

Wyatt regarded me, curious. "How long you been practicing, braggart?"

I smiled. "I lost my virginity when I was fourteen, during Juhannus."

"Yu what?"

"Juhannus." I thought about it, but it didn't translate into anything meaningful. "It's a day in June—the longest day of the year."

"The summer solstice?"

"That's it!" Maybe it *did* translate. "In Finland, the summer solstice is a holiday. Poppa and I went back every year to celebrate, but we went back that year mainly because Poppa was dying, and he wanted to spend his last days in his homeland. The problem was, I didn't want to spend the whole holiday watching him die, so I found this boy.

"His name was Mika. He was upright, like you. Upright and uptight. I had it in my head that I wanted my first time to be in the sauna, but Mika thought the idea was sacrilegious—you'd have to be Finnish to really understand that part. But long story short, I told him my way or the highway, so he gave in and did it my way. And I almost died."

"Why?" Wyatt asked, as if he expected the answer to enrage him, like he thought Mika had held a knife to my throat or something.

"It wasn't anything Mika did; it was the sauna. Having sex in a thousand-degree room is *not* a good idea. I passed out in the middle of it, and Mika had to drag me out and dump me into the lake to revive me." I laughed. "But that almost killed me too; I almost drowned."

"Sex and death," said Wyatt good-naturedly. "Like hot dogs and mustard. Hey, wait!" he said, when I would have crossed the street. "Let's keep going this way. There's a shop I need to stop at."

"It's your turn," I said, as he draped his arm around my shoulders.

"I was fifteen." He smiled in remembrance. "Shoko was my first."

"Ugh!" I pushed him away.

"What the hell?"

"Shoko? That mean green woman from administration? She's, like, ten years older than you!"

"Four." He looked thoughtful. "You think she looks old? I think she looks hot."

"Of course she looks hot, damn it! That's not the point. Why lose your virginity to *her*? She's so *bossy*. I bet she ordered you around the whole time."

"You don't even know her." When I just stared at him, he ducked his head. "Okay, she's a little bossy, but she's cool! A great fighter—really knows her shit. She took me on my first hunt, and I was so excited. . . ." His ears turned red. "That's why we ended up doing it, right there in the dark park. She figured it'd be the quickest way to calm me down."

"Sounds real romantic," I said, and kicked some thoughtless kid's half-deflated football the hell out of my way. "Are you and Shoko still—?"

"No way," Wyatt assured me. "I have better control of my nerves than I used to. Better control of my hormones, too."

"So who else?"

He laughed. "Jesus, Hanna, you want a hit list?"

"Petra?"

The laughter dried up. He shrugged. "Yeah." When I opened

my mouth, he hurried on, "But I don't wanna talk about her."

"Why not?" I demanded. "Is it too painful?"

"Me and Pet are just friends, Hanna. Seriously."

By this time we had reached a tiny herbal shop, and Wyatt disappeared inside, leaving me to brood about questions like, if Wyatt was seriously over Petra, why wouldn't he talk about her? Was the sex with her so pure and sacred he didn't want to sully it by describing it to me?

A few minutes later, Wyatt came out with a package wrapped in brown paper.

"Good thing we came down this street," he said. "I almost forgot I needed to get some stuff for the hunt."

I pulled him to a stop, my hurt feelings and unanswered questions scattering on the wind. "*Our* hunt?"

"Yeah. I'm working on it."

"When are we going?"

"I'm *working* on it."

"Before next Sunday?" The two weeks would be up by then.

"Look," he said, exasperated. "I'm having to sneak past a shitload of rules for you. Be patient, okay?"

What choice did I have? "Okay. I trust you."

He looked startled. "You do?"

"Sure. I thought you were nice the first time I saw you. Nice boys tend to be trustworthy."

"You think I'm a nice boy?" He seemed to find the idea hilarious.

"Aren't you?"

We had paused by a tall, scraggly fence pasted over with missing-person flyers of happy faces that had probably stopped being happy long ago. Arc sodium lights lent an orangey-red, almost hellish tint to the flyers and to Wyatt's eyes as he looked at me. Hellish, but intriguing. He slipped his hand up the slope of my bare shoulder around to the back of my neck, which he squeezed as he leaned toward me . . . and then his phone rang.

He groaned when he saw the number. "What, Pet? Why do I need to be there? No. *No.* Because you need to learn how to handle things on your own. I said no, damn it." He hung up. "I swear to God she's like . . ."

I watched him struggle to find the perfect words, wondering if I'd ever inspire that sort of passion in anyone.

"I can't even say she's like a four-year-old," he griped. "My little brother's four and I'd trust him to take care of himself better than Pet could."

"She's a transy too, right?"

"Not anymore. She's been here long enough to get a key of her own and everything. But she acts like she just moved here."

"Like me?"

"She's nothing like you." He leaned next to me against the fence, the package under his arm nearly poking me in the chest.

"A key of her own." I remembered the key on Petra's necklace, the key on Rosalee's red bracelet. "A silver key?"

Wyatt pulled a thin chain that snaked from one of his belt loops into his back pocket. At the end of the chain were several keys, including an old-fashioned silver key, nearly identical to Petra's and Rosalee's. "Everybody gets one," he said.

"*I* didn't get one."

"You gotta be born here." He tucked his keys back into his pocket. "Or be like Pet. If you survive long enough, like a year, I think, the Mayor comes around and gives you a key. To welcome you to the neighborhood."

Yet another thing that set me apart from everyone. I watched Wyatt pulling the edge of one of the flyers between us, ripping into some kid's fake say-cheese grin. He was deep in thought. I didn't have to guess who he was thinking about. "Are you going to leave me and go to her?"

"What?"

"Well, you seem distracted."

"Not because of Pet."

"Then why?"

He stopped picking at the flyer and kissed me, pressing me back against the fence. His tongue was cold and raspberry-flavored and, like the snow cone, seemed to melt when I sucked it. He was like an eclipse, the way he blotted out everything except the sugary taste of him, the hard push and pull of his body, the way he made me want to climb all over him.

"Let go of my arm," I murmured between kisses, wanting to squeeze him. I couldn't get a good grip with just one arm free.

He pulled back slightly, frowning. "I'm not holding your arm."

His hands were on either side of my face. Yet I couldn't move my right arm.

I looked down at a long pink . . . appendage, attached to the inside of my elbow, where all the green veins stood out so prominently—a glistening appendage as long as my arm.

"Shit," Wyatt breathed, his eyes following the attachment at my inner elbow to where it curled out of sight through a gap in the boards of the weathered fence.

"You can see it too?" I whispered, relieved that even a brain like mine wasn't faulty enough to hallucinate something so heinous.

"Yeah, but don't worry. I got it."

Wyatt backed up into the street and took a running jump at the fence, throwing himself over it like a Cirque du Soleil acrobat.

A feeling of loneliness galvanized me. I grabbed the slimy thing attached to my arm, felt its rhythmic squeeze as it sucked blood from me like a mutant leech. I could *feel* it draining me.

No amount of tugging on my part compelled it to release me. Instead the appendage tightened and did some pulling of its own, yanking me forward to smack headfirst into the huge wooden fence.

Talk about an eclipse.

Chapter Sixteen

I was on the ground, dazed, but not too dazed to recognize
Poppa, despite the fact that he was dressed in a vanilla suit
he'd never owned in life. But I recognized the purple paisley
tie I'd made for him—his favorite. He looked hale and fit, and
so tall it hurt my neck to look at him. So neat and clean while
I sprawled on the ground like a ragamuffin.

"It's not my fault," I told him, trying to straighten my dress
with my free hand. "I can't get up. This thing won't let me up."

"It's not a thing." How strange to hear his voice *outside* my
head, for the first time in a long time—how deep and perfect.
"You know what it is. Say what you mean, Hanna."

I was dying, and he was scolding me.

Unbelievable.

Of course I knew what it was. I watched the Discovery Channel. I knew leeches when I saw them, even pink ones, and I knew how I *felt*—like a girl-shaped juice box, warm and surreal.

"You're forgetting the herbs," Poppa said. He knelt next to me, all grace and blond serenity as he opened the bundle that Wyatt had dropped. Poppa went through the contents. "Here we are. Panic grass."

He tossed me a bound cluster of brownish-green grass. I caught it, and before I could wonder what the hell I was supposed to do with it, the grass burst into flames. I yelped and tossed it aside.

"No." Poppa picked up the smoking, flameless clump and held it out to me. "Take it."

Because it was Poppa, I took it, and it immediately burst into flames again.

"Steady," said Poppa, as I struggled with the urge to drop it before the flames could . . .

But the grass wasn't burning me. The flames in my palm were cool as air, but the flames engulfing the leech attached to my arm licked hotly over the creature, partly melting it.

When Poppa leaned down and blew out the gentle flame in my hand, the flames cooking the leech also blew out. The blackened leech hurriedly detached itself from my inner elbow and zipped out of sight through the gap in the fence.

If not for the stinging, penny-size hole in my arm and the grassy ashes smearing my palm, I would have been sure I'd hallucinated the whole thing.

Wyatt landed beside me with a thud, startling me, a bloody switchblade in his hand that quickly disappeared into his pocket and a familiar penny-size hole on his left forearm. My relief that he was still alive left me shaken. That or the blood loss.

He gathered his bundle under one arm and me under the other. "We gotta piss off. There's a whole nest of 'em in there. And the mother's none too pleased about losing an arm."

"A nest of what?" I asked as we jogged down the street. I felt dizzy, too dizzy to jog. I wondered how much blood I'd lost. Well, not lost. How much I'd had *stolen*. "A nest of leeches?"

His brow furrowed. "I don't think so. It fed on us with its tentacles. Leeches don't have tentacles."

"Leeches don't fly, either," Poppa said behind me. "But this one does. You might want to jog a little faster."

I looked back. Poppa was pointing at the sky, at the wide, glistening, pink *weirdness* spiraling over the fence like a horrific party favor, lashing its tentacles about as if it meant to bleed the air itself. A wingless abomination, and yet it attracted me, the way a grizzly would. Or a pouncing tiger. Who could resist being wanted, even if only for a meal?

It rushed us.

Wyatt pushed me to the sidewalk and out of harm's way, but the leech was content to settle for the tall, half-green target standing guard over me. Wyatt had just enough time to pull a red card from his pocket before the leech snatched him off the ground and entwined him in its long, pink coils.

"Wyatt!" I scrambled to my feet as the leech U-turned against the starry sky, high above the street, and flew Wyatt back over the fence.

To its waiting nest.

Smaller, skinnier tentacles whipped high into the air, striking inexpertly toward Wyatt's thrashing legs as the mother leech dangled him above her hungry children.

"Wyatt!" I screamed again, flitting back and forth along the fence in search of a way in, but before his name stopped echoing down the street, the leech mutated from pink to red, a rapid discoloration that reminded me of how the lure in the administration window had changed. And just like the lure, the leech exploded—not into glass fragments, but into a huge, misty ball of redness, like a burst water balloon, spraying me with fine bloody droplets.

Within seconds, Wyatt vaulted gracefully over the fence, drenched in blood as if he'd bathed in it. He grabbed my hand and pulled me into a run down the street.

He was *laughing*.

"This is the night you should've cooked those blood pancakes. I think I'm down a pint. How 'bout you?"

"At *least* a pint. What about the rest of them? The ones in the nest?"

"They're just babies," he said, whipping out his cell. "They can't even fly yet." He sent a text one-handed, holding on to me with the other. I could see the screen, see the message urging the Mortmaine to deal with the baby leeches before someone got hurt. Someone else. "In the meantime, we can go to my house. We need orange juice, antibiotics, bandages . . ."

"Is he a Boy Scout?" Poppa asked while Wyatt went on and on. Poppa didn't run like us or even walk. He skated along, his shadow looping crazily over the asphalt.

"Kind of," I explained. "But they call them Mortmaine here."

"What?" Wyatt was watching me. "Was that Finnish? Something about Mortmaine?"

"I have to stop." I *think* I said it in English. God, I was dizzy.

We had reached Carmona Boulevard, and Wyatt parked me against the wall of a music store. He used a couple of stray wet wipes he'd found in his pocket to clean the blood off me and off himself as well. He was far bloodier than I was—Carrie-at-the-prom bloody.

"You'll be all right," he said, and after a few minutes, I began to believe him.

"Good thing you thought to use panic grass. That stuff's real handy. Runyon figured out a long time ago that plants that grow near Keys tend to grow a little differently. That Runyon was clever as hell. Too bad he was such a dick. How did you know to use it?"

"I didn't."

"Lucked out, huh? My house is right down there," he said, pointing. "You'll feel better once we're inside, okay?"

"Okay."

He helped me stand. I thought my legs would give out, but they didn't. They were soldiers.

"You holding up?" People looked at us curiously as we passed them in the street. Not shocked, not horrified, not concerned. Curious.

"Why not?" I said, trying to match Wyatt's long stride. "It was just a leech. Just a huge monstrous flying leech. With tentacles."

"Is Rosalee gone freak about you getting hurt?" As though the idea of upsetting Rosalee bothered him more than the leech.

I looked at Poppa, who was keeping pace with us. He knew Rosalee better than I did. But Poppa kept his thoughts to himself. Not that it mattered. I knew the answer.

"Hanna?"

"She doesn't care what happens to me." The truth of the words coiled around me like a funeral shroud.

Wyatt blew it off. "Rosalee's a Porterene; even when we care, we don't always show it. We got good poker faces."

But I didn't want to talk about Rosalee.

I shoved Wyatt back against a telephone pole and kissed him the way he'd kissed me at the fence, only much more thoroughly, tasting his eyebrows and the wells of his ears and the scar on his chin as well as his mouth. The slight tang of blood on his tongue spurred me on to deeper exploration.

"See what I mean about sex and death?" he said, gasping when I nipped his upper lip.

"I see what you mean about death," I said between bites. "The sex part, you'll have to show me."

He grinned. "Oh, yeah?"

Chapter Seventeen

We kissed our way down Carmona Boulevard, past skinny old brick houses with high stoops and pointy iron fences that bit into my back whenever Wyatt and I leaned against them, which was often. We were determined to swallow each other whole. I wished Wyatt *could* swallow me—how comforting to be cradled within such a strong boy.

"Strong and powerful," said Poppa.

"Hm?" I deferred my exploration of Wyatt's mouth to find Poppa watching us from the stoop of one of the skinny houses.

"He's powerful," Poppa explained patiently as Wyatt kissed my neck. "His family is. They own a Key. *This* Key. No one else can make that claim." Poppa was pointing to the house's door knocker, an odd one: about a foot long, glossy black, and twisted like a cruller.

"What's wrong?" Wyatt followed my gaze up the stoop.

"That's the Key?" I looked at him. "The one from your story?"

"Yeah?"

"I thought you said it was made of bone."

"It is."

"It's *black*."

He gave me a silent, incredulous look, as though I'd disappointed him. "Anna was different. I told you that. That's why Runyon used her."

"But that's just it. Why do *you* have Runyon's Key?"

"The Mayor gave it to us."

"Why?"

"Hanna, come on." Wyatt kissed me, and though it didn't make me forget my question, it did remind me why I'd followed him home.

He pulled me up the stoop, past Poppa, and into his house.

Wyatt's parents were sitting on a couch on the far wall of the living room, companionably sharing a newspaper. They looked up when we entered but were distracted when a little boy with fat cheeks plopped onto the floor in front of the TV, a bowl of nearly black cherries before him and a rag doll with wild orange hair tucked under his arm.

"Paolo," said Wyatt's mother sharply, "what're you doing out of bed?"

"Ragsie can't sleep," said the boy, as he fed a cherry into the doll's blue Magic Marker mouth. Which opened and swallowed the cherry.

The doll, *by itself*, reached into the bowl for more, picking over the fruit with its cloth hands.

"Don't let Ragsie blow your mind," said Wyatt, squeezing my hand, startling me out of my astonishment. "He ain't even that interesting. Just eats all day like a little pig."

He strode forward and ruffled the doll's orange hair, then did the same to his little brother. "If you keep feeding Rags every five seconds," Wyatt told him, "he's gone get fat as all outdoors."

"Cherries're good for you," said the boy, stretching sleepily on the floor, uninterested in the blood coating his brother. "Can't get fat if it's good for you." He blinked his big little-kid eyes at me. "Who's that?"

"Yeah, Wyatt," said his mother. Both his parents were openly staring at me. "Introductions'd be nice."

Wyatt pulled me into the room. "This is Hanna Järvinen. Hanna, this is my kid brother, Paulie. That's Ragsie."

The doll *waved* at me, regarding me with its red shoe-button eyes. I did not wave back.

"And those're my folks, Sera and Asher Ortiga."

Sera didn't look like anybody's mother, more like the person you hired when you wanted your mother killed. She was lean and watchful, with Wyatt's clear brown eyes and a mouth like a scar, thin and unsmiling. Asher, on the other hand, looked soft and jovial.

"What happened to y'all?" he asked, taking in our wrecked and bloody appearance.

"It's nothing," I said, concentrating on not allowing my mind to be blown by the hungry little doll. "We just had to kill this . . . thing."

"Ah," Wyatt's folks exclaimed in unison.

"She handled it great," said Wyatt, slapping me on the back like we were buddies and not at all interested in getting into each other's pants. "You'd've thought she was from here."

"Good for you," Asher said, smiling at me. "Rosalee must be proud."

"You know my mother?" I asked him.

Asher shot his wife a guilty look, then disappeared behind the paper. "We, uh . . . went to school together."

Sera's scar of a mouth curdled.

So Rosalee had slept with Asher. That meant that if I had sex with Wyatt, I would be carrying on a family tradition.

Sweet.

"We're gone go get patched up," Wyatt said, pulling me away from his parents. We had to step over Paulie, who had fallen asleep on the floor, his doll still stuffing itself with cherries.

"Nice meeting you," I said to his parents as Wyatt pulled me up the stairs.

"You too," Asher called back. Sera just watched me speculatively until I was out of sight.

Once we were upstairs, Wyatt kissed me again, violently, unmindful of the hallway's gallery of family photos bearing witness.

"We should clean up first," I said at one point. I'd been running my hands under Wyatt's shirt, and he was so soaked with that leech-thing's blood, my palms were bright red.

Wyatt took my bloody hand, hauled me into the bathroom—a cramped space with fuzzy green mats all over the floor—and turned on the shower. Then he cussed out my dress in Spanish when he couldn't figure out how to get it off me. I had to show him the hidden zippers, and then I returned the favor and stripped him of his gory clothes.

The blood that had exploded onto him was partly mine; I liked the idea that he was covered in my blood, my scent. It made me feel possessive. Savage.

I backed him into the shower so forcefully, he smacked the back of his head against the green tile. He laughed it off, but I remembered my first time with Mika, how I'd bullied him. I didn't want to bully Wyatt, didn't want to do him as an antidote to nearly dying. I wanted a connection—a real one.

"What's wrong?" Wyatt backed off, giving me space enough to really see him, to see into the brown glass of his eyes, to glimpse the depth of things I didn't know about him. Which was nothing compared to what he didn't know about me. No wonder he wouldn't tell me why Runyon's Key was on his door.

What had I ever shared with him?

Almost shyly, I stepped into his arms beneath the hot

spray. "You remember asking me in what way I was weird?" I asked, letting my fingers drift along his face, careful of how I touched him.

He was focused on me, studying me. "I remember."

I took a deep breath, blinked water from my eyes. "I can see my Poppa. I can talk to him. Even though he's been dead for a year."

"For real?" He kissed my nose. "I knew there had to be a reason nothing freaks you out."

Porterene insouciance would never cease to amaze me. "That's all you have to say?"

He kissed my ear. "Cool?" He kissed my collarbone twice. "Real cool?" He pressed three more kisses into my armpit. "Double-dog cool?"

We clung to each other, laughing in the heat and steam, the last of the leech blood swirling down the drain. We clung to each other . . . and it *was* cool.

Very cool.

We stayed under the shower until the water turned cold. Then we shut it off and stayed a little longer, despite the hard, unyielding tile. We could have been lying on a porcupine and still we would have tarried. I didn't mind the discomfort, though to Wyatt's credit, I didn't notice how sore I was until after we staggered into his room. But despite how good the sex was and how well we'd meshed, I found myself avoiding him.

It was always that way for me. After I opened myself to someone, I needed a few minutes to close down again, to restore my sense of privacy.

Wyatt lay on the bed, brown as toast in his white boxers. He'd given me a ratty green robe to wear while my clothes were in the washer, but he hadn't felt the need to clothe himself. He was too busy smiling at the ceiling, lying atop the fluffy whipped cream of his bedspread like boy-shaped biscotti.

"I don't think I ever been this tired after sex," he said, in tones of wonder. "Between the leech and you, I'm all tapped out."

"That'll last ten minutes," I said, rolling my eyes. "There's no such creature as a tapped-out sixteen-year-old."

"I'm seventeen."

"Same difference."

I made myself stop smiling at him and turned on his stereo. Eerie British people singing about poems haunted me as I studied the multitude of plaster of Paris body parts clinging to the walls, like stark white bodies trying to escape into Wyatt's room from another dimension.

"I used to be into sculpture," he explained. "Arms, heads, feet. Just pieces of things. I'd stick 'em up here and there on the walls instead of played-out rock posters. I thought I was so fucking cool, you know? Real deep. Then I got into the Mortmaine thing and . . . all of it just seemed really childish. So I tried to remove 'em."

I touched the nipple of the single, perfectly cast breast near the window by Wyatt's desk. "Tried?"

Wyatt shrugged. "The house likes 'em now."

The breast throbbed against my palm, as though a heart beat within it. I yanked my hand away and backed into his desk. An avalanche of books hit the floor at my feet as I gaped at Wyatt. "Your house is *alive*?"

"It didn't use to be," he said, in what he probably thought was a reassuring tone. "The Key changed it. All that power."

"Is it changing me?" I asked as I retrieved the fallen books, glancing nervously at the walls.

He tsked at me. "If you're a weirdo, own it. Don't blame our Key."

The nervousness went away. "Smart-ass. I *do* own my—"

The title of the book I was holding seized my attention.

"*The Compleat Book of Charms and Spells*?" I gaped at him, brandishing the heavy old tome like a weapon. "You *can* do magic!"

"That book is totally bogus, Hanna," he said, eyeing it scornfully. "It's not even mine; it's Pop's. I hide that stuff in here so he won't accidentally kill us all in our sleep with his stupid rituals."

"*His* stupid rituals? What about your sticky cards?"

"*Glyph* cards."

"Aren't those magic?"

"Glyphs are just symbols. Letters, shapes, drawings. Just stuff that represents other stuff. Like the one on Melissa's door, remember?"

I could see it in my head still, a square with three squiggles inside it.

"The square represents the idea of fencing something in. And the wavy lines represent smell. Simple as that."

"But how isn't that magic? You carve squiggles into a door and suddenly horrible, noxious smells can't escape and alert the neighbors that they live next door to Corpse Central? And what about those glyph cards you put on us at Melissa's house that kept her off us?"

He rolled over onto his elbow to look at me. "You know

how spraying bug repellent on yourself keeps mosquitoes off? It's chemistry and biology, Hanna. Not magic."

"But you said yourself that the other Mortmaine can't use glyph cards. You said you'd get in trouble if they found out *you* were using them."

"They *can* use them," he insisted bitterly. "They just won't. Nobody ever uses glyphs offensively; they're too scared of what could happen."

"Maybe it's not that they're scared; it's that they don't know how to do what you do. They can slash marks into doors, but can they make your little magic cards? Or are you the only one who understands 'chemistry' and 'biology'?"

The loose lines of his body tensed. "It's only magic if it goes against the laws of nature."

"And you don't think glyph cards go against nature?"

"Not nature as *I* know it." He patted the narrow space on the bed next to him. "Come here."

"That was a quick ten minutes," I said archly, but I was in control enough to go to him, to lie in his arms. He wasn't demanding or grabby, content to lie still beneath my weight as I snuggled with him on his bed, our feet tangling together. He made it so easy to be with him.

I decided to throw him a bone. "You don't have to admit you're a witch if you don't want to—"

"*Witch?*"

"—but I like the idea that you're different from everyone. I know I am. I don't think I'll ever really fit in." I meant to say it offhand, like I didn't care, but it didn't come out that way.

"You *already* fit in. Transies usually die within the first week of moving here. Or move away. Or go crazy." With my ear to his chest, his speech sounded deep and wise. "They come here with ideas about the way the world is supposed to be, so when they see something weird, their minds break." He stroked his hand over my hair. "Your mind, though, is very bendy." The pride in his voice made me smile. "So bendy, you can even see ghosts."

"Not ghosts. Just Poppa. And never until I came here. I only heard him in my head before I came here."

"How do you know it's not in your head?" he asked reasonably.

"He knows things I don't know." I thought of the leech and shuddered, which moved Wyatt to stroke my back. "He's the one who told me about the panic grass back at the fence."

Wyatt's hand froze. "Is he here?"

"Over there." I pointed to where Poppa sat in Wyatt's desk chair, still as lake water, watching me.

Wyatt went up on his elbows and gazed at his desk, badly startled. "What's he *doing*?"

"Watching me."

His eyes widened. "For how long?"

I laughed at his old-lady expression. "Poppa's dead, Wyatt. Perfectly beyond shame."

"Wish I was." He pulled a pillow over his face.

I snatched the pillow away, and it was like unwrapping a present. Such a nice face my Wyatt had. I whispered in his ear, "You have nothing to be ashamed of," and then I kissed him.

Such a nice mouth.

"Wyatt, did you turn off your—" Wyatt and I scrambled apart as Sera crowded the doorway. "Phone?" Her gaze steamrollered over me, vindicated.

I knew then that Wyatt's mom and I would never be best friends.

"I didn't turn it off." Wyatt sat slightly in front of me, shielding me from his mother's eyes, even though he was less clothed than I was. "I left it in my pants."

"Where did you leave your pants?" Sera asked pointedly, eyeing the pillow in Wyatt's lap.

"In the hamper." His ears smoldered like embers.

"Your elder had to call *me* to tell you that you're going hunting in the dark park tomorrow night."

"*We're* going?" I whispered in Wyatt's bright red ear, heart pounding with excitement.

"No," he whispered back. "Not with Elder there."

"Wyatt!" Sera barked. When his head snapped forward she said, "Go get your phone. And your pants."

Wyatt rolled off the bed and grabbed a pair of jeans from his closet. He flashed me a rueful grimace as he yanked them on, and then he fled the room.

When Sera and I were alone together, she gave me the once-over, studying me like I was a shiny new toaster she wanted to take apart. "You look just like Rosalee."

"Thanks."

"That wasn't a compliment." Her eyes clouded over with dark memories. "Certain women don't handle beauty well." She refocused on me. "I hear your father's a Swede or something?"

"Finn."

"I'm surprised Rosalee didn't get knocked up by some guy around here. Lord knows she's had plenty of opportunities."

Was it a cultural thing, this Porterene penchant for tactless commentary?

"Did Asher give her an opportunity?" I asked, oh so innocently.

Watching Sera's scarlike mouth deform in anger was a distinctly unpleasant experience, but even though Rosalee didn't deserve it, I had to defend her honor. And my own.

Luckily, before Sera could challenge me to a smackdown, Wyatt came back. "I put your dress in the dryer," he told me, and tried to get by Sera's outstretched arm blocking the doorway. She wouldn't let him. Instead she started fussing at him in Spanish. And then they were going back and forth and forth and back until Wyatt yelled, *"Basta!"*

He looked at me apologetically. "I'll make us something to eat, all right?"

"Great," I said, but I was looking at his mother. "I'm always hungry after a good *shower*."

Sera slammed the door, shutting me alone in the room, the best thing she could have done if she wanted to punish me.

I was sick of being alone.

"You're not alone." Poppa sat at the desk, white and still, like one of Wyatt's sculptures, one that had managed to cross fully into the room.

"And you *are* like Rosalee," he continued. "She liked to use sex as a weapon too. You're going to hurt that boy the way she hurt me."

"No, I'm not," I said, appalled by the very idea.

Poppa turned away from me. "It wasn't a question."

I got home later that night to find Rosalee in the living room in a glitzy, skintight dress, transferring items from one purse to another.

When she saw me, she did a doubletake. "What happened to you?"

"Giant leech attack. I lost a lot of blood. Do we have any orange juice? Wyatt said I should drink lots of orange juice."

She ran to the kitchen—ran!—and returned with a quart-size bottle of orange juice. She sat me in the chair near the metal floor lamp, which she used to spotlight my wounded inner elbow and the bruising on my head and legs.

Visible injuries, like a real Porterene.

Wyatt had done an excellent job patching me up, but the extra fussing sent me over the moon. Rosalee cared about me so intensely, the heat of it had melted her cold shoulder.

"Why didn't you come straight home?" she asked, after listening to the story of the leech attack.

"It's not that bad," I said, bouncing in the chair. "Just a few scrapes. Did you make dinner? I know it's late, but Wyatt made me an omelet." I made a face. "It had eggshells in it, though, and too much salt."

Rosalee had the funniest look on her face.

"What?"

"You got attacked by a giant flying leech and all you can think about is food? You should be thinking about how to make up with your aunt so you can go back home."

"I am home. I won the bet. Remember? I've made friends. I have Wyatt."

"Sleeping around doesn't count. I told you that."

I stopped bouncing. Wow. Could she smell him on me? I sniffed myself.

"You *told* me you was gone sleep with him," she reminded me, exasperated.

"Oh, yeah." I shrugged it off. "He liked me before all that, so it still counts. But what counts most is that I have you, too."

Rosalee slapped me so hard that the inside of my cheek bled. "You do *not* have me!"

She shot off the arm of the chair to get away from me, as though *I'd* hit *her*. "You don't even know me. And I sure as hell don't know you. I don't know why I even bother trying to talk sense into you. *Get* eaten. *Get* killed. It's nothing to me."

"*You* kill me."

She started, as though I'd fired a gun at her head. "What?"

"Kill me in a fit of passion. How cool would that be?" The left side of my face was hot, as if a heat lamp was trained on my cheek. "A crime of passion. Do they call it a crime of passion if it's your daughter? It doesn't matter, because I know you would only go through the trouble of killing me if you felt passionate about it, right? If it was important to you? I'd like it if I were important to you. Would you like me to get you a knife? Or you could strangle me. How would you like to do it?" I couldn't see her expression. The tears made everything run together. "Just tell me how."

Before Rosalee could decide, a horn honked out on the street. She turned to flee, but I grabbed the strap of her purse.

She wrenched away, leaving the purse in my hand as she scrambled for the door as though I were giving chase. I was glad I hadn't caught her hand. She might have chewed through it and left it with me as well.

I watched her through the window, watched her throw herself into a black Lexus and speed away. Poppa drifted up beside me like a summer cloud in his vanilla suit. His purple tie was reflected in his gray eyes so that they seemed bruised, as though it literally hurt him to look at me.

As I moved to bury my face in his chest like I used to whenever I felt bad, he removed a knife from his jacket and held it between us, held the blade to my face.

"*I* would have done it," he said, which only made me cry harder.

"You still could," I said, trying to talk and sob at the same time. I didn't even have my hanky; I'd lost it stripping in Wyatt's bathroom. "I don't care."

"You have to do it. Then we can be together."

I took the knife, eyes squinted against the fiercely glowing blade . . . and then Swan bit my hand.

"Ow!" I dropped the knife. Before it could hit the floor, Swan's long neck shot forward, and she swallowed it. Then, with a heave of her wings, she flew at Poppa, whooping angrily as she clawed him with her sharp black talons.

Poppa screamed in surprised hurt, Swan a heavy weight on his face, driving him to his knees. She scratched off most of the left side of Poppa's face, his cheek and temple, his hair and scalp. The excised pieces, like confetti, drifted slowly to the floor and melted away, reminding me of Melissa.

But Poppa wasn't like Melissa. He wasn't a villain, a thing to be exorcised.

"Stop!" I cried, trying to shoo Swan away. "Please don't drive him away. He's all I have. He won't say anything like that again." I looked at Poppa down on his knees, nearly half his face gone. "Will you?"

The last time I had seen Poppa look so defeated was in the last days in the summerhouse, before bone cancer took him. "I won't ask her again," he said. "Please stop."

Swan did stop, landing heavily on the floor between Poppa and me.

Poppa trudged to the chair by the floor lamp and put his ruined face in his hands.

I would have gone to him, but Swan herded me upstairs, poking me in the backs of my knees with her beak to get me moving, but when I reached my room, Poppa spoke in my head, private-like.

You're all I have left too.

I remained awake the rest of the night missing my parents, both dead to me in different ways. Swan flew in slow, watchful circles above my bed, but as much as I loved her, I couldn't help wishing that I was dead too.

Chapter Eighteen

I spent the rest of the week awake and depressed. I had no desire to sleep or eat, so I didn't—Rosalee had stopped cooking for me anyway, so not eating was easy. As usual, I countered the depression with tireless activity. I did enough homework to cover the next two units in all my classes, and I sewed two new dresses, all in the space of two days. Amazing how much you could get done when you didn't have to waste time sleeping.

Wyatt rescued me from my low mood on Friday during one of his rare appearances at school, the first time I'd seen him since we'd showered together. The Mortmaine were training him into the ground, he told me, but he would be free to hunt on Sunday. He said it was all set.

When Wyatt picked me up around sunset that Sunday, I was no longer depressed, just wide-eyed and buzzing. After I proved beyond any doubt that I could take care of myself, Rosalee would stop hating me—that was enough to lift anyone's spirits.

"That's what you hunt in?" Wyatt asked, pulling out of the driveway. "A dress and heels?"

I was wearing a backless aubergine dress and matching lace-up boots that came to my knees. I'd wanted to wear something dark, and aubergine was the closest to black I had in my wardrobe.

"What should I be wearing?" I asked him.

"T-shirt. Jeans. Boots *without* heels." He was describing his own outfit.

"Blue jeans are too complicated, and I don't wear anything I don't make myself. And these aren't exactly stilettos." I raised my legs to tap my heels together. "I could run a mile in these boots."

He almost swerved onto the curb from staring at my legs, so he went all serious and eyes-on-the-road. "But can you fight in 'em?"

"Why not? It's easier to be careful in dresses. You have to be or you end up flashing your underclothes or destroying beautiful fabric. Dresses force you to be on guard."

He risked a glance at me, eyes twinkling. "Your mind is weird. Come here."

"Gladly." And I was glad. Wyatt's friends were fun to hang out with, even Petra when she kept her fat mouth shut, but Wyatt understood me. With him, I could be myself.

He pulled away from my kisses, laughing. "Cut it out before we end up in a ditch." I stole a few more kisses just the same, and Wyatt, trouper that he was, somehow managed not to wreck the truck.

Wyatt drove to Avispa Lane and parked in the parking lot of St. Michael's, a weathered, slightly gothic church that huddled bravely in the shadow of a great, rolling forest, its huge old trees growing wild together, its dark green canopy mocking the fall season.

I walked around the truck to Wyatt's side, staring at the tangled expanse of piney woods. "Is that the dark park?"

He nodded grimly.

"It isn't so bad."

"You don't know anything about it," he said almost pityingly as he led me to the church steps, where we sat holding hands in the warm, quickly fading sunlight. Cardinals whistled at one another in the eaves of the church.

"A long time ago in Finland, I got lost in the woods on Easter. When I was five or six. It was freezing, and the snow was deep along the paths. I thought a real witch had cursed me to lose my way, to punish me for pretending to be one of them. So I'm not totally oblivious about how dangerous the woods can be. How misleading."

"Why were you pretending to be a witch?"

I shrugged. "It was Easter."

Wyatt fell over laughing. "Finnish people dress up as witches on *Easter*? I don't remember no trick-or-treaters in the Old Testament."

I snatched my hand from his grip. "I don't laugh at your stupid culture. You and your doors and keys."

"Come on." He bussed my ear. "I didn't say it was stupid. What do I know? Maybe there *were* witches and goblins at the Passover."

"Goblins? Who said anyth—?"

Shoko appeared out of nowhere, derailing my train of thought. First an unobstructed view of the empty parking lot, and then Shoko all in green, tossing her long black hair over her shoulder as she strode toward us. "I'm here."

"How—?"

"Just more of our stupid culture." Wyatt patted my knee in this condescending way I'm sure he thought was hilarious.

"*You* can do that?" I asked, preparing myself to be impressed.

"Not yet," said Shoko, as tall and imposing as I remembered. "We gotta teach him. And then we gotta teach him not to invite civilians into the line of fire."

And just as mean.

"Come on, Shoko. You used to be cool. You used to take me on hunts before I was even initiated."

"Well, I obviously taught you some bad habits," she said, glaring at me. "Let's get this over with before I change my mind." She crossed Avispa Lane and was swallowed by the tall pines.

"How can she appear and disappear like that?"

"She's not. She's using the hidden doors." Wyatt flapped his hand when I started to speak. "Don't get sidetracked by all that now. The sun's nearly gone. The hardheads'll be out soon."

"Hardheads?"

He kissed me. It stung, as though I'd kissed a light socket. "You'll see."

When we got into the forest, he was all business, tramping ahead like he knew the way. It was only sunset, but in the woods it might as well have been midnight. Trees loomed in the dark like fairy-tale giants, spindly branches interlacing overhead like fingers twining. I stuck close to Wyatt as he straight-armed the branches aside and led us into a clearing lit with several lanterns emitting a harsh white light. Beyond the clearing, darkness pressed around us, cut us off from the rest of the world; we might as well have been the last three people on the planet.

In the center of the clearing was a hole in the ground bordered with stones. Shoko knelt near the hole, oiling a small pair of metallic pink . . . maces? Each had a short handle with a single spiked ball dangling at the end of a chain.

Wyatt knelt beside Shoko, unzipped a nearby duffel bag full of blades, and armed himself with a machete and several of his favored push daggers.

"Where are the other Mortmaine?" I asked.

Wyatt looked at me. "What others?"

"She means the foxes and hounds," Shoko said, rolling her eyes. "And the asshole in a red riding coat screaming, 'Tallyho!'"

They laughed, revealing an irritating rapport.

"It's just us," Wyatt told me. "If the Mortmaine knew

about this, about *you*, they'd disown me. We're lucky to even have Shoko."

"Damn straight," she said, swinging her shiny weapons like nunchaku.

How Wyatt had managed to get close enough to Shoko to have sex with her amazed me. She was like her maces—pretty but deadly. I backed away from her, nervously eyeing the blur of the spiked balls, so busy keeping out of her way that I nearly fell down the stone-bordered hole.

I dropped to my knees beside it and peered into earthy-smelling darkness.

"Don't worry," Wyatt told me. "Only Shoko and me are going down the tunnel."

"Is that where the hard hats are?"

"Hardheads," Wyatt corrected. "And yeah."

"How many are there?"

"About fifty."

I stared at him. "Three against fifty?"

"We know what we're doing," said Shoko. "Relax."

I studied the array of weapons spread between the two of them. Of them all, Shoko's were the cutest. "Do you have any more of those pink maces?" I asked her.

"They're flails, not maces," she said. "And you'd only put your eye out." Shoko strapped her metallic pink flails into a holster at her waist. Then she picked up a wooden club covered in spikes. "*This* is a mace."

As I reached for it, Wyatt intercepted it and said, "Never mind maces." He handed me a short-handled ax.

"I want a mace."

"But you *need* an ax."

I took the arm-length weapon and swung it experimentally; it was surprisingly heavy, the blade sharp but pitted and worn, as though it had been put to serious work.

"What about a gun?" I asked. "Or a bazooka?"

Shoko said, "We don't use guns."

"Why not?"

"Same reason you don't wear jeans," said Wyatt. He held up his push daggers. "It's easier to make one of these than a bazooka."

Wyatt and Shoko were so cool and together, I decided to put my fears aside and imitate them. "So," I said brightly, "what's the plan?"

"Shoko and me go down through the tunnel."

"And where do I go?"

"You got the easy part." Wyatt pulled something from his pocket and threw it to me. "Drink that."

He'd tossed me a small vial fizzing with a clear liquid, like seltzer. "What is this? More chemistry?"

Shoko said, "It lures the hardheads to you so that they'll take you into their lair. While they're busy with you, we can get the drop on 'em."

I didn't like the sound of that. "Busy with me *how*?"

"They'll be taking you to their queen," Wyatt explained. "Like a gift. That's why you'll be able to take her out—easy access."

"You want me to destroy the *queen*?" My blood zinged at the idea. "Do you think I can?"

"Absolutely," said Wyatt. He squeezed the back of my neck and touched our foreheads together.

I thought of Rosalee, the look on her face after I'd told her about tonight. "Okay!" I drained the vial in one gulp and nearly choked on the burning sweetness within.

"Better spray her now," said Shoko, tossing an aerosol can to Wyatt.

He took me by the back of the neck again and sprayed me head to toe with a warm, sharp-smelling substance.

"Hey!" I tried to dodge him, but he was quick and thorough. "What are you doing?"

"This'll counteract the stomach acid," he said. "So it doesn't burn you alive."

"*Stomach acid?*" I finally managed to pull away, only to fall over backward into Wyatt's arms, an insidious creeping numbness inching over me, a stiffness that was frighteningly unnatural.

Wyatt lowered me gently to the ground. "Make sure you hold tight to that ax," he said.

I knew I was holding it—I could see it in my peripheral vision, the ax head laying against my chest—but I couldn't feel it. I couldn't feel anything. "What's happening?" The words fell strangely from my stiffening lips.

Shoko said, "You're dying."

"*What?*" It sounded more like *Whuuuunn?*

"Did we forget to mention that part?" Shoko waved her hand. "No worries. You drank an infusion of ghoul's delight. Drink too much, you'll be a corpse for real, but in small doses it just mimics death, so that you'll look and feel and smell just like a fresh corpse."

"Ghoul's delight? Is that what you bought at the herbal

shop?" That's what I wanted to ask, wanted to scream, but I couldn't. My lungs were no longer under my command.

Wyatt's face hovered above mine, studying me so passionlessly that I couldn't help remembering what Petra had once said, about how nothing came before Wyatt's duty.

I hadn't realized that included my life.

"Hardheads love fresh meat," he said, actually smiling at me, "but they can't feed it to their queen. *She's* a carrion eater, and the only way they'll feed you to her is if they think you're dead. Hanna?"

"Damn," Shoko said, out of my line of sight. "Already? How long's it been?"

"I think it just kicked in." Wyatt put his head close to mine. "Ghoul's delight wears off in, like, fifteen minutes, so once you're inside her body, hack your way free with the ax. When the queen's toast, the others'll be easy pickings."

Shoko leaned over me, her hair falling into my face, though I couldn't feel the dark strands. "Okay, she's ready. Let's go!"

Wyatt and Shoko disappeared from view. I was alone, without even my own heartbeat to keep me company.

What I had instead were flies.

They landed on my open eyes, their busy little bodies blotting out the trees. I wanted to scream. I wanted to *run*, but I couldn't. I was worse than alone. I was helpless.

A rhythmic thumping resounded beneath me, like someone beating the ground with a sledgehammer, shaking me. I couldn't feel the shakes, but the trees above me, the sky, seemed to be shuddering. As I sucked in my last few breaths, a terrible smell filled the air. I recognized it this time—the smell of death. Melissa had taught me well.

What if a zombie horde was rising up from the ground beneath me? Was that what all the thumping was about?

Jesus.

And then they were bending over me. Not zombies . . . things. Veiny, cone-headed creatures with the bluish-gray skin of an asphyxiation victim. They studied me the way Wyatt had, passionlessly, with their white, lidless eyes. The stench emanated from them, from their huge, gaping mouths.

And then the view changed. The dusky sky disappeared, replaced by soil and rock as the cone-headed things, the hard-heads, dragged me beneath the earth.

Chapter Nineteen

The scuffling crowd of hardheads herded me through a narrow black tunnel that eventually opened out into a massive cave. Weird shadows, dull and greenish, bent and rippled along the cave above me.

The hardheads had to be carrying me on their backs. None of them had arms, only many, many legs, like spiders or centipedes. They scurried forward on either side of me, crawling over each other in their haste. One of them crawled over me, briefly surrounding me in a cage of wriggling, mis-jointed legs.

The crowd of hardheads carrying me stilled, and my view tilted sickeningly from the cave ceiling to a widening hole, twice as wide as I was, a hole that grew bigger and closer as I fell into it.

A dark blue space enclosed me; I heard the rushing of fluid like an ocean. I could *feel*—heat and damp, an unpleasant squeeze and deposit. Then another squeeze and deposit, as though I were being birthed and rebirthed into one hellish, wet pit after another.

I could *move*, so I thrashed within the deep blue pit, and the ax in my hand bit into something soft.

The ax.

I gripped it in both hands and hacked into the cocoon of slick meat surrounding me, gasping, sucking in a fetid, animal stink. I hacked an opening wide enough for fresh air to waft in and tantalize my newly functioning lungs. I forced my head and shoulders through, and finally I was free to the waist.

An unearthly chorus of insectile chittering greeted me. The greenish cave was full of motion, hardheads scrambling to and fro like cockroaches caught in the light. Actually the hardheads looked more like fleshy scorpions than insects, only instead of tails curling up from their bodies, their cone-shaped heads did, whipping to and fro on the long stalks of their necks like malevolent wrecking balls.

Wyatt and Shoko flew among the creatures, attacking them while simultaneously defending themselves against the hard-heads' rock-breaking skulls. The two of them moved with such quick, easy grace that, if not for the spurting blood, they could have been dancing.

Wyatt, his fists curled around the handles of his push daggers, stabbed one hardhead after another in the neck or back, while Shoko bashed them on the backs of their curved necks with her swinging flails.

"Hanna!" called Wyatt, far down below me, alien in the green light. "Kill the queen!"

Queen? My view of the cave and its inhabitants was limited and would remain so until I got free of this hole. As I attempted to wiggle out, a buzzing screech sounded behind me.

I turned and realized I didn't have to look for the queen; I was *in* her, poking up from her school-bus-length back. She was ten times bigger than the others, her cone-shaped head nearly half the size of my own body and glinting with a hard metallic sheen.

"For Christ's sake, Hanna!" Wyatt screamed. "Kill her!"

I had to laugh at the absurdity of it, my upper body shivering in the coolness of the cave, even as my lower half baked within the queen's warm body. Might as well ask an ant to kill an elephant.

But I tried. I brought the ax down onto her back.

An ugly screech bubbled from the queen's sickeningly wide mouth and unnerved me. But when she whipped her head at me, I was ready with the ax; I swung it right at her skull . . . and the blade snapped clean off the handle.

The force of the blow numbed my hands, and the numbness brought me alive all over, alive and ready to stay that way. When the queen swung at me again—her head wasn't even scratched!—I took a deep breath and ducked back inside her.

I no longer had the ax, but I had built-in tools—my hands, with their lovely opposable thumbs, perfect for snatching and ripping anything that pulsed. Deep inside the queen, I rediscovered the childhood joy of destruction. With no Lego Space Station or Malibu Dream House to crush underfoot, the queen's organs made an excellent stand-in.

A long, messy time later, the queen quivered around me and fell, an impact I was cushioned against, encased as I was in her flesh.

I popped out of the hole in her body, the pleasurable zing

of destruction still speeding along my veins, but the vibe in the cave had changed; the hardheads shambled aimlessly, their piss and vinegar lost. No fun at all.

Wyatt and Shoko stayed busy, however, picking off the now tame creatures, putting them out of their misery. Sort of. Wyatt was a considerate executioner, usually requiring only one blow to their necks to fell them, while Shoko left several twitching in agony.

I wriggled free of the queen, covered in goo and trying not to stumble in the loose piles of animal bones, wet rock, and mounds of hardhead eggs. Wyatt bounded over to me, dodging long pillars of color where the stalagmites and stalactites had grown together.

"So how was it?" he asked.

I puked.

Wyatt and Shoko laughed.

"Yeah," he said. "It's intense, right?"

Shoko swatted me on the back. "Especially once you get past that first stomach."

I wiped my mouth and reached to straighten my dress out of habit, but it was a slimy ruin; I straightened my shoulders instead. "Do either of you have another ax?"

"Nope," said Wyatt. "Just this." He pulled the machete from the back of his pants.

I took it and stumbled back to the dead queen. Her long, whippy neck was surprisingly easy to saw through, considering the hard head it had had to support.

Wyatt and Shoko watched knowingly, like maybe they'd hacked their own share of trophy heads.

I lifted the queen's head and balanced it against my hip. It was heavy and so wide I could barely wrap both arms around it, but I was determined to carry it home with me, even if I had to roll it through the streets like a barrel.

After destroying all the eggs, we climbed out of the stone-bordered tunnel, and then out of the dark park, crossing the street back to St. Michael's. The night seemed magically bright after the crushing darkness of the woods, the stars like disco lights, everything abnormally loud, as though the volume had been turned to eleven: Shoko's slow heartbeat, the click and buzz of gears inside Wyatt that made him tick.

Because he wasn't human. He couldn't be.

"So how we gone celebrate our victory, kids?" Wyatt asked at the truck, which glowed like swamp fire in the lit parking lot.

Shoko leaned against the fender like a chick in a low-rider magazine, only way overdressed. "There's another hive upsquare we can tackle," she said.

"*Hell*, yeah." Wyatt grinned at me. "You wanna help us with the new hive?"

"You killed me."

His grin faltered.

"You made me drink that stuff. You killed me."

He rolled his eyes, like my death had meant nothing. It hadn't, of course, not to him. Robots couldn't feel. "It only seemed like it," he said. "And it was just to fool the hard-heads. How else were you gone do any damage? You're not a fighter."

"I can't believe Poppa warned *me* not to hurt *you*!" I hitched the head higher on my hip and stormed off.

"Where're you going?"

"Away from you, murderer!" I began to jog, the heels of my boots ringingly loud against the sidewalk.

"You can't run around in the streets this close to the dark park! Are you crazy?"

"What do you care? Afraid I'll get killed? *By someone else?* Do you own that privilege, Wyatt?"

He grabbed me from behind and hustled me across the street toward the dark park. Probably to push me in with all the monsters and let them finish me off. When I whirled on him, to clobber him with the head, I realized I was about to take my anger out on Shoko, not Wyatt.

I also realized that she and I weren't anywhere near the dark park, but down the street from my house. She must have taken me through a hidden door; I hadn't even noticed.

But my stomach noticed. The disorientation made me hurl again.

Shoko watched me unload all over the sidewalk, impassively, and when I was done she marched me up the street to my house.

She said, "I don't give a damn one way or another, but Wyatt would be crushed if something happened to you, and then he'd be no good to us." She looked me over. "It'd be a shame to lose a good fighter over something stupid."

She pushed me toward my porch, and I nearly toppled over, the weight of the head unbalancing me. She waited for me to go inside, so I did just to get away from her.

Rosalee sat in the living room, reading. Pretending to read. Whenever she was home and I was out, she always waited up for me in the living room. Seeing her reminded me why I had put myself through all the past weeks of danger and weirdness. Because I *knew* she cared deep down, and now she could admit it.

"Catch." I heaved the head at her, and she dodged out of the way. A good thing, as something in the chair snapped beneath the weight of the hard head.

Rosalee stared at it wide-eyed, watched it leak onto the chair. "What's that?"

"I went on a hunt with the Mortmaine." Just Shoko and Wyatt, who was only an initiate, but Rosalee didn't need to know everything. "I killed a hardhead queen. That's her head. Now you know I can take care of myself. Now you can stop treating me like a ghost."

Rosalee put her hands over her mouth, the way beauty queens do just before they burst into tears. Had I moved her to tears?

I reached for her. "Momma?"

Her hands fell away from her face. She wasn't even close to tears. Just the same stony expression as she grabbed my slimy arm and pulled me toward the front door.

"Where are we going?"

"Dallas. I'm driving you there right now."

I felt as though I were inside the queen again, upside-down and suffocating. *"Why?"*

Rosalee brought me to a halt and shook me. "You went alone into the dark park—"

"I wasn't alone!"

"—and fought a monster! You think that's what I want? You think that makes me happy? That after Joosef went through all the trouble to bring you up right, two weeks with me and you become *this?*"

She took me in, the goo and filth. "Maybe you think this is an improvement, but I don't. You're going back to Ulla. I'll work something out with her so she'll—"

"Aunt Ulla doesn't want me!"

"I don't care what she wants! I don't care what *you* want!" Her stony expression had cracked wide open, her true feelings plain to see, but none of those emotions was happiness. Or love. Only fear. "You're not staying here in this goddamned town!"

As Rosalee yanked me toward the door, I snatched up a table lamp and swung it at the back of her head, hard enough for the bulb to explode.

She hit the front door and bounced off it, falling over backward to the floor.

I froze, the lamp cold in my hands.

I was caught in an endless loop—first Aunt Ulla, now Rosalee. Maybe I would always come back to this place—a weapon in my hand, a body at my feet.

Poppa stepped up from behind me, a cold presence in his vanilla suit and violet tie. "This is your hell," he said, "and this time an ax won't free you."

Chapter Twenty

Pieces were still missing from the left side of Poppa's face, as though something had been nibbling on him. But he was a welcome sight just the same. "Oh, Poppa, what did I do?"

"You bashed your mother over the head," was his prompt reply.

"Oh my God." I dropped to the floor beside Rosalee's body, beyond grateful to see the rise and fall of her chest. I scrambled to my feet, hauled her closer to the end table, and positioned the broken lamp beside her head, careful of the squishy dent I'd made in it.

"Now when she wakes up," I whispered, "she'll think she tripped, fell, and hit her head on the end table. She won't know *I* did it. She won't blame *me*."

"Who says she'll wake up?" Poppa said, with his fearless ability to face facts.

Not like me.

The anger, the fear, everything fled, whooshing out of me as though I were a tire and someone had run up behind me and slashed me with a knife. I escaped upstairs, sank into bed, and pulled the covers over my head so that no one would see me. I stank of blood and sweat and hardhead gloop. Maybe the gloop was toxic; maybe it would poison me, like radon.

Poppa crowded next to me on the bed, the way he did sometimes when I was scared. He said, "We have to talk."

"What's there to talk about? Rosalee's dead. That's why you're here, isn't it? To take her with you?"

"Then why I am up here with you?"

"Because I'm going to die too. Because I'm going to slit my throat. Better death than a hospital for the criminally insane."

"You need to fix this."

"How?" I was surprised he wasn't in support of the throat-slitting idea. Then I remembered his run-in with Swan, how she'd altered his views on suicide.

Or maybe Poppa had changed his mind about wanting to

be with me. After what I'd done to Rosalee, I couldn't blame him. I didn't want to be with me either.

Poppa said, "Remember what Wyatt said about the door knocker on his house?"

"He said it's a Key."

"What else?"

I had to think about it. "He said . . . it opens doors?"

"That's not all it does. It grants wishes. All Keys do."

"Like a stupid fairy tale?"

"It's no fairy tale."

"It *is*. You're not even here. You're not real. I'm dreaming. It's all a dream. Please?" I thought of Rosalee lying downstairs, and a layer of ice formed in my belly. "Please, be a dream."

"In Portero, many strange things are real. And so if everything is real, why not wishes?" Such logic my Poppa had. "Wouldn't it be nice to wish away the crater you put in Rosalee's head?"

"Really nice." I hardly dared say the words. Hardly dared believe it could be true.

"All you have to do is touch the Key and make a wish."

"That's all?"

"Well"—he ripped the covers off me and shooed me out

of bed—"there are always complications, aren't there?"

"Like what?"

But he was too busy rifling through my armoire to answer. "All this purple is ridiculous," he told me, handing me a nightgown. "You don't even like purple."

"*You* like it."

"I never immersed myself in it the way you do. You need to learn moderation, Hanna."

"I know." I removed my sticky dress and boots and washed up in the bathroom. I wasn't embarrassed for Poppa to see me naked. We'd sauna'ed together, after all. What was nudity between family?

I put on the nightgown and went downstairs, careful not to look at Rosalee sprawled on the floor—if I couldn't see she was dead, she wouldn't be.

I went to the garage for the bike. No. Where would Poppa ride? The handlebars? I went back inside and snagged Rosalee's car keys from the rack by the front door.

I remembered the way to Wyatt's house and soon found myself on Carmona. Poppa rode shotgun, less animated than before, light snaking over his pale face.

"What's it like being dead?"

"Like anything else."

"Are you . . . did you go to heaven, at least?"

"There's no such thing as heaven. Or hell. Not for me."

"So what do you do all day?"

He turned his gray gaze on me. The longing in his eyes was bottomless. "I think about you. And Rosalee." He looked out the window. "We're here."

I slammed on the brakes, surprised, and hit the steering wheel hard with my chest because I had forgotten to buckle up.

As I went up Wyatt's stoop, the stone beneath my bare feet still warm from the day's heat, I heard sounds from the open windows of his neighbors: a sitcom laugh track, people arguing about a burnt roast.

The smell of the burnt roast turned my stomach, and I realized I was frightened. The twisted Key swam before me, gleaming darkly. If this didn't work . . .

"It will." Poppa stood at the curb near Rosalee's red Prius. The light from a nearby streetlamp gave him a weird broken shadow. "Make your wish."

I touched the Key, and a hideously unpleasant zap rocketed through my elbow, as though someone had whacked my funny bone with a ball-peen hammer. But I held on. "I wish—"

The pain was immediate. Searing. I screeched and skipped backward, but I couldn't skip far. My hand stuck fast to the Key, sizzling.

"Poppa!"

No answer. I looked back for him, but he was gone. Of course Poppa was gone; he'd never *been*. But I wasn't alone. Someone raced up the stoop toward me.

Wyatt's dad.

He dropped a flat box at my feet, spilling leftover pizza near the door. The aroma of sausage and garlic eclipsed the burnt roast smell. He put his hand on the door above the Key. "Let go."

"I can't!"

But he wasn't talking to me. It was weird, but the Key let go of *me*. I collapsed to the stoop, cradling my hand to my stomach.

Wyatt's dad crouched beside me. "Let me see." He coaxed me to uncurl my hand. The skin of my palm was blackened and peeling like charred paper. Inflamed tissue peeped here and there, red and angry-looking.

Sera climbed the stoop and joined her husband, Paulie asleep on her shoulder, a blue balloon tied around his tiny wrist. She rolled her eyes at me. "Stupid transy."

Chapter Twenty-one

Asher retrieved the dropped pizza box, opened the door, and stepped aside to let his wife and child move past him into the house. He took me by the elbow. "I think you'd better come in too."

"My hand." He seemed confused until I showed him my burnt flesh again.

"We can take care of that," he said as he took me inside.

Even worse than my hand was the pain of knowing that I'd failed, that Rosalee was dead or dying and I hadn't even made the wish.

Wyatt's dad parked me in a chair, shushing me and patting my back because I was crying and useless and alone.

A moment later a cool, soothing tingle settled over my burnt palm. I wiped my eyes as Asher knelt before me and slathered the popcorn-colored contents of a brown jar into my hand. "Better?"

I nodded. Much better. Only a vague memory of pain remained. I fingered the paste. "What is this?"

Asher frowned at me, and I understood then that he was confused because I was still speaking Finnish. I had been all along with Poppa and hadn't switched gears. I repeated myself in English.

"Just something Wyatt whipped up." He looked chagrined. "Did he tell you about making wishes on our Key?"

Actually my dead father had told me, but I knew better than to say that aloud. "It came to me in a dream," I said, almost truthfully.

Sera came downstairs. She'd changed clothes and, as if she weren't scary enough, now looked like a ninja. She went to Asher. "Paulie's fast asleep, so I'm gone join Wyatt and Shoko, okay?"

"Where are they?"

"Upsquare near the mill. Depopulating hardheads. How did she know about the wishing?" She frowned at me. "Did Wyatt tell you?"

"It came to her in a dream," said Asher, impressed.

Sera was not. "Well, don't think you can get a bigger allowance or a new car by sneaking wishes off our Key."

"I wasn't—"

Asher said, "I'll handle it, dear."

Sera gave me one last glare, then kissed Asher's forehead. "Please yourself. I'll see you later."

"Have fun." When the door closed behind his wife, Asher shot me a conciliatory look. "Trust me. You do not want to get her riled. Now." He rubbed his hands gleefully. "With her and Wyatt out of the way, there's no one to interfere."

"With what?"

He shot to his feet. "There's a spell I've been wanting to try out. If it works, it'll fix the unfortunate *sticking* side effect of the Key. You want a cool drink?"

I nodded, and after some time, he returned with a cart, wheeling it over to the couch. A number of items littered the cart, including a pitcher of lemonade, several bundles of herbs, a mixing bowl, a long, thin knife, and several jars.

One of the jars rattled.

"A feisty one," said Asher.

"A feisty what?"

He poured my lemonade. "Even with the Key *outside* the house, sometimes a door opens in here and something gets through. Fortunately," he nodded to the rattling jar, "we have ways of trapping them. Now, listen up."

He gave me a stern look. He didn't do stern well—discipline was obviously more his wife's thing. "I don't want to have to explain this again: The Key isn't there to be misused."

"By wishing for cars and bigger allowances?"

"And old girlfriends back and rivals to die or loved ones to come back from the dead. You have no idea how chaotic things would get if people started getting their wishes granted willy-nilly. You use the Key to knock on the door, fine. You use the Key to make a wish, forget about it. As you saw, Keys have built-in defenses to keep them from being abused."

"If it's your Key, couldn't you give me permission to make a wish?"

"Of course!" he said brightly. "But I won't, so don't waste your breath. Nobody's made a wish on that Key since 1989." I guess he must have heard every excuse, seen every trick, every angle.

He probably thought he had.

"I'll have to insist, Asher. I'm in a real bind."

He seemed to really see me for the first time. I must have looked like a Dickensian orphan, with my dirty bare feet and voluminous nightgown. "You don't have to stare," I said, tucking my feet away. "I know what I look like."

"You look fine." His voice was deep with feeling. "You look—" He cleared his throat. "You look like your mother."

I had seen that look on Poppa's face too often not to recognize it. "Do you love her?"

"Yes." He didn't even hesitate.

"I bet you'd give *her* a wish."

"You're not your mother," he said, gentle but firm.

I decided to back off. Temporarily. "How did you get control over the Key?"

"I don't control it. No one does. I watch over it and protect it, but I don't control it."

"But why you?"

"It's been in my family for generations. It was fashioned from my great-grandmother's bones."

I thought back to Wyatt's story.

"The creature Runyon tortured was your *aunt*? How's that possible?"

"She wasn't a *creature*," he said indignantly. "She was

human. Human enough for him to get her pregnant."

My mouth dropped. "Runyon *raped* her?"

Asher blinked at me, abashed. "Wyatt said he told you."

"Not that Anna was raped. Jesus."

"Oh, yeah." His smile was bright and bitter as poison. "Runyon got Anna pregnant so that if his Key-making scheme didn't work, he'd have a backup in place. A spare to practice on. But a year after Anna's daughter was born, the Mayor got wise to what Runyon had done and paid him a visit. She took the Key and Anna's daughter and put them in the hands of the Mortmaine.

"Eventually the daughter grew up and had daughters of her own, one of whom was my mother, who got possession of the Key. It used to be there, over the mantel, but having it inside the house opened too many doors. Couldn't even open the pantry without something leaping out at you. Do you have a feather, by chance?" he asked, patting himself down.

"No. Sorry."

He pulled a feather from his own pocket and dropped it into the mixing bowl, turning its contents a hideous hot pink.

I watched Asher with new respect. "Wyatt said there's no such thing as magic."

Asher harrumphed. "Typical teen. Thinks he knows everything. Doesn't understand that the world's full of mysteries. 'You only call it magic when you don't understand it.'" His mockery of Wyatt was spot-on. "If the world is full of mysteries, can anything ever truly be understood?"

He shook his head at his son's presumption, running the knife along his finger, letting his blood drip into the bowl. The contents turned from hot pink to the crystal clear of spring-water. Then he wheeled the cart to the front door and opened it. The heat outdoors quickly sucked the cool air from the room as he painted the Key with the clear mixture, making it glossier.

Asher then used an oven mitt to lift a red licorice-length needle from the cart. It smoldered when he touched it to the door and carved a small ring of shapes. Glyphs.

He tossed the stick onto the cart and, without looking, reached back for one of the jars, the rattling one, which he smashed against the door as if christening a ship.

A concussive boom blew him out of the doorway and flung me and the yellow chair I was sitting in backward to fetch up against the wall.

Standing in the open doorway was a freakishly tall man-shaped creature that was so much taller than the ceiling, it had to curl downward like a hooded cobra. Red, lobsterlike armor covered it, except for its maggoty white arms and lower legs.

Lobsterman observed Asher lying stunned on the floor and fell on him, trying to bite Asher with its teeth like razor blades—sharp, white, and unbroken. Asher managed to hold it off, but he wouldn't be able to for long.

I left the chair and crept to the cart, assessing the situation and pleased by how calm I was. I think I was smiling.

"Asher?" I said, lifting the knife Asher had used to cut up the plants. I rolled it thoughtfully between my fingers. "Why don't we make a deal?"

Chapter Twenty-Two

"I know you don't like people wishing on your Key, but just this once, why don't you make an exception?"

Fear had rounded Asher's eyes, giving him an interested, focused look as Lobsterman tried to eat his face.

"I'm going to help whether you agree or disagree, but I want you to consider the great favor I'm doing you, particularly since I'm putting my life at risk to save yours. And since I'm only sixteen, my death would be the greater tragedy."

As I talked, I circled behind Lobsterman, who whipped around to face me, blood on its odd, bladelike teeth from where it had managed to nick Asher's cheek. Its yellow eyes glowed like sunlight. If I closed my eyes, I'd see spots.

I backed off and dropped carefully to my knees, still close enough to Lobsterman to see mites crawling in the gaps of its red-orange armor, but not close enough to cut it. I was, however, close enough to cut Asher.

I grabbed one of Asher's thrashing legs and pared a substantial slice of hairy white skin from his calf muscle. Asher screamed, but I ignored him.

"Oh, Lobsterman." I waggled the bit of flesh in the creature's face and just managed to toss the skin into its mouth as it lunged at me, snapping.

I sliced another piece from Asher's leg and fed it to Lobsterman as well. "Good boy," I said, because there was something oddly doglike about the creature, the eagerness it displayed for the paltry scraps in my hand.

But after I'd sliced a third piece, instead of feeding it into Lobsterman's wickedly sharp mouth, I turned and flung the meat.

I had meant to throw it out the door, but it landed *on* the door, on the Key, which was still sticky from Asher's ministrations, and hung there like grisly, overcooked pasta. Lobsterman sprang after the meat with the helplessness of a dog going after a stick and lunged into the Key, face-first. While Lobsterman stuck to the Key, trapped and howling, I crawled to it and stabbed it in its soft, armorless parts.

Ripping the queen apart had been fun, but this was something else—killing something after you've fed it isn't exactly a carnival.

Finally Lobsterman quieted, and its dead weight unstuck it from the Key.

Asher looked away from Lobsterman lying in a heap in the doorway and stood awkwardly, lifting his pant leg to examine the bloody area where I'd peeled his skin away in neat strips.

He frowned at me. "I don't know whether to thank you or backhand you."

After meeting his wife, Asher didn't scare me. I tossed the bloody knife on his cart. "I'd rather you thanked me, if it's all the same."

"*Thank you.* I guess you earned it. In the most half-assed, unethical way possible."

"I would have saved you, no matter what. I told you that."

He was quiet a long time. "Go on," he said, after he'd bound his wounds. "Make your wish. But you only get one!"

I had to tread on Lobsterman to get to the Key, which I reached for gingerly, afraid of more pain. But I touched it despite my fear, ignoring the zing in my elbow, hoping it wasn't too late.

When I saw Asher staring incredulously at his cart, wondering where he'd gone wrong, paying not the slightest attention to me, I whispered, "I wish Rosalee's head wasn't damaged."

A brightness bloomed behind my eyes, like a camera flash.

When my vision cleared, I said good-bye to Asher and rushed to the car. After I finally made it home, I dropped to Rosalee's inert form on the floor of the living room. I tested her head, the way I tested melons, feeling for overripe patches. Finding none, I whispered, "Rosalee?"

No response. Her head was perfectly sound, but she was as still as a corpse. Why hadn't I wished she were alive instead of that her head not be damaged? Jesus Christ, how stupid was I?

"Rosalee?" I shook her, knowing it was futile, but helpless to stop. "Rosalee!"

Her eyes opened and locked on me. They were bright blue. Electric. She sat up and immediately seemed to regret the move, grabbing her head in her hands. "You're not Bonnie."

I recoiled, not from Rosalee—from her voice. It wasn't Rosalee's voice. Not her eyes and not her voice.

"And you're not Rosalee," I said.

"Ahh, yes," said the voice, the intruder. "*Her.*" Rosalee slumped over to her side, unconscious.

Chapter Twenty-Three

I pried opened my mother's eyes, desperate to prove to myself that I hadn't seen and heard what I'd just seen and heard, but her eyes had rolled to the whites, their color hidden.

I put Rosalee over my shoulder like firemen do. I had no idea I could do such a thing until I did it. But I was a sturdy enough girl. I hauled her to her bed and settled her in.

She looked like a sleeping princess against the fluffy pillows, cursed to lie dormant, to be admired but not met. I kissed her mouth. She tasted like cherries. "Momma?"

And like that I was staring into her own starry black eyes, stunned that such a fairy-tale ploy had worked.

"What?" she slurred, before drifting back to sleep.

I was so relieved she wasn't comatose, so relieved to hear *her* voice, that I collapsed to my knees beside her bed and wept.

The weeping left me drained and tired, but I couldn't sleep. I'd read enough to know that I couldn't let a person with a possible concussion fall asleep without risking coma. I would have to watch over Rosalee all night and keep waking her at intervals.

But at least she was alive to be woken.

I shook her shoulder. "Momma?"

"What?" she grumbled, turning to her side away from me.

I stroked her hair rippling blackly across the pillow. Her curls were softer than mine, as if she brushed her hair more than I did, as if she didn't mind battling our island-girl tangles.

"Momma." But I didn't say it loud enough for her to hear.

I just liked saying it.

When I opened my eyes, Rosalee was out of bed and it was seven in the morning. I rose to my feet from the hard floor, rubbing my sore neck, and went to the kitchen, where Rosalee was making breakfast, looking cheery and awake and Stepford mom-ish in her red apron. She glanced up from the boiling pot to look me over. "Hungry?"

I had to resist the urge to look over my shoulder; I couldn't believe she was talking to me. "Yes."

"Go shower and get dressed. Breakfast'll be ready when you finish."

I didn't want to move, afraid I was dreaming and that if I even blinked, Rosalee would revert to the sullen, tight-lipped person from yesterday.

"Go on now!" Her voice brooked no argument, so I got on.

I showered and dressed in record time and went back to the kitchen. Rosalee set a full plate before me and joined me at the table. She sat in the red chair, but she'd brought in the garden chair for me.

"Are you okay?" I asked.

She swept her shadowy hair from her face, inviting me to look my fill. "What do you think?"

I thought she looked great. The feebleness of last night had sloughed away and left her glowing and bubbly as ginger ale.

"You up for school?" she asked. "If you wanna cry off, no problem; I know you had a long night."

I had awakened her every thirty minutes before dropping off myself at six a.m., barely an hour ago, but my continued insomnia sustained me.

"I'm fine." A sudden thought occurred to me. "Where did you put that head from last night?"

"Buried it under the sweet gum," she said, as if she did such things at least once a week. She poured me a glass of milk. "I'm surprised you stayed. After you hit your aunt, you ran away."

"Where would I have run?"

"Back to her."

"For the last time, she doesn't want me."

"You sure?" Rosalee said, handing me a cream-colored envelope. "That came in the mail yesterday."

It was from Aunt Ulla. I read it, then laughed, muscles unknotting. "She just wants to know if I still want to go to Helsinki with her for Christmas."

"Do you?"

"Of course."

Rosalee stared incredulously. "I thought y'all hated each other."

"We do, but that's no reason to ruin Christmas. If you wanted, you could come with us."

"I could do a heap of things." Rosalee stabbed her fork at my plate. "Why ain't you eating?"

I looked at the food: sausages, biscuits, some white stuff.

I tried the white stuff first. "What is this?"

"Grits." She shook her head sadly at my blank face. "Figures you wouldn't know about grits, that I'd have to feed you your heritage a spoonful at a time. So to speak."

"Ah," I said, making the connection. "It's a black thing."

"Mm." Rosalee sipped her coffee. "Next week I'll show you how to cornrow your hair. By the end of the month you'll be ready for the naming ceremony. Hanna won't do. Maybe LaJonda or Tyroniqua?"

"I didn't know you had a sense of humor," I said, pleasantly surprised.

"Well, I'm still not sure you have one. You're like your father. The funnier the joke, the blanker his face would get, until I just had to smack some understanding into him. Maybe I should try that with you."

"Smacking me?!"

"Sure. Aversion therapy. I'm not averse—ha, ha—to beating a sense of humor into you. If you're gone stay with me, you'll need one."

"What about partiality therapy?" I offered, eager for alternatives. "Instead of smacking me, you could reward me. With gold stars and cupcakes."

But Rosalee was implacable. "Not a cupcake in the place. No snacks. Just smacks. How 'bout I owe you one?"

"A snack?"

She smiled. I'd never seen her smile before. She was *smiling* at me. "You wish."

When Wyatt showed up at the bike rail after school and begged me to let him take me to Smiley's, I agreed, keen to go anywhere with anyone willing to listen to me talk about Rosalee.

Smiley's, as always, was packed with kids yelling happily over one another and over the rusty old jukebox that played nothing but rusty old songs. A rich, battered smell permeated everything, as though the whole building had been deep-fried.

I was starving, so Wyatt and I split three orders of shrimp ceviche—unusual fare for a diner, but it was Smiley's specialty. As I ate, I told Wyatt about Rosalee. Not about hitting her, but about how nice she'd been that morning. I had just launched into an explanation of partiality therapy when Wyatt began to laugh.

"Sorry. I just never heard anybody go on and on about her *mother*."

"I'm boring you?"

"No, it's great. And Rosalee's great. I wish I got along with Ma like that."

"Last night was so bad—you have no idea how bad—but today . . . what a difference. She likes me!"

Wyatt looked baffled. "What's not to like? You're amazing. Even though you were pissed at me last night, you still helped my dad. Even though the Key burned you." He took my hand gently. "How is it?"

"Almost completely healed." I shrugged it off. "How's your dad?"

"He's all right. Ma and me patched him up when we got home." Wyatt took a deep breath and squeezed my hand hard enough to hurt. "Look, when I gave you that drink, I wasn't trying to kill you. We all take turns being bait; I should've explained it first. I take all this shit for granted—hunting, all that—and I didn't think how scared you might be. I'm sorry."

I shrugged that off too. I just couldn't dredge up any anger. Rosalee liked me.

What else mattered?

"Apology accepted." I celebrated with another mouthful of ceviche and noticed him staring. "What?"

He looked thoughtful. "What were you gone wish for?"

I choked on the lime-flavored shrimp. "Pardon?"

"Touching the Key wouldn't've burned your hand unless you tried to make a wish."

"Jailhouse Rock" blared through the diner, soundtracking my scramble for an explanation.

"Tell me the truth," Wyatt said, his eyes narrowed suspiciously. "Did you go to my house to turn me into a frog?"

I laughed and so did he. We laughed for a long time, but he was still waiting for an answer. Before I could think of one that wouldn't be incriminating, a crash overrode all the noise.

A busboy had dropped the tray he'd been carrying, and its contents were now splattered across the peach and white tile. He turned red amidst the whistles and mocking applause. "You better stop clapping and start watching those milkshakes," he yelled. "A milkworm's loose."

The taunting ended in a hurry as the diners inspected their food.

I frowned at Wyatt. "What's a milkworm?"

"A parasite," he said calmly, "that likes calcium. The kind in milk, but especially the kind in your bones. Trust me, you don't wanna swallow one of those. Gotta be careful drinking milk or anything made with milk."

"First I had to give up coffee; now I have to give up milk?"

"You don't have to give it up," said Wyatt. "Milkworms're easy to avoid. If your food or drink looks like it's boiling or bubbling, toss it."

We only had ceviche and slushies at our table, not to mention the fact that I was sitting with sharp-eyed Wyatt, so I stopped worrying.

"So what were you gone wish for?" Sharp-eyed and persistent. But I couldn't tell him I'd bashed his hero on the head.

Wyatt's annoying persistence made me feel crazy reckless. I couldn't tell him about Rosalee, but I could tell him about *me.* When "Tell Him" started playing on the jukebox, I took it as a sign.

"Hanna?"

"I'm manic-depressive, and sometimes when I get really worked up I hallucinate."

"*What?*"

Did he really want me to repeat it?

"You hallucinate?" he said, like he was testing it. "You mean, you only think you see things? Like your dead father?"

"No. That's real. He's the one who told me about wishing on the Key and about the panic grass. Poppa was only a hallucination before I moved here. That's why Aunt Ulla sent me to the psych ward that first time. I kept telling people he wasn't dead because I could still talk to him. So they locked me away."

"Damn, Hanna." He looked stunned. "In an insane asylum? What was that like? Were there mean orderlies? Did they tie you in a straitjacket?"

"It's only like that in the movies. I was there a whole month this one time, and the worst that ever happened was some kid threw a tantrum when a bee got onto our floor. That kid did *not* like bees." I took a sip of my slushie. "It's like nursery school. Except even nursery school kids get to go to the bathroom without adult supervision."

"So it's not that bad?"

"It's horrible! People telling you where to eat, when to sleep, when to bathe, what you can have, what you can't have. People even telling you how you *feel*, like they have any idea. All they do is make guesses. Mostly the wrong ones. Do you know how many times I was misdiagnosed before they finally figured out what was wrong with me? But Aunt Ulla didn't care how incompetent the doctors were. She used any excuse to send me back to that place."

"Why?"

"Because she hates me. And because . . ."The old bitterness was forced to scooch over to make room for chagrin. "Sometimes I think I'm okay, and so I stop taking my pills. And when I stop taking my pills, sometimes I do bad things."

"Like?"

A slew of criminal and immoral activities stirred in my memory. So many that I was surprised at myself.

It had been a busy year for me.

"What?"

I smiled at Wyatt. "I don't want to blow your mind—"

"Aw come on."

"—but the last thing I did that set Aunt Ulla off wasn't even that bad. About a month, maybe two months ago, I decided to start wearing purple to honor Poppa's memory—because it was his favorite color. And so I needed to buy purple fabric. I borrowed Aunt Ulla's credit card and bought five thousand dollars worth of purple everything. When she got the bill, all hell broke loose and she tried to send me back to the psych ward. Forever."

"What did you do?"

"I ran away to Rosalee," I told him, skipping the part about the rolling pin. He didn't need to know everything. "I figured small-town life would be restful and restorative."

We had a good laugh over that one and then sat in a comfortable silence. For me, a relieved silence. It felt good to disclose your darkest, innermost secret to someone and have him still like you after hearing it. Almost as good as having a *mother* who liked you.

Wyatt smiled at me speculatively. "I bet you have some kick-ass pharmaceuticals."

"Define kick-ass."

"Valium?"

"No."

"Prozac?"

"No."

"Ritalin?"

"Yes."

"Score!"

"It's old, from when I was thirteen. That's when they told me I was hyper. And then one day I smashed out all the lights in our house and all the lights up and down the street because I was scared all the light would attract something bad from outer space. Like a giant alien moth or something. That's when they decided I was suffering from *anxiety*, if you can believe it, and started feeding me Xanax. Stupid doctors."

Wyatt was highly amused. "Alien moths?"

"Don't make fun of me, Wyatt. I remember thinking that night in the dark park that you were a robot. I remember wanting to cut you open with the machete to see the gears with my own eyes."

He gave me such a look.

I sighed. "Maybe I shouldn't have said that out loud."

He laughed hard. "Jesus Christ. You *are* insane! You really are."

"Yes, but it's okay," I assured him, taking my emergency stash of pills from my purse to show him. "This is what I take now. Lithium. And this one's Seroquel. They keep me nice and even." When I took them, of course.

When *had* I last taken my pills? Not since Rosalee had asked me to, maybe a week ago. I liked waiting for her to insist that I take them. Hopefully I wouldn't have to wait too much longer.

Wyatt was still chuckling and shaking his head. "So many things about you make sense now."

I moved my chair next to Wyatt's so I could kiss him real

good, kiss him for laughing instead of running for the door. His mouth was sweetly acidic from the shrimp.

"A lot of my old friends turned on me when they found out," I told him. "I'm glad you're not like that."

"Hell, I can't exactly throw stones," he said, smooching my ear. "I'm only sorta human. Pop said he told you?"

"*You* could have told me. You know I like freaks."

"Well, how freaky is this?" He held out his hand under the table, angled so that I could see it. I gasped when the skin turned melty and receded toward his wrist, leaving the bones of his hand bare.

Like the Key, Wyatt's bones were glossy and black.

Seconds later, his hand reshaped itself and was once again whole and normal. Normal-*looking*, anyway.

"You're lucky you have me, freak boy," I told him, sliding my hand over his prickly scalp. "Who else would put up with you?"

"I would."

Petra stood beside our table, holding a glass bowl of strawberry ice cream too big for her skinny hands. She frowned at me. "*Anybody* would. Don't let her bad-mouth you, Wyatt."

Wyatt looked touched. "You sticking up for me, Pet?"

She sat at our table as though she had been invited, making eyes at Wyatt. "Friends look out for each other, right?"

He was sitting with me, with his arm around *me*, and it was like I'd vanished.

Petra noticed my pill bottles on the table and grabbed one. "Lithium?" she read, shocked. "I thought they only gave this stuff to whack jobs." She peered at me. "Are you a whack job?"

I snatched the bottle from her. "Absolutely." Since Rosalee and Wyatt didn't care, I didn't care what other people thought.

Petra looked at Wyatt. "So that's what you're into now? Whack jobs?"

"Pretty much," he said, and smiled at me. "But I knew she was crazy when she begged me to take her hunting."

"Shut up." Petra turned her amazed eyes on me. "You went on a hunt?"

"Last night," I told her, mollified.

While she gaped at me in wonder, her spoon halfway to her mouth, I noticed the milkworm curled in the bubbling dollop of ice cream. I grabbed the spoon, but she didn't let go of it as easily as she had my pill bottle, and the contents of the spoon spilled all over her black camisole: the ice cream and the fat, white, finger-length milkworm.

Petra jerked backward and screamed as it slithered over her chest and up her pale throat. It probably would have made it into her open mouth had I not slapped the worm against her neck as if it were a mosquito, not thinking about how gross it would look—the stuff that came out of the milkworm was cheese-colored.

Petra squealed as she scrubbed her neck with paper napkins from the dispenser on the table. I took a few for myself before she used them all. *I* was the one who should have been squealing. My hand felt as though a garden slug had exploded all over it.

"It's just a milkworm, Pet," Wyatt said, when her whining didn't end soon enough for him. "Don't be so—"

"Cowardly?" she screamed, hurt. "Is that what you think? Is that why you sat there on standby waiting for me to swallow that thing?"

"Pet—"

"Screw you! I don't even care anymore. I found somebody else. Did you know that? He's tall and muscular and *he* doesn't mind taking care of me."

"The way you took care of Michael?" said Wyatt in a low voice.

Petra stilled, as if his words had killed her.

"I'm trying to help you," he said.

She slapped him across the face; the sound was loud enough to draw every eye in the diner. "Shit on your help!"

Wyatt reached for her and Petra flinched, as though she thought he was going to return the slap. He didn't, of course. He lowered his hand and looked so disappointed in her that she ran from him, right out of the diner.

"Who's Michael?" I asked, when the dust had settled.

"Her younger brother." Wyatt absently rubbed the red handprint on his face, staring down at his empty plate. "He died while they were walking home from the movies. A cackler bit his legs off, and you know what Pet did? She left him there. Alone on the street, in the dark, with a cackler snacking on him.

"I was patrolling with the Mortmaine when it happened and I was the first one there. I *saw* her run. If the other Mortmaine had seen her run, they'd have put her down the same as they put down that cackler.

"I tried to save Michael, but he'd lost too much blood. I tried to save Pet, too, in a way. I thought maybe she just panicked, and if she had it to do all over, she'd step up. Maybe take an interest in helping other people, since she failed with

Michael. Out of guilt if nothing else. But now, I don't know. To scream over a *milkworm*?" He gave me a desperate look, as though I could explain Petra to him.

"Maybe she just doesn't like creepy-crawlies."

"Then she shouldn't have moved here," he said sharply, as though I'd given the wrong answer. "Here, there's nothing *but* creepy-crawlies." He spat out the word. "So many, there's no room for cowards.

"No room at all."

Chapter Twenty-four

After the diner drama, I was glad to go home to Rosalee, who was in the kitchen in her red apron and bare feet. I couldn't believe she was home so early in the afternoon. "Go take your pills," she said. "I'll put dinner on."

I took my pills gladly, because I had a mother who cared whether I was sane, and then went down to the kitchen with my schoolbooks. "What are you making?"

"Tortilla soup. And before you ask, no, it's not a black thing."

"Sounds great." I was still hungry. I hadn't been eating right the past few days, and my stomach was determined to make up for lost time.

I dropped my books on the table. "There's about fifty messages on the machine."

She paused from chopping bright red peppers to look at me. "I know."

"I bet most of them are from that snake." I poured myself a glass of milk.

"Which snake? I know several."

"That Jaguar snake. The one who likes to smack you around."

She tilted her head to the side, pretending to think about it. "The one whose balls I crushed?"

"Maybe it's not him," I conceded, and pulled out the purple chair . . . and nearly dropped my milk to the floor. "You bought a new chair! For me!"

She shook her head sadly. "Ain't very observant, are you?"

I'd been so right to go on that hunt. Now that she was over the initial shock of seeing me covered in blood and guts, she understood that I could take care of myself. She had accepted me. The chair proved it.

I sat in the bright purple chair, which almost perfectly matched my dress. Perfect, perfect, perfect. Sitting had never felt so awesome.

"What's the homework?"

"Geometry," I said.

"Only thing I was any good at in school was math and languages. There were set rules. You followed them. The end. You never had to give an opinion about quadratic functions."

"I know. My old English teacher once asked me why it's important that the character of Iago in *Othello* is motiveless. And I thought, who said it was important? It's so arbitrary."

"Joosef loved Shakespeare. Any play. He was a drama freak. I hate all that stuff."

"Did you have anything in common with Poppa?"

"We were both good-looking." She munched one of the red peppers thoughtfully. "I thought he was beautiful. I used to take pictures of him. Wanna see?"

"Do you have to ask?"

Rosalee rushed out of the kitchen, then rushed back with a Candies shoe box full of photos. She tossed the box at me and then went back to her post at the chopping block.

I looked at the pictures: Poppa young and skinny and half-naked on a beach, hair bleached almost white by the sun; in a purple sweater with white breath issuing from his laughing mouth; on a ferry, his eyes as gray as the sea.

I stroked my fingertips across the pictures, across Poppa's face. "Why aren't there any of you together?"

"We weren't together," said Rosalee, so abruptly that for a long moment I was too abashed to speak. But one question wouldn't be denied, one I'd always wanted to ask.

"Why didn't you abort me?"

"I knew Joosef would want you. Least I could do for him. He was . . . nice."

"He loved you."

"Many men do," she said matter-of-factly. "It's a Price thing, this ability to fascinate."

"Could your mother fascinate?" I asked her as she bewitchingly stirred the soup pot.

"Oh, yeah. Daddy wouldn't let her outside unless he was with her. I kid you not. Me either, after I hit puberty. I had to sneak out. I wasn't exactly a model daughter." She pressed the back of her hand to her lips, as if wanting to press the words back into her mouth.

"That doesn't mean you won't be a model mother." Her unhappiness weighed on me, but I didn't have the skills to deal with my own problems, let alone hers. "You can be one."

"It's nice you think so." She lowered her hand, her lips red from the pressure she'd put on them. "Obviously, you won the bet. You can stay. I know you already know that, but it needed to be said."

It wasn't ladylike to whoop, so I just bounced in my chair a little.

"You seem like a sweet girl, but sweet turns sour in this town pretty damn fast. Why you wanna be as sour as all the rest of us Porterenes is beyond me, but . . . what's funny?"

"When did you decide I was sweet: before or after I hit you with the lamp?"

She grimaced. "Hey, that reminds me—if you're gone stay here, you need a shrink."

The bouncing stopped. "Why?"

"Because last time I checked, manic depression don't just clear up on its own. You need therapy."

"Therapists don't know anything. They can't even decide what flavor of crazy I am. This year it's manic depression. Next year it'll probably be senile dementia. The only thing I need is my pills, and I can get those from a regular doctor. I can handle my situation *by myself.*"

"I seen how you handle situations *by yourself.*" She made a big production out of rubbing her head.

"You just want to put me in a hospital like Aunt Ulla. Admit it! I swear to God if you try to put me in a hospital, I'll . . ." What? Bash her again? Hamstring her? Nothing seemed bad enough.

"I don't mean for you go to the hospital," said Rosalee gently. "I just got back from visiting a woman named Dr. Geller. She works outta her home. It's nice, and you'll only have to go on Wednesdays."

I knew intellectually that I needed a shrink, but Aunt Ulla had always foisted me off on them for every little thing. Much easier than dealing with me herself. What if Rosalee developed the same strategy?

Fucking shrinks.

I hadn't been in a hurry to revisit downsquare after the Melissa situation and the hunt. It had taken on a horrific cast in my memory: corpses, noxious smells, hardheads. But as Rosalee and I ambled about, I realized that downsquare was just another part of town, not as pretty and historic as the area where I lived—the square, Wyatt called it—but it had its charms.

"It's divided into two parts," Rosalee explained, jumping onto the base of a streetlamp. "Come up here."

I did, feeling like the guy in *Singin' in the Rain.*

"See that gazebo way in the distance? That's Portero Park, so this area is the part of downsquare called parkside. Now, see the trees way *way* beyond the gazebo? That's the dark park. The other side of the dark park is where darkside begins. It's darkside you have to watch out for—that's where all the weird shit happens."

"That flying leech didn't attack me darkside."

Rosalee hopped off the lamp. "*Most* of the weird shit."

She took me to an eatery with no signage on or over the door, but they had the best taquitos ever, crispy and spicy, well worth my scorched tongue.

As we walked the food off, my elbow twanged periodically, as it had since the wishing incident. I ignored it, the way I ignored all the unsettling things that had occurred that night. I ignored it and focused on the joy of being with Rosalee.

Poppa and I had often taken walks together, but walking with Rosalee was different. Whenever Poppa and I had traveled anywhere, people scrutinized our mismatched skin with suspicion or bewilderment, wondering at our relationship. But with Rosalee, the resemblance was so obvious, who could doubt our kinship?

Rosalee pointed out a cool fabric store, and I went inside and bought three yards of green angora to make Wyatt a coat, never mind that it was October and still too hot for even a sweater.

People sat or swung or rocked on porches, watching their kids playing, watching one another. Watching us. No, not *us*. Rosalee.

Several people whipped out their cells to snap her picture as we went by, and not just because of her tight clothes. I felt like I was the only thing keeping them from rushing her, as though she were a rock star and I her matronly aunt. But despite the attention, Rosalee only had eyes for me.

On one street, however, we weren't quite as welcome, a street with trees marching along either side of it with military precision. People crouched in the shade beneath the trees, watching us with guarded suspicion; walking past them was like walking past poorly leashed Rottweilers.

"What's their problem?" I asked, moving closer to Rosalee.

"This is Dark Peach Street," she said, unruffled by the behavior of her fellow Porterenes. "The peaches that grow on these trees are good luck, but they're jealously guarded. Unless you aim to get stoned with peach pits, don't ever take any unless offered."

In honor of Dark Peach Street, we walked to Alcide's Cajun Market and bought a bag of regular peaches from a strapping white-haired man in suspenders. Rosalee spoke to him in German and he answered back, grinning ear to ear as he flirted with her.

"You did use to live in Germany, didn't you?" I asked when we'd moved on, the peach warm and sweet and welcome within my taquito-ravaged mouth. "I remember Poppa said you guys met on a plane in Hamburg."

She didn't say anything. I hoped she hadn't gone close-mouthed on me again.

"Why did you move to Germany?" I prompted.

"I went to school there, in Heidelberg. It was different, so opposite of what I'd grown up with here. Germany was changing—the Berlin Wall had fallen. Seemed like a good time for change."

"Did you change?"

"No." She shrugged fatalistically. "Once a downsquare girl, always a downsquare girl."

"Is your family still downsquare?"

"Nope. Moved up to Lamartine."

"They live on our street?"

Before I could get excited about the idea of grandparents and cousins, she said, "Yeah. In the cemetery."

"*All* of them?"

"Wasn't very many to start with. Just me, the folks, and a couple of great-aunts. Wanna see my old house?"

It was just down the street, a one-story with orange shutters and a kid's bike lying forgotten on the lawn.

Rosalee seemed to empty as she stared at the house. "See that tree?" She pointed to the cottonwood shading the lawn. "When I'd get in trouble, Daddy'd make me come out here and rip a branch off that tree, and he'd switch me with it."

"Switch?"

She pretended to whip at my legs.

"He *hit* you with it?"

"Corporal punishment." She stared at the house grimly. "You didn't miss a thing not growing up in the South."

"We moved to Dallas when I was seven," I said to distract her. "I've lived in the South for nine years."

"It's not the same." Her black eyes melted a little. "You were with Joosef far away from here. Happy. Free."

"I would have been happy growing up here."

"It's dangerous here." Her hands drifted up to hide in

her armpits. "I always thought that was why Daddy was the way he was. Because he was so desperate to protect me. And when you showed up, I thought, now I'm gone have to be like Daddy; how else can I keep her safe? But I couldn't be like that. I couldn't hurt you."

Strange how she didn't understand that her coldness had been more hurtful than any beating would have been.

"So I figured if I bided my time, you'd be scared away on your own. My hope was that you'd only *see* something scary and not get eaten by it. My hope was that you'd give up.

"Then you came home from the fucking *dark park* with a severed head. And you were so nonchalant about it. God, that pissed me off."

But she didn't look pissed. She didn't even sound pissed. The more she talked, the deader she looked and sounded. As if her childhood home was drawing something vital from her.

"You were afraid for me?" I said, touching her arm.

"Partly." She pulled away from my touch, her eyes never leaving the house. "But mostly, when you managed to keep yourself safe, I realized that the way I'd been raised was so *unnecessary*. All the switchings. The beatings. The spying. The interrogation.

"I'd go out for five minutes and it was where'd you go,

who'd you see, who saw you, why'd it take so long? Daddy'd ask me about boys I knew or boys he thought I might know and whether I'd ever let them do this or that to me, all these detailed questions. Guys ask me all the time, where'd you learn to fuck like that? I tell them, from my father. He gave me a lifetime of great ideas with all his questions."

It was like free-falling through slime just *listening* to her, so I couldn't imagine what she must be feeling. I would have taken her hand, but she was still hiding them.

"Grandpa . . . he molested you?"

"No," she said, her voice disturbingly wistful. "But maybe he should've. Maybe then he wouldn't've hated me as much.

"But he didn't like me like that. He didn't want *anybody* to like me like that. I had to sneak out if I wanted to be with anybody, and I always got caught."

She was shivering, goose bumps popping out on her arms, despite the heat. "I thought it'd be so great when I finally escaped that house, but it's like I'm still trapped in the back room alone and—"

I stood before her and blocked her view of the house—its view of her. "You're not alone anymore. You're not trapped. Or should I burn down that house to prove it to you?"

She was so startled, she dropped her hands. "Don't talk crazy."

"I *am* crazy. That's the point; I have a ready-made alibi."

The thought of fire thawed the cold cast of her face and lit the dark oil of her eyes. "*Would* you burn it down?"

"Got matches?" Her interest was firing me up. "Because if that's what you need, I'll do it."

She *wanted* me to do it. I could see it. *Just ask me.*

Ask me!

She opened her mouth. I was prepared for anything, except the shrill voice that interrupted.

"Hey! Rosalee? Is that you?"

A dried stick of a woman stood on the porch of the house next door to Rosalee's childhood home, a woman with inexplicable old-lady hair, parted on the right and slicked to the side in a weird white bouffant.

"Hey, Miz Holly." Rosalee had regained her balance, all the burning anticipation of arson drained out of her; her hands came to rest lightly on her hips. "Ain't seen you in a long time." She didn't sound upset about it.

Miz Holly pushed up her glasses, all the better to see me with. "This the daughter I been hearing about?"

"Yes'm."

"She's so pretty. Just like you. Hope she only takes after you in looks. Or is she running wild in the streets the way you used to?" To me, Miz Holly said, "I could tell you stories about this one—"

"G'night, Miz Holly," Rosalee said, bright and mean. "Tell your son I said hi. And your husband."

"I . . . okay."

We walked back the way we'd come. "I guess we won't be sending her a Christmas card," I said.

Rosalee threw an evil look over her shoulder at Miz Holly. "She was always ratting me out to my folks."

"So you got back at her by sleeping with her son *and* her husband."

Rosalee's laugh was as evil and gorgeous as a serpent's tooth. "Am I that transparent?"

"It's what I would have done," I admitted. "When I was back in Dallas, I decided to sleep with all the boys in my class in alphabetical order, and they totally went along with it. It's like you said—it's easy to fascinate men."

She looked at me, half-shocked, half-amused. "You went to bed with all the boys in your class?"

"I never even got to the *B*s," I said, swinging the bag of peaches. "Too many *A*s for little ole me. I got bored after Armbruster and called it off."

"You're definitely my daughter," said Rosalee, chuckling, halting conversations midsentence as people marveled at the sound of her laughter.

I wanted to burn something for her so badly I felt sick with it. I wanted to tell her I'd do anything for her, but my heart was too full to speak.

I was her daughter.

Definitely.

Chapter Twenty-Five

On Wednesday I tried not to think about the trip to the shrink all day, but after school, when I could no longer avoid it, I began to shake. When Wyatt asked to drive me home, I let him, but a few blocks from my house, I made him detour into an empty lot so I could drag him into the backseat.

I wanted to eat up some time before I had to go home, but not much time was eaten.

"That didn't take long," I griped, retrieving my discarded underpants from the footwell.

Wyatt zipped up his pants, grinning and sweating and vibrant beside me on the leather seat. "Wasn't supposed to," he said. "Afternoons and backseats are for quickies. Everybody knows that." He slung his arm around my shoulders and kissed me hard on my throat, hard enough to stop my breath for a second. "I like your neck."

The way he said it made me smile, as though he were admitting a shameful secret. "Really?"

"Mm." He kissed my jugular. "It's swanlike."

"I love swans." I pulled away from his admiring kisses and rested my chin against the top of the backseat, staring out the rearview window at the high yellow grass and pine saplings bending in the gusty wind.

I watched the gray sky and prayed for a tornado. "If I were a swan, I wouldn't need a tornado."

"What?" He was no longer touching me, but he watched me, waiting for that after-sex wall to come down.

"If I had wings I could fly away."

"Why you wanna fly away?"

I looked at Wyatt, shocked by the sting of tears in my eyes. "I don't want to go home yet."

The threat of my tears didn't worry him—he was beyond worry. Something bright and irrepressible crackled deep in his eyes, like fireflies in a beer bottle. "I don't aim to take you home yet. I wanna show you something."

He pulled me out of the truck, and the wind nearly stripped off my dress. The air was moist and unstable and promised rain. I stayed by the truck, trying to keep my hair out of my face while Wyatt surveyed the lot.

"There," he said, and ran through the brilliant yellow grass to a flailing sapling ten yards away. When he reached the tree, he turned to face me and stepped sideways into the wind . . . and disappeared.

My first thought was of Runyon's daughter and how she'd vanished off the sidewalk one day, vanished and was never seen again.

"Wyatt!" I ran forward, screaming, and when he reappeared in mid-sideways step, I ran smack into him. We both hit the ground on our butts. Unlike me, Wyatt was laughing.

"How cool was that?" he said.

I crawled through the yellow grass toward him, my right elbow jingling and jangling as I clutched the front of his green shirt. "You used the hidden doors, didn't you?"

"They finally showed me how," he said, so full of good cheer I wanted to shake him. "I only just got the hang of it."

I shook him. "You scared the shit out of me! And do you even know how many laws of nature you just totally destroyed?"

"Not nature as *I* know it!" He lifted me off my feet and twirled me around the lot.

"Is this a happy dance?" I yelled, not wanting to laugh, but laughing anyway. "This is so transy. I'm telling everyone."

"Tell 'em!" Wyatt set me back on my feet and kissed me all over my face. "When they start clowning me, I'll just make my escape." He slid to the right with a flourish and vanished. Seconds later he reappeared, sliding to the left. Then he started strutting around like he owned the planet.

I smacked the back of his head. "Stop showing off." But I was grinning as I said it; his excitement was catching. "How are you able to disappear like that?" I asked as the happy dance worked itself out of his system.

"I didn't disappear," he corrected. "Not the way you mean. I didn't pop out of existence. It's more like . . . taking a short-cut. But instead of going down an alley, you go through a door."

"A *hidden* door."

"It's funny, though, cuz they're not hidden." He was crazy excited, like a lit firecracker before the moment of explosion. "They're *everywhere*."

"But why do you have to go through them sideways?"

My cluelessness prompted him to give a demonstration.

We walked back to his dusty green truck, and he opened the driver's-side door. "If you tried to go through this door like it was the front door of your house, you couldn't get in. To get through this truck door, you gotta climb in. Hidden doors are the same way; they're all doors, but they ain't all shaped the same. Some of 'em you can only go through sideways, like that one over there."

He gestured toward the sapling where he'd disappeared, obviously seeing something I couldn't. "Or for *that* door"—he pointed past the front of the truck at thin air—"you'd have to fall through."

I scanned the city-block-size lot, empty except for Wyatt's green truck. "Are they all over the lot?"

"There's six here, just in this one bit of space." He shut the truck door and leaned back against it, regarding me with eyes as electric as any lightning bolt. "You know how many times I been dead-ended by some nightmare-looking thing and had to fight my way free? Fight to the death? But now I know— there's always a way out."

"There always was for you. It's in your blood. In your bones, anyway." I settled next to him and pinched his side, because I could. Because he was there and because he was real. "Have you ever left the world the way Anna did?"

He pinched me back, smiling. "I don't aim to go out of the world. The last person who did was that prick Runyon. To hell with that."

"Do the hidden doors lead to weird places? Weird flying-leech places?"

"The elders told us to watch out for the doors near the Keys, cuz doors near that much power could lead to any damn thing. The other ones, though"—he waved his hand around the lot—"they just lead to places around Portero. The Mortmaine've mapped 'em over the years, but I don't exactly have 'em all memorized.

"The door by the tree led upsquare to Torcido Road. But that one . . ." He was pointing beyond the front of his truck, a teasing glint in his eyes as he turned to me. "You wanna see where that one leads?"

To his startlement, I grabbed his hand and pulled him around to the front of the truck. Hell yes, I wanted to see where it led: Fountain Square, Detroit, Narnia. Any place was better than therapy.

He laughed. "Atta girl."

I thought of the time Shoko had taken me home. "I hope I don't hurl this t—" I gasped and grabbed my elbow. It didn't hurt, but it was crawlingly uncomfortable.

Wyatt put his hand on my shoulder. "Feel like something just whacked your funny bone?"

"Yes! It's been doing that ever since the hunt."

He smiled knowingly. "The night you made a wish—the Key changed something in you. You'll get that tingle every time you pass a hidden door." He pulled me back, away from the door I couldn't see, and the tingle became easier to bear.

"Holy shit, Hanna." He looked at me as though he'd never seen me before. "If you were marked, you could probably go through a hidden door on your own."

He showed me a fresh, almost wet-looking glyph on his well-defined upper arm, a green tattoo of a door with an eye in the center.

"No, thanks. I prefer my skin smooth and untouched."

He bit my lip. "Liar."

"Stop that." I pushed him away, laughing. "Or did you change your mind about the door?"

"Hell, no." He grabbed my hand and pulled me into the horrid tingling. "Step forward on three."

My hand trembled in his as I gazed at the yellow grass whipping against our legs and the hidden door only Wyatt could see.

"One, two, three."

We stepped forward and fell through the grass.

Everything went black for a second, my stomach in free fall . . . and then my knees buckled as gravity caught up with me on a sidewalk somewhere downsquare.

Definitely downsquare, I decided, noting the seedy shops in need of paint squatting next door to saggy-porched houses. The people looked as worn and lived-in as the shops and were wholly unimpressed with our sudden appearance.

Except one girl, halfway down the block.

She'd fallen against the beige wall of a dollar store, holding her hand over her chest as she watched us with bugged eyes. I took her in at a glance: yellow shirt and blue jeans, no visible scars, innocent eyes.

"Stupid transy," I said gleefully, when she turned and ran. At least I was no longer *that* person.

"I know where this is," Wyatt said, looking around. "There's Gourmandise." I followed him across the street to a sweet-shop, whose display of sticky treats and chocolate confections made me want to press my nose to the window and lick the glass.

Wyatt dragged me around to the back of the shop. "I saved the owner's nephew once," he explained, "and so she gives me free goodies. But she don't want people seeing her be nice; it'd kill her repu—"

His words died away as we both beheld Petra on the back stoop of the sweetshop, kissing a boy.

The spark that had been blazing in Wyatt's eyes all afternoon fizzled out. "Pet?"

Petra came up for air, flushed and merry; she became even merrier at the sight of Wyatt's shock. "Well, hey there," she greeted him. "The freaks don't only come out at night, I see." She looked at me. "Or the loonies."

I sighed. "Hi, Petra."

"God, curb the enthusiasm, Hanna." She turned to the huge brick of meat in the floury apron she'd been making out with. "Babe, that's Wyatt and his girlfriend, Hanna. Guys, this is Francis Allen, but call him Frankie. Otherwise he gets pissed. And Frankie, watch out for that one." She pointed at me. "She's got a few screws loose."

Frankie was a real bruiser, at least six feet tall, with hands big enough to palm the moon. He looked at me with interest, his eyes small and penny-colored. "Loose screws, huh? What are you? Schizo?"

"Manic-depressive," I told him.

Frankie turned to Wyatt. "You don't mind that your girlfriend's got loose screws?"

Wyatt didn't even look at me; all his attention was focused on Petra. "She's not my girlfriend."

Each word fell on me like a whip, each syllable laid open my skin.

"That's smart," said Frankie. "Commitment is for old married people. Pet here knows I'm just using her for sex."

Petra gave her man a fond squeeze. "You're such a bastard."

"Girls are like the ice cream at Baskin-Robbins," said Frankie, enjoying his bastard role. "You have to try 'em all before you can pick a favorite."

"I know Wyatt's favorite flavor," said Petra. "Chocolate-vanilla swirl. With nuts, right, Hanna? Uh-oh. Frankie, look at her. See the steam coming outta her ears? Go get us some lattes, quick! That'll cool her down."

"We don't want anything," said Wyatt, feeling free to speak for me.

"Your loss," said Frankie. "One latte coming up, babe." He hustled into the shop.

"Why're you being so rude?" Petra skipped down the stairs toward Wyatt, ballerina-like in her black tights and flat shoes. "Frankie works here. He can hook us up."

"Where'd you find that guy?" Wyatt asked heatedly. "Under a rock?"

"He just likes to kid," she said, her eyes lighting up at the mere thought of him. "Frankie's really very sweet."

"As toe fungus. Why don't you just admit you're trying to make me jealous?"

Petra laughed in his face, a good long laugh that knocked Wyatt down a peg or three. "Like I knew you were gone come sneaking around in the alley behind a shop where my boyfriend works. *Qué una* ego, Wyatt. I am so over you."

Wyatt tried to pretend he wasn't hurt. "*Be* over me, but I hope you don't think for one second that that prick is gone look after you."

"Which prick would that be?" said Frankie. He stomped down the steps; the latte in his giant fist looked like a sippy cup. "This prick?" He passed the drink to Petra and hauled her to his side, where she posed like a little kid next to a mountain. "You need me to squash this guy?"

Petra tut-tutted. "Wyatt ain't easily squashed, babe. Besides, Hanna'll do a better job than you ever could." The two of them looked at me.

But not Wyatt, still not Wyatt, who was frowning at the gray sky stretching over the alley. "You hear that?"

Frankie looked up, alarmed, like he could hear it too. Whatever it was. Petra and I exchanged clueless looks.

"Hear what?" she asked, sipping her latte.

"A flapping," said Wyatt, straining to hear. "Like wings. Like—"

"Blech!" Petra spat out her drink and dropped the cup; its contents exploded redly onto the ground. "The *fuck*."

"Sorry," said Frankie. "I must've given you one of the red teas by mistake."

"That didn't taste like tea! It tasted like bl—"

Frankie kissed her. For a bruiser, he had an intriguingly delicate technique. "I'm sorry," he said, cuddling her close, their blond hair tangled in a windblown knot. "Next time I'll let *you* make it. Okay?"

"Okay," Petra said, in this blissed-out tone. As she pulled Frankie back for more kisses, the strong wind blew her cup to my feet. The liquid coating the paper cup was pale and frothy, not at all red like I'd seen. Or imagined.

When Wyatt looked away from the sky to find Petra and Frankie all over each other, he grabbed my arm and dragged me out of the alley back to the hidden door that—oddly—we had to drop through again.

Back in the lot with the yellow grass, we climbed into Wyatt's truck, and the whole time he didn't say one word to me. He just drove me home in silence, smoldering volcano-like on the edge of eruption.

When he pulled up to the curb on Lamartine and waited for me to get out of his truck, I finally spoke. "If you're not over her, you should just say so."

"I don't wanna talk about her."

"Why? Because she's not into you anymore? Because she couldn't care less if—"

The volcano erupted. "You think she cares about that *asshole*? That he cares about her?"

"You don't know anything about him, Wyatt."

"You saw the way he spoke to her."

"He didn't say anything worse than what Petra says on a daily basis," I reminded him. "If you ask me, they're perfect for each other."

"Nobody did ask you!"

So unfair that my happy-dancing Wyatt was being held hostage by this sore-headed prick.

He turned away from me and gripped the steering wheel so hard it creaked. "Something about that guy is wrong."

"And I know what it is," I said. "It's that he's sniffing around your property, and you can't stand it."

"I'm over her, Hanna." He said it to the steering wheel. I was glad he was unable to look me in the eye when he lied to me.

"You wouldn't even admit that I was your girlfriend."

"Are you?" He looked at me then, and his eyes raked over me, a stranger's eyes. "We never even talked about it."

"I didn't think we had to. I thought you liked me as much as I like you. Am I wrong?"

He muttered something that sounded like "Stupid fucking question," but otherwise refused to answer.

"You've shared all these hard-core secrets with me, secrets even your best friends don't know. Or Petra or Shoko or any of the girls you've—"

"Hanna, I like you, okay. There, I said it—I like you!" He glowered at the dashboard. "You can be my girlfriend if you want."

"I don't need you to do me any goddamn favors, Wyatt!" I said, reduced to shouting at him. "What do *you* want?"

He didn't answer. Just sat, silent and unhappy. A herd of laughing kids zipped by the passenger-side window on Rollerblades. I hoped they never went from laughter to heartache as quickly as I had.

"Indecisiveness is a very unattractive trait in a man," I said, quoting my grandma Annikki. "Even when he's just a boy."

"I don't like to give up on people," he said at last. And that was all he said.

"Then don't give up on her. She needs you. I don't." I grabbed my pack and hopped out of his truck, feeling as though I'd left a part of myself behind with him—hopefully, the part that gave a damn. To hell with him.

To hell with everyone.

I slammed into the house and then froze when I found it much too dark. All the windows had been shuttered. A dim beam of light from the floor lamp, however, was aimed toward the hall leading to Rosalee's room. A deep, slow scratching rasped from the hallway, like a lazy dog begging to be let in, one scrape at a time.

I crept toward the hall, unnerved by the odd scratching, and came upon Rosalee in her sweats, hunkered down on one knee before the door of the linen closet, as graceless as I'd ever seen her, caught in the single beam of light like a burglar picked out of the darkness by an intrepid homeowner.

She even had a weapon, a knife she was using to carve a glyph into the door of the closet—a series of jagged peaks, like a child's drawing of mountains or the sea. A name was also carved into the door: Bonnie.

Rosalee lowered the knife and reached for the doorknob. It rattled briefly beneath her shaking hand, and with a quick twist, the door was open. Whatever she saw inside, or didn't see, seemed to deflate her.

"Rosalee?"

The look she gave me startled me, her eyes like cat eyes, reflecting the light of the lamp; but then I realized her eyes weren't reflective, they were *blue*, the same electric blue I'd seen after I'd made my wish.

"Rosalee?" Fear made my voice sharp.

"Bonnie?"

She blinked, and between one blink and the next, her eyes were black again. Puzzled. She stood and turned on the hall light. "What're you—?" She was brought up short by the knife in her hand. She flung it to the floor, just missing her bare toes.

She scurried away from the knife, from the hall, brushing past me. "Uh . . . Hanna . . . you're back early. How'd you like Dr. Geller?"

"You're possessed!"

"Hanna—"

"You are!" I yelled, following her as she went all over the house, turning on lights. I grabbed her arm at the stairs, brought her to a stop. "Did you hear me? You! Are! Possessed!"

She gripped the banister, as if it were the only thing that could keep her upright. "I know."

"*You know?*"

"After you hit me on the head, it came back to me." Her voice was small. "*He* came back. You woke him up." But she didn't say it accusingly; she was more bewildered than angry.

I was afraid to ask, but I had to. "Who did I wake up?"

"Runyon Grist."

The name hung in the air between us, like poison.

Chapter Twenty-six

Rosalee fled the house, seeking more light than a hundred-watt bulb could provide, but once on the porch, she slumped into the corner, hiding there like a shadow.

I sat across from her beneath the shelf of red chrysanthemums and tucked my feet under my dress, waiting for her to speak. I waited a long time, watching her face slip from composed to exalted to scared and then back. Weird seeing such emotions on a face normally devoid of all feeling.

"I guess I was about your age," she began haltingly. "I snuck out with this boy. Billy. Or Benny. Whatever. We drove to Houston to go to this Digital Underground concert, and I didn't get home until maybe two or three in the morning. I didn't have a house key, so I had to sneak in through my window. But I couldn't. Daddy was at my window, waiting for me. Told me he'd slut-proofed the house and that I'd have to spend the rest of the night elsewhere. I remember it was raining that night, because Daddy stuck his hands out the window and said he washed his hands of me. He was always saying stuff like that."

She trailed off in thought, perhaps remembering other stuff he'd said.

"Since he wouldn't let me in," she continued, "I just walked around, letting the rain fall into my eyes and down my throat, hoping I'd catch some sickness from the clouds and die. But I didn't die." I couldn't tell if the thought amazed or saddened her.

"You went to Runyon's house," I prompted her.

She began to fiddle with the key on her red bracelet. "Not on purpose. I don't think so. I just ended up there. This was right before the Mortmaine put down the wards to keep people out. I knew the Mayor had forbidden anybody to go inside, but that's why I went inside, *because* it was forbidden. I figured the Mayor'd strike me dead or something. I was hoping she would."

The Mayor who, according to Wyatt, could force a man to stick around even after he was dead. "What did she do?"

Rosalee snorted. "I never even saw her. It was Runyon I saw, sitting in the living room like something from a daguerreo-type, old and sad and faded. I'd heard all the stories about him." She grimaced. "How he raped and tortured some transy woman."

I thought of Anna and what I'd been told. "Is that what everyone thinks? That she was a transy?"

Rosalee removed her sweatshirt; she kept it a lot colder in the house than Portero probably ever got, even in winter. "Well, she wasn't from around here, that was for sure; nobody knew where she'd come from." She looked at me. "Why? You know something different?"

"No," I said quickly. The Ortigas and the Mortmaine had to be keeping Anna's origins secret for a reason. At any rate, it wasn't my secret to tell.

"So I knew all this bad stuff that Runyon had done, but seeing him just sitting there in his little house, it was hard to imagine him hurting anybody. He was just so average, you know? Not to mention he'd been dead for a zillion years already."

"Was he . . . rotting?"

"No." She thought about it. "He looked the way he had when he'd been alive, I guess. Except not as fit. He used to be Mortmaine, but when he was confined to his house, he let himself go. So by the time I saw him, he looked like an accountant or a file clerk. Pudgy and white, like somebody who sits inside on his ass all day. He had these long sideburns down to his jaw, and an old-fashioned Oliver Twist outfit—all he needed was a top hat."

"Did you talk to him?"

"Yeah. I said, 'You must've really loved your daughter.' Because the idea of it blew me away, the lengths he'd gone to just to make a way to get her back.

"He said, 'I *still* love her.' So I walked to the couch and sat next to him."

"You sat next to him!"

"He was a ghost," she assured me. "He didn't have a real body, just an image of one. He didn't even make a dent on the couch. And anyway, I had this big thing inside me I had to say, and I knew I needed to be sitting down when I said it."

"What did you say?"

"I said, 'I wish Daddy loved *me*.' And then I started crying."

She paused again for a long time, like the words were still big enough all these years later to choke her. "I cried for a long time. But it was the last time I cried. Cuz Runyon told me—I'll never forget it—'Love is a trap. Don't ever get caught.'

"When I asked him how to avoid it, he said, 'I can show you.' His eyes got huge like tunnels and sucked me in, but *he* was the one who came into me.

"Almost right away I felt a change. I walked out of his house, and it was like I could do anything. I didn't care what Daddy thought or what the neighbors thought. Not even the Mortmaine, who were out in the dawn light carving glyphs into the sidewalk to make the ward. You should've seen how they looked at me. Normally I would've been apologetic, but I just walked right by 'em. From then on, I was gone do what I wanted when I wanted."

Rosalee's lip curled humorlessly. "That lasted about five minutes. While I was walking home, a car lost control in the rain and plowed right into me. I fractured my skull. I think I was in a coma for two months? Something like that? I forgot all about Runyon and my trip into his house, but I never forgot what he said: Love is a trap."

I picked at the porch screen. "Pop Goes the Weasel" tinkled

merrily in the street as the ice-cream truck made its daily rounds. "Do you still feel that way? That love is a trap?"

"Yeah. But I can't seem to make it apply to you." She nudged my knee with her foot and smiled tiredly at me. "Maybe because I carried you inside me. Maybe that shit really does make a difference. Even Runyon agrees; it's different when you have a kid."

Runyon agrees?

"He's *talking* to you?"

"Yeah."

Her insouciance was mind-boggling.

I sat forward and grabbed her ankle. "Isn't that a bad thing? That you're *possessed*? Shouldn't we tell someone?"

"It doesn't feel bad," she said, using her other foot to pry my hand off her ankle. "He's not a monster, you know. Like I said, he used to be Mortmaine; it's just that when he lost his daughter, he went off his head."

I looked for any sign of strangeness—a forked tongue, slit pupils—but I saw only Rosalee, with her big, dark eyes and unhappy mouth, awaiting my judgment.

"Is he the reason you're being nice to me? He misses his daughter and it's just . . . rubbing off on you?"

Rosalee looked offended. "He doesn't control my feelings. He doesn't control *me*."

I exhaled a deep, relieved breath. "Then I guess you know what's best for you ... but just know, if your head starts to spin around, I'm calling a priest. Deal?"

"Deal." Her smile nearly singed my eyelashes.

When she smiled like that, it was hard to care that she was sharing her body with someone else, impossible to care about anything but making her happy.

As long as she was happy, what else mattered?

The following Sunday evening, I was in my room taking Rosalee's measurements as she hummed along to her Billie Holiday CD. I listened to the morbid recitation of "Gloomy Sunday," uneasy as I noted Rosalee's hip size, handling her like nitroglycerine ...

... wondering whether Runyon was looking out at me through her ear.

I'd barely thought about him since she'd told me her story, but these weird imaginings crept up on me at the most random moments.

When I'd finished with her, she went to the dress form near

my sewing machine and stroked the black jersey fabric that draped it. "I can't believe you're almost finished with this. How can you sew so fast?"

Since my hair was twisted into an intricate knot atop my head, I could only pretend to flip my hair over my shoulder. "I'm extraordinarily gifted."

"And extraordinarily big-headed." Rosalee's expression turned thoughtful as she fingered the dress. "This don't really seem like me."

I followed her to the dress form and sat before it. "It is you. You're beautiful. Why not wear beautiful things instead of . . ." But I didn't have to finish the sentence—she knew how slutty her clothes were. "I'll make you some other things too."

"You don't have to."

"Sure I do. I need something to take my mind off stupid Wyatt. He wasn't in school Thursday or Friday. I was all prepared to freeze him out, but he didn't even have the decency to show up."

I glared at the green angora coat I'd made him, hanging on the metal clothes rack against the wall. I'd like to put *him* against the wall, with a firing squad at his back. "I hate boys."

"That's my fault." Rosalee sat on my platform bed, watching me pin the hem of the dress. "Boy hating is genetic."

I gave a heartsick sigh. "So I won't grow out of it?"

"I haven't, and I'm thirty-six. Maybe by the time I'm forty?" She gave me an ironic look. "Or maybe by the time you stop being so chickenshit about going to therapy."

I pricked my finger on one of the pins.

"Don't think I didn't notice that you missed your appointment last Wednesday," she continued. "You know when you miss your appointments, I still gotta pay for 'em?"

She did her Easter Island thing, waiting for an answer. "I'm sorry," I told her. "I'll go this Wednesday. I promise." An easy promise—Wednesday was days away.

My cell beeped.

"You gone answer that?"

"After I finish this hem," I said. "People who hang up quickly—"

"Never want anything important." Rosalee snorted. "Järvinens."

I finished the hem and snatched the persistently beeping phone off the nightstand, falling onto the bed next to Rosalee.

"Who is it?" she asked, looking over my shoulder.

"Wyatt." I showed her the text message.

"What's RUT?" she asked.

"Are you there," I explained. I typed NO!

The phone beeped again. "IMS?" Rosalee asked.

"I'm sorry." I typed SO!

When he texted me back, Rosalee said, "Jesus, ain't the boy ever heard of vowels?"

So I translated for her.

"'You don't need me, but I need you. Only girl I trust. Only girl I can talk to. Only girl who understands my freakish ways.'"

"Freakish?" Rosalee sounded intrigued.

"Long story," I said, then continued translating. "'Please be my girlfriend? You won't have to share me.'"

"Share him with who?"

"Petra," I explained. "His ex. He's having trouble letting go." I frowned down at the cell's glowing screen. "But that's just it. How can I know he's really over her?"

"Make him invite you to church," said Rosalee. "No guy invites you to church in front of God and his folks and everybody unless he's serious about you."

I typed Rosalee's suggestion, and Wyatt immediately responded, with OK.

"No hesitation, see? That's a good sign."

"'Next Sunday,'" I read. "'Eleven a.m. Mass.'"

Maybe I wouldn't make him face that firing squad after all.

"Come to church with me and meet him," I said, tossing the cell on the nightstand.

Rosalee raised her eyebrows. "I already met him."

"When?"

"On the porch."

I had to think back. "You mean after you kneed that snake in the groin and breezed into the house without saying hi or even looking at Wyatt?"

She shrugged. "That's how I meet people." When I just looked at her, she said, very ungraciously, "*Fine*. I'll meet him." She fell onto her back in an elegant sprawl, plumping the comforter. "I ain't been to church since I was your age. I don't even *have* any Sunday clothes."

I pointed at the dress form. "The little black dress?"

"I don't want to waste it on *church*. Besides, you can't wear black to church."

"Really?"

"It's the one day of the week when it's okay to draw attention to yourself, okay to sparkle. Reasoning is, if you can't be safe from monsters in the Lord's house, you can't be safe nowhere."

"Then I'll make you a red dress."

She lit up. "I love red."

"I noticed." I grabbed a notebook, stretched out beside her, and did a sketch to show her what the dress would look like. But the more I sketched, the more her face fell. When I finished the design, she looked like someone had died.

"I'm gone look like Carol Brady in this thing."

"It's church." I brushed her cloud of wild hair to the side and gave her the bad news. "You're *supposed* to look like Carol Brady."

She shied away from my hand and stood, pursing her lips. "I don't know. Maybe it'll look less prissy on a full stomach. You hungry?"

"Starving." And spurned. Why would she never let me touch her?

"Smiley's makes these chili cheese corn dogs." She made a yummy sound. "Want me to pick us up some?"

"Sounds good." I put on a happy face. After all, I couldn't expect miracles. Touching aside, things were great between us, especially compared to the way things had been when we'd first met.

She'd stop flinching from my touch one day.

I continued to work after she left, running on adrenaline and happiness, much more potent than caffeine. I finished her black dress and then got to work on the red church dress. I had the perfect fabric—scarlet silk chiffon, which I'd bought in the days before I'd gone all purple.

I'd just meant to start the dress, but when I finally looked up from the sewing machine, I realized I'd finished it.

I hopped up and put the red dress on the rack, neck sore, fingers sore, eyes tired, but *I* wasn't tired. I could have made ten more dresses, but I was beyond starving. Where were those corn dogs?

I checked the time and then rechecked it. It was midnight. More than six hours had passed.

Forget the corn dogs; where the hell was Rosalee?

She might have come up to eat with me, but then hadn't been able to get my attention. Sometimes when I was working on something, I didn't connect with what was going on around me.

I went downstairs and switched on the stair light. Two bags from Smiley's lay abandoned by the front door. Even cold they smelled good, and my stomach rumbled, but my hunger had been superseded by growing fear.

"Momma?" I found her once again in the hallway before the carved-up linen closet, kneeling before it as if in prayer. Only she wasn't praying or carving; she was whimpering.

I turned on the hall light and knelt beside her. "What happened?"

Her eyes were wet, but she wasn't crying—even though her hands were wrapped in blood-soaked bandages.

"*What happened?*"

"I don't remember." Her face was a study in pained bewilderment. "I went to get the food . . . and then I was holding this door knocker. Only it's not really a door knocker—"

"It's a Key," I said, understanding then what must have happened to her hands. "Wyatt's Key."

She looked surprised. "You know about the Ortiga Key?"

I nodded and left it at that. "What did you try to wish for?"

"Not me. *Him.* All I wanted was food. He wanted the Key. *Wants* it. He says it's his. That it's the only thing that'll get him into Calloway."

"Into where?"

She paused, head cocked in a listening pose. Listening to *him.* I tried not to shiver. "He says he thinks that's the world his little girl disappeared into."

"I thought he was over that. What happened to his 'love is a trap' philosophy?"

"That was for me, not him. It's too late for him."

"But you said he couldn't control you."

"He's not controlling *me*, just my body."

"Just?" I looked at her bloody hands and decided not to split hairs. "What did the Ortigas say when they saw you?"

"They didn't see me. I don't even think they were home. I had to pull and pull to get free." She studied her mangled hands as though they'd let her down.

"The Ortigas have some kind of paste that'll fix your hands," I told her. "Just tell them—"

"I ain't going back there! You think I want them to know what I tried to do? God, how fucking *humiliating*."

"Then I'll get the paste for you."

"How?"

I looked at my perfectly healed hand and made a fist. "I'll figure something out."

I was sitting in the same yellow chair as before, only facing Sera instead of Asher. I felt like I was facing the firing squad I'd wished on Wyatt.

For Sera, Christmas had come early. She scooped the paste from the brown jar and spread it ungently into my burnt palm, wallowing in my every wince of pain. At least I'd played it smart and used my left hand this time around.

"What did we say about trying to make wishes?"

"Not to."

"Did you try to be clever and wish for an infinity of wishes?" Her eyes never left my face, not just listening for a lie, but looking for one too. "So you could come back here and make wishes at your leisure? I guess you found out the hard way that old trick don't work."

"Busted," I said, glad she was doing the work of making excuses for me.

"You're not the first one to try," she said grimly. "Won't be the last, either. Some idiot was here earlier getting scorched. He was gone by the time I got to the door, but he'd left half the skin of his hands behind. At least you had the sense to wait and be released, so I hope you have sense enough to listen."

She leaned into my face so I could see her contempt of me right up close. "This is the second time you tried to wish on our Key without permission. You do it a third time, you don't get your hand back. Understand?"

I nodded. Tried to swallow. "Can I have a glass of water, please?"

She leaned back, amused to have intimidated all the spit from my mouth. When she went into the kitchen, I hurriedly removed the small jelly jar from the roomy pocket of my apron dress and transferred a substantial amount of the popcorn-colored paste into it. By the time Sera came back with my water, the jelly jar was filled and once again stashed away.

In order to account for the amount missing from the brown jar, I was slathering what was left of the paste onto my sore hand like butter.

"That's enough." She snatched the jar away.

"It hurts." That was the honest truth.

She sat across from me. "Using up the whole jar ain't gone make your hand not hurt faster." She handed me the glass of water and watched me drink. "And I hope you don't think you can hang around here drinking water while you dream up a way to con me out of a wish the way you did Asher."

I sputtered. "I didn't con Asher!"

"The hell you didn't. It's all over town that you're some kind of head case, but if you wanna plead insanity, you came to the wrong person. I know a user when I see one."

"I saved your husband's life. How is that a con?"

"You refused to help him until he gave you what you wanted."

"That was a *negotiation*. There's a difference."

"You ever try 'negotiating' like that with my son's life, I'll cut up your face." She said it so calmly that I believed her. "I have a score to settle with your mother anyway; taking it out on you'd work just as well. We understand each other?"

First Poppa and now Sera. Why did everyone think I was going to hurt Wyatt?

"Perfectly," I told her, setting the water on the coffee table, looking her dead in her eyes. "But if you think that physical pain is the worst kind of pain, I envy you."

Sera opened her mouth to speak, but she couldn't; I'd surprised all the words from her mouth.

I thanked her for the first aid and left; I wasn't afraid of pain, but I was still happy to leave with both hands intact.

When I got home, Rosalee was full of questions, but I only told her that I'd had to improvise a little.

"Improvise my ass," she exclaimed, as I covered her hands

with the paste. "You burned your hand for me. How do I even say thanks for that?"

She kissed my cheek. Her lips were cold. Her kiss burned. Her smile was like starlight.

Who needed thanks?

Chapter Twenty-seven

The following Sunday, Rosalee and I were sitting on the steps of St. Teresa Cathedral overlooking Fountain Square, waiting for the service to finally be over.

At school that Friday, I had explained to Wyatt that Rosalee wanted to come with me, but not into the church itself. I told him she was having a crisis of faith, when really Rosalee was afraid that since she was possessed, she might drop dead on the spot if she tried to enter a church.

Wyatt had been understanding about how I'd burned my hand for a second time on his Key—even about the confrontation with his mother. "I know you wouldn't've just let my dad die that day, and Ma knows it too. She's just overprotective."

It pleased me that he had so much faith in my integrity. Strange, though. He hadn't asked me what I'd tried to wish for this time around. Maybe he was scared to ask. The last time he'd asked, he'd found out I was mental—he probably wanted to quit while he was ahead.

I patted the shiny green gift-wrapped present I'd brought for him. He deserved a truckload of presents for putting up with a girl like me. I decided to kiss him when he came out, to give him a big wet one in front of God and everybody, but especially in front of his mom.

I hoped she choked on it.

Rosalee nudged me with her elbow, grinning at me. "What's with you and that smile?"

"What smile?" I asked, smiling. I let my head fall back and watched a flock of blue jays fly across the low, overcast sky, wishing the birds were closer so their wings would fan me.

"It's that boy of yours, right?" Rosalee persisted. She took me by the chin and made me look at her. "You could be in there with him, you know? God ain't gone throw any lightning at *you*."

"You're my God." I wrapped my arms around her, breathed her sweet, clean scent. "'Mother is the name for God on the lips and hearts of children.'"

She wriggled out of my grasp. "Don't lean against me. It's too hot for that." Before I could feel hurt, she grabbed my chin again. "*Look* at me."

"Why?"

"Your eyes remind me of winter. Like two clouds full of snow. I could sure go for some snow right now." She touched her forehead briefly to mine. "Poor little Nordic girl. I'm surprised you ain't melted yet."

I tried to hug her again when she called me her little girl, but she wouldn't let me. Ever since she'd kissed me, she'd been less shy about touching me, but *she* still didn't like to be touched—the heat was just an excuse. There was always an excuse.

When the church bells rang, Rosalee shot up and pulled me down the stairs, barely giving me time to scoop up Wyatt's present.

"What is it?" I asked, as she led me down the steps, the skirt of her red dress swishing pertly around her tawny legs.

"Standing in front of the doors of a Catholic church when service is over," she told me, "is a good way to die young."

Before the noon bells had even finished ringing, a rush of brightly dressed people poured from the heavy double doors.

For once, my purple dress no longer stood out—every color was represented. Except green.

I was so busy looking through the crowd for Wyatt that I didn't notice Asher until he was right in my face.

"Oh, hi!" I said.

"Hi." But he wasn't looking at me. I was used to it by now; whenever I was with Rosalee I became Invisible Girl.

Rosalee shook his proffered hand. "Hey. Andy, right?"

"His name is Asher," Sera said, coming up beside him, Paulie in tow. Her bright yellow dress made her seem washed-out. But to be fair, with Rosalee standing next to her, Sera would have looked washed-out no matter what she'd worn. "Must be hard to keep all the names straight," she added.

Rosalee ignored her but kept hold of Asher's hand. When Sera started to turn purple, I took Asher's hand from Rosalee—the last thing I needed was a Jerry Springer–style situation. "Where's Wyatt?"

"He couldn't be here," Sera said while Asher gawked at Rosalee—right in front of her!—like he was insane . . . or fascinated.

Rosalee hadn't been joking.

"He had to train." Sera seemed more than happy to give me the bad news.

My eyes dropped to the present. I hadn't realized until now how much I'd been looking forward to Wyatt's public declaration of affection.

Rosalee said, "Don't feel bad. That's how it is with the Mortmaine—they're always on call." She turned to Sera. "I'm Rosalee Price, by the way. Hanna's mother."

"I know who you are."

"My daughter's your son's girlfriend."

"I *know*."

"He been telling everybody," Paulie said, peeking around Sera's arm. "He called our grandpa in Argentina and told him. He called our cousins in California and told them. He even told the mailman."

"That's enough, Paulie," said Sera.

It was enough, all right. Enough to boost my spirits and send a big smile stretching across my face. "Could you give this to Wyatt?" I handed the present to Asher, since he was closest. "And tell him I'm sorry I missed him?"

"Anything you say."

"Thank you," Rosalee told him, since his declaration had been addressed to her.

Sera grabbed his arm none too gently and dragged him off.

"Did you sleep with him before or after he was married?" I asked, watching the Ortigas disappear into the crowd.

Rosalee scrunched her nose in this really cute way that I immediately decided to practice in the mirror. "Both, I think. That was a long time ago."

"Hey, Hanna."

Lecy, wearing blue poppies in her hair that matched her dress, descended the cathedral steps with her group of friends: Petra in pink, Petra's mountainous boyfriend Frankie in a dark blue suit, Casey of the orange braces and formerly see-through skull, and a bunch of other kids from school all in their church finery.

None of whom were looking at me.

"Hey, Miz Rosalee," they exclaimed in unison.

"Hey," said Rosalee, before turning her back on them to ask me, "Wanna go sit by the fountain?"

Before I could open my mouth to reply, Lecy said, "Hey, guys, come on! Miz Rosalee asked us to sit with her!"

In no time Rosalee and I were sitting near the bottom tier of the sunken amphitheater, near enough for the clear fountain water to splash us, surrounded by Rosalee's adoring fans.

"Miz Rosalee," said Lecy, "lemme get you something to drink."

"No, I'll get it," said Casey.

"Let the girl get me a drink if she wants," Rosalee told Casey, the spray from the fountain sparkling in her hair like diamonds. "In the meantime, *you* can rub my feet."

"Cool!"

Everyone fell over laughing, watching Casey fumble with the complicated straps of Rosalee's lipstick red stilettos.

"I was just kidding!" she said, exasperated, shooing him away from her feet.

"I don't mind," said Casey, who refused to be shooed. "Believe me. I always wanted to—"

The rest of the sentence was drowned out by loud, pained moaning.

Petra was moaning.

She'd doubled over on the tier above us, arms wrapped around her stomach. My first thought was that she was jealous of the attention being lavished on Rosalee and wanted some for herself, but she was making such horrible, plaintive sounds, such an *ugly face*, that I knew she couldn't be faking it.

Everyone quieted as Frankie rubbed her back with his huge hand, worried. "Baby, what's wrong?"

"Stomach," she gasped, eyes squeezed shut. "My stomach—"

"Holy hell, y'all," someone screamed, *look at the fountain!*"

We looked. The formerly clear pool had become a thick red soup. All the people dangling their feet in the water jerked them out at once. The smell that arose from the fountain was unmistakable, as though a vein had opened beneath us and the Earth was spewing its heart's blood.

Hardly anyone screamed or panicked. No one spoke, and yet the Porterenes rose as one and fled Fountain Square in a rainbow-colored exodus. There was something Animal Planet about it, like a herd of zebra fleeing the presence of a hungry lion.

"They're well-trained, aren't they?" said Rosalee, only it wasn't her voice.

I sidled away from Runyon, from his blue eyes blazing from her face. "Are you doing this?"

"Me?" He removed Rosalee's complicated shoes and waded into the ankle-high pool that had turned the same color as Rosalee's dress. "If memory serves," he said sardonically, "turning water to blood was God's specialty."

I stood, the fountain spray staining my dress. "Shouldn't we go too?"

"And miss all the fun?" He put out Rosalee's tongue to catch the bloody droplets spewing from the fountain, like a kid trying to catch snowflakes.

I couldn't stand the intrusion. Couldn't *stand* it. "Momma?"

She blinked those blue eyes away. "I'm here." She was herself again, but for a person up to her ankles in blood, her cheerful expression was disconcerting. That and the fact that she continued to hold out her tongue.

"It's okay," she said, noting the look on my face. "It's not really blood, despite what it looks and smells"—she finally caught a fat splash of blood in her mouth—"and tastes like. Blech!" She spat out the blood. "Runyon says it's a sign."

"Of what? The *apocalypse?*"

"No." She looked up at the cloudy sky. "A breeder's coming."

"Breeder?"

She nodded. "Breeders track other breeders by scent. If any of their kind is near water or any liquid, really, the liquid takes on the appearance and scent of that breeder's blood. The more liquid there is, the better the scent given off. This fountain, for instance? A breeder could smell all this from miles away."

"Is Runyon a breeder?"

"Not Runyon," she said, exasperated. *"Him."*

She pointed at Frankie, sitting behind us with Petra, the only people left in the square besides Rosalee and me. Petra didn't look fit enough to go anywhere, chalky and sweaty as she was. Frankie was cradling her in his lap, cooing to her. All the while he watched the sky. Just like Rosalee.

I looked up and saw why.

A huge flying man dived out of the gray clouds, zooming directly toward us. As he approached, the flap of his transparent wings beat the air, blowing my dress against my legs.

Rosalee grabbed my arm and dragged me up the amphitheater, leaving bloody footprints on the pale gray tiers. I thought we were finally leaving, but she only led me halfway up and then pulled me down to sit beside her.

"What are you *doing*?"

"Runyon wants to watch. Besides, that breeder ain't after *us*."

She was right.

The flying man alighted before Frankie and Petra. He had dirty-blond hair and huge crystalline wings like a fairy. Like Frankie, he was stocky and had a certain pugnacious quality, the kind of guy who'd smash his own wings with a crowbar just to destroy something beautiful.

"I've been searching for you for two weeks." His deep voice shivered my bones, and he didn't speak English like it was his first language.

"I'm sorry," said Frankie, still rocking Petra on his lap. "I didn't dare face you until I was sure it took."

"Were you successful?"

"Yes." I could tell he was grateful as all hell to be able to answer affirmatively.

The flying man looked surprised and then pleased. "Well. Perhaps I will be successful as well." He turned his wild, sky-colored eyes on Rosalee, zeroing in on her like a bull spotting a red flag. He stomped over—I'm sure I felt the ground shake with every step—and towered over us like a Philistine, burying us in his shadow. He grabbed Rosalee.

"No!" I tried to grab her back, but he knocked me aside with a careless swipe of his huge hand and left my head ringing. He lifted Rosalee as though she were weightless, both hands easily spanning her waist.

"Dad," said Frankie, faintly derisive, "I don't think you're human enough. Remember the last woman?"

"But we're here now," argued the flying man. "Amongst an entirely new species." He grinned at Rosalee with angel-white teeth. "I think I should like to see how human I am."

"Well, I shouldn't." Rosalee removed a knife from the garter beneath her Carol Brady dress and sliced through the arm holding her. The flying man dropped her, his now useless arm dangling at his side, tendons severed and gushing blood onto the stone.

Rosalee skipped back to me and helped me sit up. "I ain't into bestiality," she told the wounded flying man as casually as if he'd asked for her phone number in a bar. "Sorry."

The flying man roared in pain and fury, but before he could do anything, the appearance of squealing emerald trucks on the square above us distracted him. Scores of Mortmaine, several of whom literally appeared out of nowhere, converged on the amphitheater. Green all over the square; green for safety.

The flying man didn't know what hit him. Mortmaine rushed down into the amphitheater and swarmed over him like ants, hacking and slashing and eerily silent as the flying man was forced backward into the red pool beneath their full-on attack. Once he was dead and torn asunder, the fountain went clear again, except now it was cloudy with real blood.

As he watched his father fall, Frankie released Petra and shot to his feet. He flexed his shoulders and, with a great tearing sound, unfurled his own wings, ripping his nice Sunday jacket all to hell. His wings were easier to see than his father's—a translucent bluish green—and with one mighty flap, Frankie was airborne.

Only he had a passenger.

Petra had caught him by the foot as he left the ground, and she held on like a kite string, her pink skirt billowing prettily, her negligible weight dragging him down just enough for the Mortmaine to catch her legs and use her to reel Frankie in.

"Wait," Frankie screamed, throwing a desperate glance at the Mortmaine closing in on him, and at Petra, who was once again lying curled up on the ground, Frankie's church shoe clenched in her hand. "I'm the only one who can care for her. She'll die without me."

"She's already dead, breeder," one of them said before they engulfed Frankie like a strangle of kudzu, ripping off his wings, and when the Mortmaine climbed out of the amphitheater, they each held a bloody piece of him.

They built a huge bonfire up on the square and tossed both

Frankie and his father onto it. The smell of their roasting flesh was weirdly delicious.

A Mortmaine stepped down toward Petra, an older man as skinny as she was, but not fashionably so. He'd simply stripped away his nonessential parts until he'd made a weapon of himself. "Initiates!" he called in a ringing voice.

A small group of younger Mortmaine came down the tiers, all wearing green shirts. Wyatt, my Wyatt, was among them, bloodstained and as radiant as I'd ever seen him.

"Gather round," said the older Mortmaine. "So you can see what happens when a breeder impregnates someone. Katie! Cut off the girl's head."

One of the initiates, a short, pigtailed girl carrying an ax almost as tall as she was, hopped down to Petra's tier, raised the ax, and—

"*Stop!*"

Wyatt pushed Katie back, almost into the fountain, and dropped to his knees beside Petra.

She dropped Frankie's shoe, and her tiny hand gripped the front of Wyatt's shirt. "Did that man say . . . impregnated?" she asked in a small voice.

"What's the holdup?" demanded the older Mortmaine.

The bright radiance had drained so quickly from Wyatt, I was surprised not to see a puddle of light beneath him. "Elder . . . I know this girl."

"*Knew* her," said Elder, grabbing Wyatt by the scruff of his shirt and hauling him to his feet. "Katie?"

The pigtailed girl shot Wyatt a vindicated look as two of her fellow initiates came to her side to unfold an unresisting Petra and hold her flat on the ground. Again Katie raised the ax.

"Wait!" Wyatt cried, struggling against Elder's tight grip.

But Katie didn't wait. She swung the ax. The blade sliced cleanly through Petra's pale neck; the sound of metal hitting stone was fearsomely loud.

When Wyatt screamed, Elder shook him like a terrier with a chew toy until he stopped. "Katie! Lift the ax."

She did. And everyone gaped. Not only was there no blood on the blade, Petra's head was still attached to her neck. To prove it beyond a doubt, Elder tossed Wyatt aside, marched to Petra, and pulled her head by the hair. Petra whimpered in pain, but somehow she still had a head to whimper with.

When Elder released her, her whimpers changed to laughter. Hysterical laughter.

Once again, Wyatt dropped to his knees beside her, pushing aside the initiates who'd been holding her down—once they let her go, she immediately curled into a ball again. "I'll be a hit at parties, Wyatt," Petra said, giggling unpleasantly as she held her stomach. "Me and my uncutoffable head."

Wyatt looked up at Elder, pale with horror and shock. "There's gotta be something we can do for her."

"We *are* gone do something for her," Elder told him. He turned to address the other initiates. "We're gone put her out of her misery. As you saw, when Katie lifted the ax from the girl's neck, the mortal damage she'd inflicted was healed instantly. The breeder spawn in her belly have advanced enough to have taken complete control of her body; enough to do whatever it takes to keep her alive until they no longer need her. You do notice the way she's curled in pain, don't you? That's because her children are eating her from the inside out. When she's used up, about four mini versions of the breeders we just eliminated will come bursting out of her. Literally."

"But—"

"No, Wyatt. Either we kill her now, or her children will kill her later."

"We should definitely kill her now," said Katie matter-of-factly.

"Fuck you, Katie!" Wyatt screamed. "She's my friend!"

"A Mortmaine's only friend is his duty," said Elder. "Now cut open her stomach and remove the spawn."

"Gladly." Katie stepped forward.

"Not you," said Elder. He removed a knife from his belt and held it out to Wyatt. "Since Wyatt cares so much about her, he'll ensure that it's done painlessly. Take the knife, Wyatt."

Wyatt just looked at him disbelievingly, stroking the damp yellow hair at Petra's temple.

Elder's face darkened. "Take it!"

But Wyatt wouldn't.

"Do it, Wyatt," said Petra.

"No." Wyatt was looking at her like even her tiniest pore was worthy of intense scrutiny. "I can figure something out. I can *make* something, a card." The desperation in his voice was painful to hear. "I just need time to—"

Petra reached up and smacked Wyatt across the face. It made a sound like a thunderclap. "Stop it, Wyatt." Her voice was strained but strong. "The one time I need you to be brave and you're wigging out on me. Take the knife."

He took it. It trembled in his hand.

"You heard him. I'm dead no matter what." Petra was almost beatific in her agony. "I always figured I'd come to a bad end. Because of what I let happen to Mikey. I don't even care. Just . . ." Her hand tightened on Wyatt's shirt. "Can you tell everybody I went down fighting? You saw me, didn't you? Saw me grab his foot?"

"I saw you," Wyatt said. Pride threaded his words, puffed them with momentous weight. "You were badass."

Joy superseded the pain in her waif's eyes. "Really?"

Wyatt chose that moment to knock Petra unconscious with the hilt of Elder's knife. And then he quickly sliced through her pink dress . . . and her stomach.

Like that, Petra became unreal. No longer a person, but a thing full of stuff that needed removing.

Due to Petra's ability to heal quickly, Wyatt had to work swiftly and ungently to find what he was after, reopening her stomach several times before hitting pay dirt.

What Elder had called spawn, grotesque things the size of Ken dolls, had fused to several of Petra's organs and spine so that when Wyatt pulled them free, howling and irate like bratty toys, most of Petra's innards came with them.

Wyatt smashed each of the spawn beneath his boot,

grinding them into the gray stone. His face was dead as he worked. He could have been carved from wood.

Elder inspected his work and called the other initiates over. "You and you, put the girl's body on ice; y'all can deliver the news to her people, find out how much fun that is. You and you, scoop up this spawn mush; y'all get to take it back to Nightshade and analyze it. Who knows, might be a cure for the common cold in all that goop. Or a pheromone that would make me irresistible to the opposite sex." Elder was looking at Rosalee as he said that last bit.

"Hiya, Rosalee," he said, climbing the tiers to greet her. "Been a long time."

Rosalee smiled and waved. "Hey, Steve."

Elder cleared his throat. "It's David, actually." When the initiates sniggered, he silenced them with a thunderous frown.

After Elder had called attention to our presence, Wyatt locked eyes with me, his wooden mask slipping to reveal the horror and shame underneath.

Elder clapped his hands. "Okay, everybody, back to your regularly scheduled programs!"

Wyatt turned away quickly, along with his fellow initiates, and fled the amphitheater.

The Mortmaine departed the square just as quickly as they'd arrived, leaving no trace of their massacre behind, other than the lingering scent of roasted flesh.

"How thrilling was that?" said Rosalee, clapping her hands together.

I opened my mouth to speak, having no idea what would come out, but Runyon spoke first.

"Very thrilling," he answered. "God, I miss being Mortmaine. The *ruthlessness* of it—"

"Momma!"

"What's wrong?" she asked, with her own voice. She turned to me, surprised.

"Don't let him out like that." After filling my eyes with so much ugliness, I relished the act of burying my face in my hands.

Rosalee squeezed my shoulder, concerned. "What is it?"

"Ruthless is right. Don't you see?" God, how could she not see? "If the Mortmaine find out about you, about *Runyon*, they'll kill you, too."

Chapter Twenty-eight

Petra's funeral was held the following Wednesday afternoon in the graveyard behind St. Michael's, in the shadow of the dark park. I felt guilty being glad that going to the funeral meant I wouldn't have to go to therapy yet again, but there it was.

Wyatt, in a black suit with a green waistcoat, stood apart behind the sea of mourners. He wasn't crying, but the pain in his face had its own liquidity. For him this was real, not a respectful way to avoid therapy. Petra had been his friend. A clingy, whiny friend, but still.

After they lowered Petra into the ground, I looked back at Wyatt, and he looked at me. I watched the horror of that day in Fountain Square twist across his face; I watched his shame.

He *let* me watch.

"Hey." Rosalee followed my gaze to Wyatt. "Should we go to him?"

"No!"

Wyatt winced, as though the word were a blade and I'd flung it into his gut, but I couldn't afford to care about his hurt feelings. The last thing I wanted was for Rosalee to go anywhere near the Mortmaine, even an initiate.

"Let's go, then," said Rosalee, pulling me along behind her. She was wearing one of her own dresses, not as tarty as some she owned, but even still, she looked less like a mourner and more like a merry widow. "I'm freezing out here."

It had gotten cooler, a lot cooler, but the wind blowing down from the north was hardly arctic. When we got in our car, I asked, "You like to travel, don't you?"

"Yep."

"Then why don't we travel? Like, to the other side of the planet. Just for a few years or so."

Rosalee laughed and rummaged through her purse. "You need this more than I thought."

"Need what?"

"Did you take your pills today?"

I unclasped my own purse. "No, actually—"

"Good!"

"But I have my emergen—" I blinked. "Good?"

"That way your meds won't interfere with this." Rosalee waved a small brown bottle with an eyedropper under my nose. "Tilt your head back. Open your eyes wide."

I did, and something wet splashed into both my eyes. "What was that?"

"Tears of Happiness," she said, wetting her own eyes. "Something to chase those oh-no-my-friend-just-died, the-Mortmaine-are-plotting-to-kill-my-mother blues away. I bought it off your friend Carmin a while back."

"Don't joke. If they find out—" I had to stop being shocked by anything she did. "You buy drugs from Carmin?"

"Lotta people do." Her smiling eyes were dark and lustrous. "He's a *very* talented boy. And stop worrying about the Mortmaine. I know what I'm doing."

Instead of driving away, we sat with the heater on until the last car had pulled out of St. Michael's. When we were alone, Rosalee grabbed a black trench coat and a wicker basket from the backseat and grinned mischievously. "Let's go."

I followed her as she threw on the coat and hurried across

Avispa Lane, plunging into the looming dark park.

"What are we *doing* in here?"

"I need a spindle." From the basket, Rosalee removed a flash lantern that was barely strong enough to beat back the darkness. "Don't look so worried. Runyon knows this place like his ABCs."

Rosalee spied about, while I clutched her coattail like a scared little kid. Everything the light touched seemed to cringe. I was wearing an aubergine-colored dress I'd made especially for the funeral, and I blended in so well with the surrounding darkness, I felt invisible. Ghostly.

"Mushrooms!" Rosalee dropped down and picked several from the base of a dead tree. In the light of the lantern, with her basket, she reminded me of Little Red Riding Hood gathering treats for Grandma.

Something about it struck me as funny, and I laughed until I was literally sick, vomiting into the undergrowth as tears of laughter poured down my face.

"Oh, dear." Rosalee tsked. "Maybe I gave you too much Happiness."

"I'm okay." I wiped my mouth with the hanky from my bra, giggling. "What're the mushrooms for?"

"Medicinal purposes. But we didn't come into the dark park for mushrooms we could get anywhere. Check it out." She pointed to a short tree, a midget among all the towering pines, a midget with its own brand of needles.

"The spindle tree," said Rosalee. "They call it Satan's Fountain Pen."

"Why?"

She pulled on a pair of black gloves, snapped a red thorn the size and shape of a knitting needle from the tree, and used it to carve into a neighboring pine. The thorn scorched the bark from the tree as Rosalee wrote HANNA + ROSALEE = HOT. She stood back to admire her work. "Look at that perfect spelling. The Little Rascals'd be so disappointed."

"Who?"

"Never mind, young'un." She tossed the used, sizzle-less thorn aside and snapped off another, wrapping it in sacking I hoped was fireproof before placing it into the basket. "Let's go."

In the car I had another laughing fit, one so bad Rosalee had to pull over. But she was cracking me up. She kept cocking her head and listening to Runyon, *arguing* with him. Saying "no" and "make me," like a little kid. A crazy little kid. Just like me.

When she noticed me laughing at her, *I* noticed that she

had one blue eye and one black eye. Looking at her like that almost killed me. I seriously almost died laughing.

"Sorry," I wheezed.

She had to blink really hard to chase that blue eye away, make it black again. "Don't apologize," she said, as she wiped my eyes and nose clean. "I think your mania is heightening the effect of the drug. I should've thought of that."

"I don't feel manic. It's just . . . everything is so great. You're great. I'm great. Portero is great. I used to feel like such a freak, but I'm not a freak here. I don't even register on the freakometer."

"Freakometer" threw me into another fit of giggles.

Rosalee held my face, an unfamiliar look of tenderness and warmth in her eyes. Protectiveness. It would have been sweet if everything hadn't been so goddamn funny.

Her eyes flashed blue. "No!" she said, and made them go black again. She let go of me and punched the steering wheel. "I said no! *I'll* find someone."

If I could have stopped laughing, I would have asked her what the hell she was talking about. But the laughing continued almost unabated until we reached the lake.

As night fell, Rosalee drove us to a rural area with unlined roads snaking through trees and rolling hills. By this time, the laughter had tapered off enough that I could pay attention. "Where are we?"

Rosalee gave me a strained smile. "Way upsquare."

We got out of the car and walked down the road to a huge lake circled with houses, like the lake at my old summerhouse in Finland, only the bloated McMansions surrounding *this* lake weren't at all like the simple, rustic cabins I was used to.

The deep blue sky was clear and the stars were bright. The moon was out, just a sliver of light. I laughed at the moon and the moon laughed back, a high, whistling sound like the wind blowing over the tundra.

Rosalee was on her knees near the edge of the lake. "You okay over there?"

I twirled, finally finding a use for those long-abandoned ballet classes. "Perfect."

"Do you see?"

"See what?" Air blew cool off the lake; unseen things sang in the dark and hopped in the grass at my feet. "Oh, it's pretty up here."

"Hanna," said Rosalee sharply. "Pay attention. Do you see the swimmer?"

Starlight stippled the lake and reflected eerily on the lone figure cutting slowly through the dark water. "I see him."

"Hanna." Her voice compelled me to look at her, her eyes fiery in the golden light of the flash lantern she'd set on the ground. "Bring him here."

"Okay."

I walked down the long pier, teetering in my heels. When I reached the end, I dropped to my knees, bruising them on the wood. The pain made me laugh.

"Hey!" My voice carried clearly across the water to the swimmer, who paused midstroke and then swam toward me.

The lights at the end of the pier made it easy to see him once he was close enough; I got quite an eyeful, actually.

"You're skinny-dipping!"

"Sorta." His deep, almost sexy voice didn't match his appearance. He was my age, give or take, with too many zits.

"Who goes skinny-dipping alone?" The thought made me laugh. "Come up and talk to me."

"Um . . ." He was eyeing his discarded clothing next to me on the pier.

"Aw. Are you shy?" I took pity on him and shimmied out of my clothes and shoes and threw them atop his. My nipples, like two big goose bumps, brought home to me how truly cold it had gotten. "Now we're even," I said, through my chattering teeth. "Don't be scared."

The wooden slats beneath my icy feet creaked and groaned as he climbed the ladder onto the pier. The harsh white light revealed him. His entire body was covered in zits—red, angry ones. Even his toes. He flushed beneath my scrutiny.

"Moonlight is supposed to help," he mumbled, edging around me to get to his clothes. "Gran says . . ."

"You don't have to explain." The boy was nothing to look at, but Rosalee wanted him, and that made him sparkle. When he reached for his clothes, I kicked them into the lake, his and mine, and fell over laughing at the look on his face.

"Hanna!"

The boy ducked down behind me. "Who's that?"

"Don't worry," I said, chuckling. "It's just Momma."

"Your mother?"

"She's very sympathetic," I assured him, "and she really wants to meet you. Come on."

We walked to where Rosalee was sitting, the boy hesitant and dragging his feet and kind of hiding behind me the whole way. My giggling had tapered off in my efforts to coax the boy along, but when I saw Rosalee, I started laughing all over again.

Rosalee's bare skin was so honeylike I was surprised not to see a swarm of bees buzzing around her. The wind blew off the water and played fetchingly in her hair. She had spread a blanket on the ground, and with the wicker basket nearby, it looked like we were about to have a picnic, nudist-style.

"Here he is, Momma," I said. "I would have gift wrapped him, but there was no time."

Rosalee smiled at the boy. "Nice work."

The boy, like a peeled shrimp, looked from her to me and then back, trying to hide his erection. "Are y'all . . . witches?"

"Do we look like witches?" Rosalee asked.

"Y-yeah."

We laughed, and the boy backed away from us.

"No, you don't." Rosalee held out her arms to him, and when he didn't rush into them, I gave him a push.

"Go on; she won't bite."

Rosalee took his shaky hands before he could bolt and drew him down to the blanket. She offered him a drink from a silver cup, which rattled briefly against his teeth as he drank.

He immediately gagged and spat a mouthful of brown liquid onto the blanket.

"What *is* this?"

"Magic," I said, stifling my giggles so he'd take me seriously. "A potion. Much better than moonlight swims."

"Really?"

His hopeful expression made me reach out and pat his wet head. "Of course."

He drank deeply.

Rosalee and I exchanged a conspiratorial grin, never mind that I had no idea what the conspiracy was. "*Is* it a magic potion?" I asked Rosalee while the boy choked down his drink.

"There's no such thing as magic, Hanna. You're worse than he is." She plucked the cup from the boy's hands and pushed him onto his back on the blanket while he sputtered in surprise.

"Why'd you take your clothes off?" she asked me as she straddled him, moving his erection aside so she could sit comfortably on his stomach.

"So he wouldn't be embarrassed to come out of the water. Why did you?"

"Because *you* did. I wasn't sure what you promised him, but

I figured you might need help." Rosalee smiled down at the boy. "You?"

He had to swallow several times before he could speak, his eyes glued to her breasts. "T-to get rid of my zits?"

I explained, "A moonlight swim in the lake is supposed to help."

She pulled on the black gloves once again and removed the spindle from the basket. "Green tea would have done more for his zits than lake water."

The boy's gaze sprang from Rosalee's breasts to her eyes. "W-would have?"

Rosalee fed a towel into the boy's mouth. Her eyes briefly flashed blue as she cut into his zitty forehead with the red-hot spindle. "Should've waited for the mushroom juice to kick in," she muttered, and when the boy began to fight her, she dug her knees into his sides as though he were a fractious horse and continued cutting.

Who knew a person could scream while gagged? The boy was making an odd *eeeeeee* sound in his throat that was hilarious.

Rosalee flipped her hair from her face, smiling at me. "Wanna help?"

I smiled back. "I don't want to hurt anybody."

"Just me and your aunt?"

"It's easy to hurt people you love."

"Is it? I could never do this to you." Rosalee's fingers pressed the boy's face so tightly that his skin had turned paper white. He would have her handprint marking his face for years if she ever decided to let go.

"Why are you hurting him?"

"Cuz Runyon wants him marked. And cuz it's fun." She laughed. "Sure you don't wanna get in on this?"

I shook my head, giggling.

Rosalee tsked at my squeamishness. "Can you at least do something about his erection? It's distracting the hell outta me."

I laughed so hard, I had to crawl away and vomit again into the high grass edging the lake, to the startlement of several crickets.

I fell onto my back on the cold ground and laughed until I cried, hope bubbling within me. If it was okay for a boy to hold on to his erection while being tortured, then it was okay for me to hold on to my love for Rosalee.

No matter what she did.

Chapter Twenty-nine

I awoke to pink dawn light, a soft light that nonetheless stabbed my eyes and threatened to split my head open. I buried my face in my pillow, but the stickiness of the pillowcase repelled me. Tacky red smears stained it. Tacky red smears everywhere: my hands, the sheets. The dead boy on my—

I sprang to my feet, dragging the sheets with me, exposing the body.

I remembered the boy from the lake, remembered his zits. He still bore the glyphs Rosalee had carved into his forehead—tiny, precise shapes like chains. I remembered his ordeal, how he'd fought, but I didn't remember the boy having no arms.

Laughter startled me.

I whirled, and although Rosalee sat naked across the room in my plum-colored reading chair, it was Runyon who looked out at me sniggering, blue eyes full of mockery.

"Momma!"

She blinked, and like that, he was gone. She looked around my room dazedly. "Uh . . . good morning . . ."

I crept over to her, as if one hard step would shatter me into a million pieces. I pointed at the boy in my bed. "Is that good?"

But she was already staring at him, tugging at her red bracelet. She seemed horrible to me. Unknowable. The most horrible thing was how much she reminded me of myself.

"What happened at the lake?"

Rosalee explained, starting and stopping, listening, telling me a story that she was also hearing for the first time.

"Runyon needed someone to remove the Key. So he had me carve special glyphs into the boy's head that would make him do whatever he was told. When Runyon told him to pull the Key off the Ortigas' door, the boy had no choice but to try and try again. Until his arms ripped off. It took a real long time, but after his shoulders dislocated, they just pulled right off, like drumsticks off a chicken. But the Key never even budged."

I tried to imagine it, the effort it must have taken the boy to tear away from his own arms. "Why wouldn't I remember something so . . . ?" The horror of it stole my voice.

"You passed out at the lake," said Rosalee. "This happened afterward." She smiled humorlessly. "The Happiness was a bad idea, I guess."

"You guess? *Why is he in my bed?*"

The smile fell away, was shamed away. "Runyon thought it would be . . . funny."

"Did *you* think it was funny?"

Rosalee tugged on her bracelet so hard the key snapped off. "No."

"But you let him anyway."

"He wanted to use you," she said, fiddling with refastening the key so she wouldn't have to look at me, wouldn't have to see what she'd done to me. "He wanted to use you, put the glyphs on *you.* For convenience's sake. I had to nag him into finding somebody else."

"Should I congratulate you? For making me help you lure a boy to his death?"

She struck her fist against the chair arm. "He wanted to use you! Don't you get that?"

"*You're* the one who doesn't get it! What about next time?

I'm assuming he's already planning another way to get the Key, right? So what is it? Does he want you to scare up a few babies for him to strangle?"

"I can't be responsible for the whole world. I'm only responsible for you."

"You're doing a kick-ass job so far!" I threw out my arms so she could drink in the naked, bloody state she'd left me in. But she refused to look at me. "You're not responsible; you're a puppet. *His* puppet."

"I'm just me."

"Then tell him to leave."

Instead of telling him to leave, she cocked her head and *listened* to him.

I stormed into the bathroom. Turned on the shower. Turned around and saw her standing in the doorway watching me, but now *I* couldn't look at *her*.

"You need to trust me, Hanna," she said softly. "I won't let him hurt you. I promise. After last night, he knows how I feel about that. Knows what I'll do and what I won't do. So please don't worry. Okay?"

But it wasn't okay.

Everything was a zillion damn miles from okay.

Wyatt stood in his doorway holding a Pop-Tart; he looked shocked. "What're you doing here?"

I had thrown on a sundress before fleeing my house, a thin, summery thing unfit for the change in the weather. I stood shivering on Wyatt's stoop in the early morning air, my elbows thrumming like crazy so close to his damnable Key. "I saw a dead body."

"Yeah?" He bit into his Pop-Tart, waiting for me to get to the bad part. When I said nothing more, he stepped back to let me inside. "Well, that'll happen, won't it? Dead bodies?"

Instead of stepping inside, I stepped into his arms, but he shoved me away as if we were strangers and hurried away from me.

"Paulie, c'mere."

I followed him dejectedly into his house as his little brother came out of the kitchen, still in his pj's and nibbling his own Pop-Tart, with Ragsie curled around his leg. Wyatt pushed Paulie toward me. "Hold her till I get back, all right?"

Paulie shrugged, as though he had to hug freaked-out girls at least once a day. As Wyatt marched off, Paulie held out his arms to me. I had to get on my knees so we'd be the same height.

Holding on to a four-year-old boy wasn't weird, as it should have been. It was comforting. Like holding an incredibly sticky teddy bear.

Ragsie clambered up Paulie's leg and sat on my shoulder as Paulie patted my back and said, "There, there." Ragsie's little arms circled my head. Was I that pathetic, that even a stuffed doll felt sorry for me?

"Why're you crying?"

"Am I?" Was I?

"See?" Paulie swiped one of my tears with his crumb-specked hand and showed it to me.

I squeezed him and let his little-kid scent of Play-Doh and sunshine tranquilize me. "I'm having a bad morning."

"Me too. There was arms on our doorstep." He briefly halted his comforting pats to take a bite of his Pop-Tart. "Bloody arms not even attached to anything."

I thought of the lake boy helplessly dismembering himself and shivered. "Were you scared?"

"They was just arms." Paulie looked into my face, reading me. "Are you scared?"

I nodded.

"Of what?"

"My mother."

His round face filled with shock, as if the idea of being afraid of one's own mother was somehow worse than finding bloody arms on the doorstep.

Eventually Wyatt came back and took over. "You go on upstairs and play," he told Paulie, shooing him out of the room.

Wyatt sat me in the yellow chair and handed me a cup of tea, something lemony and herbal. "Why're you here?" he asked again. "I know you're not crying over a dead body. It's not like you ain't seen 'em before."

"I need somewhere to stay."

"You wanna stay here?" His lip curled. "You ain't scared I'll kill you?"

"You already did," I reminded him. "At the dark park. The suspense is gone."

But he was dead serious. "You should be scared."

"You won't hurt me."

"Wanna bet your life on that?"

"Yes." I wasn't afraid for myself, but for Rosalee.

The quickness of my reply seemed to startle him. The coldness melted away, and he just looked confused.

And then his cell beeped.

He frowned at it, then at me. "I gotta go."

"So go. I'll stay here."

"Ma'll throw you out if she catches you here," he said, exasperated.

"She won't catch me. Your dad won't either."

"He's at work. I ain't worried about him."

"Are you worried about me?"

The question seemed to piss him off. He shot to his feet. "So come on, if you're coming. I can't sit around here all day."

He snuck me upstairs and led me down the hall, past the raucous harmony of Sera's singing voice and the whine of the vacuum.

But once I was safely inside his room, he ignored me and gathered some daggers and a fresh stack of glyph cards from the shelf near his desk and shoved them into various pockets. Then he grabbed the hunter green coat I'd made him and shrugged into it. It fit him perfectly.

I tried to put my arms around him again, but he pushed me away. Again. Why were people always pushing me away?

"Don't touch me," he hissed, mindful of Sera's proximity. "How can you even wanna touch me?"

"I saw what happened, Wyatt. Petra asked you to do it. I wish I had the balls to ask someone to put me out of my misery."

"What misery?" he exclaimed. "You got zero problems, Hanna. You can do whatever you want. You never gotta make hard choices like—"

I burst messily into tears. I was too tired to even be embarrassed. Too unsettled and clueless about what to do to help Rosalee. I held my hanky to my face to muffle the noise.

For a long time, Wyatt stood awkward and unhelpful in the face of my unhappiness. But then a burst of inspiration crossed his face.

"Hey. Look. Look what I got for you." He grabbed something off a dresser from which clothes sprouted like half-eaten spaghetti. He shoved something into my hands—a purple, gift-wrapped box.

I sniffled and opened the box, uncovering a silver necklace from which a teeny swan—no bigger than my thumbnail—dangled.

"I was gone give it to you that day at church," he explained. "But then I got called away, so . . ."

I held the swan to the light beaming through the window

and watched it sparkle. "It's sweet." I sniffed. "Really sweet, Wyatt."

He shuffled his feet, pleased, but not wanting to be. "You told me you liked swans. In the truck that day?"

When I put my arms around him this time, he didn't push me away. But he didn't hug me back. He stood still and stiff and quiet. "I wish you wouldn't do that," he whispered. "You shouldn't."

I silenced him with a kiss. Strange how he didn't understand that his ability to do what was necessary was something I admired. I sucked at doing the right thing, especially when it was hard or painful.

His phone beeped again, and he moved away reluctantly. But he looked more like the boy I was used to seeing, although more sorrowful than I liked.

He took off, and I stayed quiet in his room and read all morning, mostly his graphic novels. I was missing school, and I would almost certainly miss tomorrow as well, but I was so far ahead in all my classes, I really didn't give a damn. I wasn't in the mood to face anyone.

Around two that afternoon, a knock at the door nearly stopped my heart, but it was only Paulie in his Superman

T-shirt, carrying a tray that was almost bigger than he was. A peanut butter and jelly sandwich, a handful of potato chips, three cookies, a huge glass of milk, and a carrot. Obviously he had put this feast together himself.

"Wyatt said to wait until Ma was doing her exercises and then bring you food, so I did," he explained as I took the tray. "Wyatt said you're a stowaway in our house and that you're a secret." He looked excited by the idea. "*Are* you a stowaway?"

"Sort of."

"Nuh-uh." He grabbed Wyatt's footboard and swung on it, eyeing me skeptically. "Stowaways hide in boats, not houses, so they can go somewhere. You can't go nowhere in a house."

"Haven't you ever wanted to be nowhere at all?"

He thought about it and nodded. "When I broke Ma's BlackBerry. I made a wish on the Key to fix it, but the Key don't work for us." The memory seemed to make him bitter. "I wanted to run away. What did you break?"

"My mother's head. I have to figure out how to fix it. *Really* fix it this time."

I watched shock fill his face again. "Is that why you're scared of your ma?"

I bit into the carrot. Nodded.

Paulie looked thoughtful. "Well, don't use Elmer's glue," he warned. "It sure didn't work on the BlackBerry."

Rosalee woke me up. I was shocked to find her standing over me. I thought she would be angry at my having stayed out all night, and especially for not calling her to let her know where I was, but she didn't seem angry, didn't even look at Wyatt lying naked beside me. She made a shushing gesture when I tried to speak and pulled me out of bed. I threw on Wyatt's ratty green robe and followed her downstairs.

My luggage was by the front door.

I turned to Rosalee, heart thumping. "What is this?"

"You have to leave now." We were the same height, but she seemed to be staring down at me from some great distance, wholly dissatisfied by what she saw. "Nothing personal. I just can't trust you anymore."

"Why?"

"You came here and told that boy my secret."

"I didn't!"

"You did," said the tall, smoke-colored man who drifted up behind her, looming over her shoulder, heaving and roiling like a thundercloud, blue eyes bright as lightning. "*I'll* be needing that room now," he hissed.

Rosalee smiled and clapped, turning to him. "We can make the bed rattle just like Linda Blair did! We can charge admission!"

"Only if you're good, Rosalee," said Runyon indulgently.

"You can't choose the devil over me!" I screamed. But they'd already forgotten me. I was a ghost.

Rosalee and Runyon danced away and disappeared into Rosalee's office. I tried to follow, but the door was locked, and despite being a ghost, I couldn't pass through the wood. I didn't have a key—one of those Mayor-issued keys that would prove I belonged.

I beat against the office door when I heard them laughing in there, beat hard until a piece of the door broke off, sharp and long enough to pierce my heart. I reached for it.

Little Swan flapped in a silver circle around my neck and got tangled in my collar. I wasn't wearing a collar, but she was tangled in it nonetheless, tugging at the back of my neck. Irritated, I reached back to swat her away.

"Ow!"

The sound pulled me from a sleep as thick as quicksand, the

room half-bright with moonlight. Wyatt turned over beside me—dressed in his bedclothes, unlike in my dream—rubbing his ear where I'd smacked him.

I hadn't heard him come in last night; I barely remembered falling asleep myself. The best part of my brain had been hard at work thinking of a way to deal with Rosalee's situation. I hadn't had enough brainpower left over to notice trivialities like the passage of time.

"What's wrong?" he asked.

I turned to my side and snuggled into his back, forcing him to spoon with me. The best part of my brain prompted me to ask, "Do spirits . . . have spirits ever voluntarily left a person?"

"That was possessed?" His voice was gruff with sleep. "Hell, no."

"Is there a way to get the spirit out without killing the person?"

"You *have* to kill the host. I told you that."

"Why?"

He yawned, and his hot breath whooshed against the back of my neck. "Because even if you remove the spirit, which is so close to impossible it might as well be impossible, the spirit leaves bits of itself behind. Like a virus that can build itself up again. What it leaves behind, the body has no way to fight off; the immune system can't handle it, so the person gets sick and dies anyway."

"If it's just a virus, couldn't you cure it?"

He was silent a long time, as though the idea had never occurred to him.

"Wyatt, if you can make a card that can blow up leeches and lure, why not a card to heal someone?"

"Healing someone and getting rid of spirit leavings . . . it ain't even in the same universe . . . unless . . ." He went silent again. I could almost hear the gears in his brain turning.

"I'd have to think about it." He squeezed me around the middle. "*After* I wake up."

"Wyatt Reynaldo Ortiga!"

I rolled over and bumped sleepily into Wyatt, who sat beside me, wide-awake and nervous, the early morning sun lightening his brown eyes. I armed my hair out of my face. "Reynaldo?"

He turned to me. "Hide! Quick!" But before I could move, he pulled me to the floor and rolled me under his bed. Seconds later, as I lay among dust bunnies and old socks, I heard Sera's voice, saw her feet encased in black Doc Martens.

"Why are you still in bed? You know you have to meet the Mortmaine."

Wyatt didn't answer.

"Loafing around up here ain't gone change what happened to that girl."

"Her name was *Petra*."

"You know the Mortmaine don't believe in pining after—"

"Don't tell me what they believe in. To hell with them. They won't even let me mourn her."

"Let her people mourn her. You don't have that luxury."

"Because I killed her."

Something thumped loudly, out of my limited line of sight. Sera yelled, "I'm sick of this self-pitying bullshit, Wyatt. Petra was dead the second she let that breeder within two feet of her; it had nothing to do with you. The only thing you're responsible for is doing your duty to this town."

"If one more person says that to me"—it sounded like his teeth were clenched—"I swear to God—"

"Do you think your nana would've neglected her duties to hide in her room and mope?"

"Of course not. Bitches don't mope."

Sera slapped him, an unmistakable sound, as loud as a

gunshot. "You don't deserve to wear her locket."

"I never said I did!" Wyatt's bare feet hit the floor as he jumped out of bed. Sera stepped back, away from him. "You want it back, take it! I'm nothing like her, and I don't want to be like her. Some hard-hearted, unfeeling—" I jerked as something smashed, broken shards falling to the floor across the room.

I held my breath in the deep silence that followed.

"Wyatt," said Sera soothingly. Her feet moved close to his. "It's okay. Calm down. I'm sorry. I know the Mortmaine push you hard, but it's only—"

"I know, Ma." He sounded defeated. "Please, just . . . stop."

Sera gave a deep sigh. "I'll talk to your elder. I'll tell him you need a day. Isn't Carmin having his party tomorrow? Why don't you go and have fun with your friends? Get some perspective back. Sound good?"

"I guess."

"So today and tomorrow, and then business as usual."

"Thanks, Ma." Wyatt's feet moved toward the bed, then disappeared from view as the mattress sank beneath his weight.

When the door closed behind Sera's Doc Martens, I came out from under the bed.

Wyatt sat cross-legged against the headboard like a skinny, angry Buddha. "I get so sick of her throwing Nana in my face, like she was a saint."

I sat beside him, plucked the locket from inside his shirt, and opened it. The photo showed a young woman, but the picture was old, from the sixties, maybe, judging from the hairstyle. Words were engraved on the back, stark and deep: *Ojos que no ven, corazón que no siente.* "What does that mean?"

Wyatt plucked the locket from my fingers and closed it, stuffed it back inside his shirt. "What the eyes don't see, the heart can't feel. If you don't see the bad things in the world, you won't feel bad about them. It's such a joke. If you knew my nana—" His voice broke, and he was silent a long time.

"She never felt bad about anything," he whispered. "Not anything."

"Why?"

"Nana was Mortmaine," he said, as though that explained everything. I guess it did.

"She had to go to this guy's house once," Wyatt continued. "This guy who'd been killing people, except not on purpose. Nobody could understand it, but everybody the guy touched died within three days. So he needed to be dealt with, because no one knew whether he was some rare kind of creature or had some weird disease. It could've been anything, so to be safe, the Mortmaine decided to send Nana after him.

"The man's sons were home when Nana showed up, these two little boys, and they begged her not to hurt their dad. But she did it anyway, stabbed him right in the heart. And then she killed the little boys, just in case what the guy had was genetic. She died three days later. Died a hero. Do you understand? That's what it means to be Mortmaine."

He had started to cry, and though he tried to choke it back, he couldn't. "Fuck."

"Cry if you want." I wrapped my arms around him. "Who cares?"

"I care! The Mortmaine care, Ma cares. I'm not supposed to be *this*. I just . . . keep waiting to feel cold or uncaring, but then I remember I ain't supposed to feel *anything*. I just gotta get the job done."

"How do you know your nana didn't cry after she killed that family? Or when she realized she had only three days to live? Maybe she felt the same way you do. Maybe she just sucked it up and did what she had to do."

A light went on in my head.

As Wyatt cried himself out against my chest, the best part of my brain found a solution to Rosalee's problem. Maybe. I had to figure out one thing first.

"Poppa?"

He came in through Wyatt's door, like he'd been waiting for my call. He sat at the foot of the bed, his ice-cream suit blending in with the bedspread. He waited patiently for me to speak.

"Is there a way to make wishes besides the Ortiga Key?"

"All five of the Keys grant wishes," he said. "I told you that."

"Which one has the quickest and"—I clenched my newly healed left hand—"least painful way to get a wish?"

I listened as Poppa explained what I had to do, but after he told me everything I needed to know, about Wet William and Evangeline Park, he frowned at me, albeit rather awkwardly— the chewed-up side of his face wasn't as mobile as it used to be.

"You could call for me to talk," he said, "and not just when you want something."

Guilt hit me like a kick to the chest. "Don't be mad at me, Poppa. You know you don't have to wait for me to call you. Just come."

He smiled and pinched my big toe. "It's been better for us since we moved here. Hasn't it?"

I wiggled my toes at him. "I think so too, Poppa."

"What're you saying?" asked Wyatt, startling me.

"Ah . . ." I looked down into his face where it rested against my breasts and had no idea what to tell him.

"All that Finnish," he said, shamelessly using my bodice to wipe his tears, his eyes as bright and fresh as a street after a hard rain. "What does it mean?"

"I was praying," I lied. "For forgiveness."

"For me?" He seemed touched by the thought.

I looked at Poppa. "For all of us," I said gravely.

Chapter Thirty

Carmin's birthday was Saturday, but he'd canceled his party the day after Petra died. "It's stupid, I guess," he explained as he, Lecy, Wyatt, and I drove way upsquare to Evangeline Park. "But what's so great about turning sixteen? Petra made it to sixteen—and look how that shit turned out."

Now it was two in the afternoon, and the four of us lay together on a blanket on the shore of the Nudoso River, tall spider lilies nodding over us, menacing and ghostly. I shivered, but not from cold.

From nerves.

"You okay?" Wyatt was warm beside me, wearing the green coat I'd made him.

"No," I admitted. "I feel weird."

"Pet made it weird when she left," Lecy said on my other side. She had on a black peacoat with white buttons, and she'd pinned one of the spider lilies in her black hair. The effect was disturbing, as though the lily was swallowing her head. "She left a hole in the world. Can't you feel it? The empty space?"

We digested this in silence, listening to the river trickle behind us.

"Pet liked coming up here," said Wyatt softly, watching the sky. "She was born near a river. The Rio Grande, I think. The sound of the water spoke to her." He grabbed my cold hand and squeezed it, his skin oven-warm. "Did you know she liked to come up here?"

I hadn't thought about it one way or the other, even though coming here had been my idea, but now that he mentioned it . . .

"I remember her saying she liked to come to Evangeline when she was scared," I said. "I thought we could all use the closure."

Lecy shifted beside me. "Where are they, Carmin?"

Carmin sat up, braving the wind, hair aflame against the cold gray sky. He removed a bundle of flowers from his toggle coat and passed one to each of us. The flowers were a lighter, gentler shade of blue than Carmin's glasses.

"These were the only fresh forget-me-nots I had on hand," he said. "I already processed the others."

I held the flower to my nose. "What are these for?"

"To remember Pet," said Carmin. "You eat the petals off it, and it helps you remember the people you loved who died."

It seemed mean to say I hadn't loved Petra, so I only said, "I hardly knew her, except that she had a mouth on her. And she was a coward."

"Not at the end," Wyatt exclaimed, turning to me. "You saw. Petra was badass at the end, holding on to Frankie's foot so he couldn't get away."

"Everybody's got some kernel of bravery," Lecy said. "Even somebody like Pet had a little." She turned to Carmin. "You should have made pills. Fresh flowers wear off quick as spit."

"I did make pills."

"Well, share, baby!"

He removed a handful of blue, liquid-filled capsules from a plastic bag and handed two each to Lecy, Wyatt, and me. "The pills last a long time. Maybe a little too long. About an hour. So only take one at a time."

Wyatt gave his two to Lecy. "Who wants to be unconscious out in the wild for a whole hour?"

"So take 'em at home, genius," said Carmin.

"I'm on call twenty-four/seven, smartass."

"Nobody's forcing you to take the pills! Why do you think I brought the flowers? Excuse me for being thorough."

"So we're going to be unconscious?" I said, interrupting their bickering.

"For a little while," said Lecy. "Like dreaming awake."

I had planned to sneak off under the guise of needing the restroom, and once out of sight, I would do what I had to do. But this forget-me-not thing was perfect.

Carmin lay back down, and they all ate the flowers. I only pretended to eat mine, holding the petals in my cheek. The flowers affected everyone almost immediately, and in minutes they were out of it, staring dreamily at the sky.

I passed my hand over Wyatt's open eyes. When he didn't blink, I spat out the petals and leaped to my feet, removing my indigo coat as a rush of anticipatory heat swept me. I trod through the cold spider lilies to the edge of the dark, colorless river, where I knelt and pricked my finger on the safety pin I pulled from the pocket of my violet pencil skirt. Remembering

Poppa's instructions, I used my bloody finger to spell out a name in the cool, gently flowing water: William.

The name hung redly in the river before slowly dissolving. I waited, gazing into the water as the wind rustled through the oaks, but for the longest time, all I saw was my reflection staring back at me, waiting impatiently.

And then my reflection came to life. Instead of lying still on the water, my image arose rippling and wet from the river, like something from a funhouse mirror. I stared at myself, and my self stared back.

Damn, I was pretty.

But then the water fell away in a great splash to reveal an older boy standing on the water, staring down at me.

He wasn't as pretty as I was, but he was all right. Eighteen or nineteen, with skin as brown as river silt. He had sad eyes, like a lost dog, and he was looking at me expectantly, like I could tell him the way home. I opened my mouth to speak.

"Hanna!"

I looked back . . . into Wyatt's eyes. He sat wide awake on the blanket, but before I could reassure him, Wet William snatched me into the river.

I went down streaming bubbles in the dusky blue water as

Wet William, his arm circling my chest, dragged me to the river bottom, the laces of my violet oxfords trailing in the cold water like sea worms. By the time Wet William set me on my feet, my chest had begun to burn with the effort of holding my breath.

Wet William was much taller than I was, his shirt billowing in the current. "I guess you know the drill," he said almost playfully, despite his sad eyes, his voice as clear as a bell. "Just take a deep breath and ask. But just so we're clear, you'd better look down."

I did, still holding my breath. Below my feet were several bones, gleaming white in the murky water.

"Those are the bones of the last girl who thought she really believed this would work."

I took a deep breath. Because it was either breathe, or faint and then drown. "Oh, I believe it all right," I told him.

Wet William's mouth dropped open, the sadness in his eyes mixed with admiration. "Son of a bitch."

"It's Hanna, actually," I said, "and I know what I want. I want you to please remove Runyon from my mother's body, *without* it making her sick."

"No problem." He cracked his knuckles. "Nice to get somebody down here with some balls for a change."

"Thank you," I said, amused that not even death could stop boys from flirting. I took another breath of water. I felt oddly congested, like I had the worst chest cold in the history of the world. My deep inhalation drew Wet William's head toward me.

His head, not his body, which Wyatt kicked to the side.

Wet William hit the river bottom, brown silt poofing around his butt in a cloud, his hands frantically patting the space above his neck where his head should have been, but wasn't.

Wyatt's machete sliced through the bloody water as he swam toward me and caught me around the waist.

"What did you do to Wet William?" I screamed, bringing Wyatt up short to gape at me in wonder, and while he gaped, Wet William's severed head chomped his arm.

Angry bubbles streamed from Wyatt's mouth as he knocked Wet William's head away.

"Wait!" I yelled, wanting to swim after Wet William's head but tethered by Wyatt's iron grip on my elbow. "What about my wish?"

"Bitch, what about my body?" screamed Wet William as the current carried him away, "You know how long it's gone take to grow a new head? Shit on your wish!"

Wyatt hauled me up through the water, and I screamed the whole way. I would have continued screaming once we were back on shore, wet and shivering on the blanket as Lecy and Carmin fussed over us, but I couldn't even breathe, not until I'd vomited all the water from my lungs. After that, it was smooth sailing.

"You all right?" Wyatt asked.

"No, I'm not!" I said into his wet chest as he held me tight. "I can't believe you killed Wet William. I can't believe you ruined everything!"

"You can't kill Wet William," said Wyatt calmly into my ear. "He's already dead."

I shoved him away. "You ruined my wish! You *ruined* it!"

"Later, guys," Carmin said, prying us apart. "Let's get in the truck before y'all turn into Popsicles."

Lecy and Carmin herded us into Wyatt's truck and cranked the heat. "What happened?" they asked, crowding into the front seat with us.

"I got Wet William to grant my wish," I said, huddled in front of the vent in the dashboard, "and then Wyatt had to go and cut his head off, and now he won't grant it!"

Wyatt at least had the decency to look miserable. "What did you wish for?"

"For my stupid boyfriend to realize I can take care of myself. I'm not Petra, okay? I don't need to be rescued!"

"I'm sorry." But as he brushed my hair from my face, he didn't look sorry. Sorry he'd pissed me off, sure, but he had no idea of the extent to which he'd screwed me.

"I can't believe you actually breathed underwater like that," Lecy marveled. "I'd be too scared to even try it."

"Fat lot of good it did me!"

Lecy gave Wyatt a stern look. "*You* oughta give her a wish. To make up for the one you messed up."

Wyatt's misery deepened, as though he *did* understand how he'd screwed me. "I can't. Wet William already granted it, technically. You can't make the same wish twice."

"But he took it back!"

Wyatt slung his arm over my shoulders. "You can have another wish. Any wish you want. Just ask me."

"I can't use your Key. Your mother swore that if I made another wish on it, she'd cut my hand off."

"And you believe that?"

I threw his arm off me. "*Yes!*"

Lecy nodded in agreement, and Carmin said, "You couldn't pay me enough to cross Miz Sera."

"Shut up," Wyatt told him.

"You shut up." I climbed into the backseat so I wouldn't have to sit next to him.

"Hanna, wait—"

"If you'd really like to grant my dearest wish, you will take me home and then never speak to me again."

"Hanna—"

"*Ever!*"

When stupid, interfering Wyatt finally dropped me home, I was more than ready to take on Rosalee. After being MIA for two days and skipping school, I was definitely expecting a scene, but I got squat. Typical. I'd spent the past two days worrying and scheming and trying to help her, and she didn't even have the decency to be home to yell at me for making her worry.

I trudged upstairs and hugged Swan.

"*You* missed me, didn't you, Swanie? You noticed I was gone."

Swan came to life in my arms and wrapped her wings around me.

"I had it, Swanie. The answer to all our problems, and then stupid Wyatt . . . God, what's the point?"

Swan tapped her beak against my chest, at the wee silver swan dangling from my necklace.

"Isn't she cute?"

Swan nodded and gave me a questioning look.

"Wyatt gave her to me. I know. It *is* hard to stay mad at someone that thoughtful."

I draped the necklace around Swan's long neck and then went to the bathroom to shower off the river water. As the warm spray relaxed me, I began to formulate a plan. Maybe Wyatt could help me after all. He wouldn't want to. Probably he would refuse to. But screw him.

He owed me.

When I came back into the room, Little Swan was fluttering before Swan; they were whooping happily at each other.

"What are you two saying?" I laughed. "Are you talking about me?"

I pulled on a lilac shirtdress and thick tights and swapped my wet oxfords for mulberry booties, but before I could leave the room Swan whooped, as if in warning, and brought me up short.

Little Swan flew at my neck, flapping and tickling me in her desire to be worn.

"Okay, okay! I just thought you two might want to hang out, that's all."

As I fastened Little Swan around my neck, the front door slammed.

My heart lurched and pumped a sick feeling through my veins. I'd never before been reluctant to set eyes on Rosalee; I hated feeling this way. But I had a plan in place now, and I had to fix things between us—today.

Rosalee slumped in the chair by the floor lamp, arms bloody to the elbow, like she was wearing long red gloves. The gore didn't even bother me; gore and I were old friends at this point.

"*Was* it babies this time?" I asked, in a surprisingly steady voice.

"Nope," she said lightly, kicking off her shoes.

"Just a run-of-the-mill killing spree?"

"Define spree."

She was making jokes while the world was shifting under me, breaking apart.

"Remember when I said I would get a priest when your head started spinning?" I reminded her. "What about murder? Who do I get now that you've started killing people?"

Her breezy humor vanished, as though it had never been. She just looked tired. "You can't share your body with someone and not make compromises. As soon as he gets the Key *stop trying to explain things, Rosalee.*"

I jumped at Runyon's sudden appearance, at his blue eyes staring out at me like radiation.

"She's afraid you're thinking bad thoughts about her," he confided, then rolled his eyes. "Her desire for your good opinion makes her tiresomely provincial."

"I'm not thinking bad thoughts about *her.*"

"See?" he said, cooing to Rosalee. "Hanna loves you. A person in love will forgive anything."

I thought about Wyatt and hoped it was true. Then I steeled myself.

"I need to talk to you."

"Me?" He seemed surprised. "What about?"

"I can get you that Key."

He looked me over insultingly. "How are *you* going to get it?"

"Never mind how. But when I give it to you, you have to leave Rosalee. You can't be doing her any good, no matter what she thinks."

The hurt in his laughter pissed me off. Who was he to get his feelings hurt?

"Will you want her, without me?" he asked, smiling grimly. "Who would she be without me? The person you first met when you got here? You think it was easy to break her open?"

Break her open?

"Is it a deal or not?"

"How you think you can succeed where I failed—," he began.

"I can go get the Key right now, or I can go upstairs and paint my toenails. I'm only going to ask you one more time: *Is it a deal or not?*"

"Fine," he said, lifting my mother's hands in surrender. "It's a deal."

Wyatt had been surprised to see me so soon after our fight, but he welcomed me in.

"My folks're in the living room," he'd whispered to me as we stood on his stoop.

"This is just a social visit," I told him. "I'm not here to sleep over."

"Damn," he said, so disappointed that it made me laugh

and truly forgive him for ruining my wish. Besides, he didn't know it yet, but he was about to make up for it tenfold.

I went inside and stayed until dark, playing ring-around-the-rosy with Ragsie and Paulie, and Go Fish with Asher and Wyatt, and nothing at all with Sera, who monitored my every movement, ensuring that Wyatt and I couldn't be alone together. Finally, in the middle of Asher's easy-listening rendition of Black Sabbath's "Paranoid," I whispered to Wyatt, "I have to talk to you. Alone."

"Good," he said, glaring at his father. "Whoever invented karaoke should be shot." He took my hand and led me toward the stairs.

"Where do you think you're going?" Sera bellowed.

"Yeah," said Asher, "I'm just getting to the good part."

Paulie snatched the mic from him. "There's never any good parts when it's your turn, Poppy. *I* want a turn."

"We're just going to talk," Wyatt said over the heated debate that had broken out between Asher and Paulie.

"You can *talk* down here."

"Can I at least take her into the kitchen? For five minutes?"

"Five minutes starting right now." Sera clicked something on her watch.

Wyatt and I hurried into the kitchen. As soon as we were out of sight, he began kissing me, stinging kisses that made my heart fibrillate.

"Actually," he whispered, smiling against my mouth, "an enterprising young man could get a *lot* done in five minutes."

I stepped away from his kisses, regretful but focused. "We really do have to talk."

"Hell." He leaned against the counter, holding both of my hands. "You wanna yell at me some more about what happened at Evangeline?"

"No." The words trembled on the tip of my tongue, *Wyatt, I need to borrow your Key*, but I couldn't say them. Because he would say no, and if I insisted, he would demand to know why, and if I told him about Rosalee, about Runyon, he would deal with it the Mortmaine way—ruthlessly.

He watched me patiently, content to let me work it out, and suddenly I hated him for being so damnably thoughtful.

Finally I said, "You said you'd let me make a wish."

He caressed my palm. "What about getting your hand chopped off?" He said it in a joking way, as if he honestly didn't believe his mother was capable of such a thing.

"It would be worth it."

He snorted. "It must be something for Rosalee."

"Yes."

"Okay. You can have your wish."

Instead of thanking him, I kissed him, but this time his kisses didn't sting; they hurt. Hurt something deep within me. I'd used boys all the time back in Dallas—they were *there* to be used—but I didn't like using Wyatt.

But what choice did I have?

"*Time.*"

We scrambled apart as Sera frowned at us from the doorway. "That must've been some talk," she said, drily.

It was dark and raining lightly by the time I left Wyatt's house, splashing out onto his wet stoop. I pushed back the hood of my indigo coat, staring at the Key hanging unremarkably from the door, my elbows thrumming like crazy. I wrapped my fingers gingerly around the Key's slick surface, wished with all my might, and then, with only a slight tug, pulled it free like a loose tooth.

I stared at the heavy black twist of shining bone in my hand in wonder, marveling at how easy it had been to take, when a spurt of blood shot from the gap where the Key had been and splatted against my throat in a warm burst.

It was like the breeders at the fountain all over again, only instead of a vein opening in the Earth, the vein had opened in the Ortigas' door.

I gasped and sputtered, but before I could duck out of the bloody line of fire, the door opened onto a bright rectangle of light that Sera immediately filled, gaping at me and the bloody hole in her door.

And the Key in my hand.

"So I was right." She gave me a smile as deadly as a scythe. "That *was* one hell of a talk you had with my boy. He say you could take that?"

I cradled the Key to my chest, ready to fight for it like a mother bear. "He said I could wish for anything."

Sera slapped me so hard, I went flying backward off the stoop. I slammed into the wet sidewalk and lost my breath; Sera gave me no time to find it. She knelt on my chest and held a machete to my face.

"What did I tell you about negotiating with my son?"

"I don't care," I gasped, struggling under her weight. "Cut off my hand if that's what you want, but I'm not giving it back!"

Sera traced the blade along my cheek. "I'm not gone cut off

your hand," she said gently. "I'm gone cut off your *face*."

I flinched from the touch of the cold blade and willed myself not to pee in my pants. "Are you *sure* you wouldn't rather take my hand?"

Sera raised the machete, rain dripping from its murderously sharp edge like blood. "Positive."

Chapter Thirty-one

"Ma!"

Wyatt jumped down the stairs and yanked his mother off me. "What're you *doing*?"

He shoved her back toward the stoop and helped me to my feet.

"What am *I* doing? She stole our Key!"

Wyatt's eyes widened in disbelief when he saw the Key in my arms. He let go of me and reached for it, but I jerked away from him.

"No," I said, breathing hard, trying to ignore the pain in my head from having cracked it against the sidewalk, and trying to keep both Wyatt and Sera in sight so they couldn't blindside me.

The look of betrayal in Wyatt's eyes was as bad as I'd imagined it would be—worse, because it wasn't my imagination.

"I don't know what's going on," he said, "but you need to give back our Key. Right now."

"I can't. I need it."

"You have stolen our Key, craven!"

We all turned to find Asher on the stoop in a ridiculous Count Dracula cape; Paulie stood behind him, staring curiously from the doorway as Asher yelled at me, "Now you must pay the price!"

Asher raised his hands overhead, screaming in Latin, his eyes rolled to the whites.

"Aw, Christ," Wyatt whispered behind me. "Ma, don't let him—"

But Sera was already running up the stairs. "Asher, don't—"

But Asher did. He was holding something in his hand, which he promptly hurled to the ground at my feet.

While Wyatt and I pinwheeled away from the exploding glass, a huge gray blob materialized before us. A blob that quickly hardened into a creature that looked like it had been carved from rock. It sprang up as tall as the townhouses bordering the street, a creature with small, rheumy eyes, boulder-like teeth, and an earsplitting roar.

Somehow Wyatt wasn't afraid to jump on this monstrosity. In his T-shirt, jeans, and bare feet he climbed the creature like a kid on a jungle gym, and the first thing he did was wrap his arms around the creature's head and poke out its eyes.

The creature's roar of anger became a roar of pain as it knocked Wyatt to the ground with one long arm and tried to stomp him. But Wyatt easily avoided the creature's dark rampage.

"Wyatt!" Sera tossed her son the machete she'd nearly used on me. He caught it, climbed the creature again, and began to chisel away at it. If he had about a hundred years, he might even succeed in reducing the bloodthirsty mountain to rubble.

"Pop!" Wyatt screamed from atop the creature. "I need backup!"

"Here I come!" yelled Asher, staring at the creature with wide, blank eyes while he patted himself down, as if the change in his pockets might counteract the nightmare he'd unleashed on the street.

"Not *you!*" Wyatt yelled back in tones of horror. "Take Paulie inside and call Shoko!"

While I was distracted by Wyatt's David-and-Goliath struggle, Sera tried to snatch the Key away from me. Without thinking, I kicked her in the kneecap, but instead of falling to the ground, she decided to show me what a real kick was—she got me right in the chest. I was the one who hit the ground, and as I did, Little Swan went skipping down the wet pavement, as well as the entire contents of my coat pockets.

I couldn't breathe for a long moment—a good thing, as I was facedown in a rain puddle.

Sera flipped me onto my back and bent over me, her eyes bright with rain and malice. "You think you feel bad now," she said, ripping the Key from my unresisting hands. "Think how bad you'll feel after I tell the Mayor what you did. When she gets through with you . . ." Thinking of what the Mayor would do to me seemed to give her some satisfaction as she stormed away.

The items from my pockets lay nearby on the pavement, including one of Carmin's little blue capsules.

I snatched it and, sucking in as much air as I could, ran after Sera, who'd made it to the stoop. She was reaching to set the Key back into the hole in her door, but before she could manage it, I leaped up the bloody stairs and onto her back, much as Wyatt had done with the rock creature.

Before Sera could react, I shoved the pill in her mouth and squeezed it. The contents burst over my fingers and down her throat. She ripped my hand from her mouth, gagging on the liquid . . . then froze, a faraway look in her eyes, a look of sadness. *"Mamá?"*

I slid off her back, snatched the Key from her, ran down the stairs—and almost got nailed by a flying speed limit sign.

I ducked just in time and saw Wyatt still picking away at the roaring giant, cleverly dodging its attempts to knock him loose. The creature had chosen to deal with its annoyance at Wyatt by destroying the street. Its car-crushing assault brought people from their homes . . . but not too far. No one was rushing to Wyatt's aid.

As I contemplated how *I* could help—call the SWAT team?—Shoko popped in from nowhere at a run, swinging her pink flails and grinning maniacally, more deadly than twenty SWAT teams. A running leap landed her beside Wyatt on the creature's back, and on that note, I ran to Rosalee's car and made my escape while I still could.

I rushed into the living room, breathless and damp from the now heavy rain thundering outside. Runyon was waiting for me, and I could tell by the look in his eyes that for him the wait had been a long one. He'd used the time constructively at least, cleaning the blood off Rosalee and letting her change into her comfy lounge clothes—a black top and yoga pants.

I tossed Runyon the shiny twist of bone. He almost fumbled it, such was his surprise, eyes widening in shock as he held it in his hands.

"If you want to hang around long enough to wish us off to Brazil," I called, shrugging out of my sodden coat and racing upstairs, "I won't stop you, but Rosalee and I have got to hit the road!"

I packed quickly, as I had before fleeing Aunt Ulla's house, but at least this time I'd have company. Maybe Rosalee would want to go to Helsinki to see the house I'd grown up in. Or maybe we *could* go to Brazil; no one would expect us to go there. But no. Wyatt had family in Brazil. Or was it Argentina? I had to stop thinking about Wyatt. I had to focus. Why was it so hard to focus?

I carried my trusty pack downstairs and tossed it at the front door . . . and beheld a second door near the metal floor lamp. Rosalee, my Rosalee with her black eyes, stood before it, a door-shaped hole that looked as though it had been stamped out of the air with a cookie cutter. Through it, the rain fell on a huge skeletal tree standing alone in the center of a field.

"That's Cherry Glade," said Rosalee, disappointed.

Her eyes changed.

"I must have got the shape wrong," said Runyon, frustrated. "Shut up and let me concentrate."

I ignored the unease spreading in my sore chest—Sera had a kick like a mule—and ran into Rosalee's bedroom. I rummaged around until I found a bright red suitcase; I shoved her clothes into it, mostly the things I'd made her. I would have packed her precious red box, but as usual, it was in the locked drawer. I carried the suitcase out and set it next to my purple pack.

The scene in the doorway had changed. The rain was now falling on a river, the same river where I'd met Wet William.

"That's not it either," said Rosalee, as though bored with Runyon's failures. "Unless they have a Nudoso River in Calloway, too."

"I know what river it is!" Runyon screeched, kicking over the floor lamp in frustration. "What I don't know is why it's not working!" He slashed the Key in a series of movements, shaping the air with precise strokes. "This is the glyph for Calloway. I know it! *Why isn't the right door opening?*"

"Who cares about your stupid problems, Runyon?" I cried, fed up. "We had a deal. I don't even know why you're still here, and I don't want to know. All I want is for you to get the hell out of my mother!"

He whirled on me, blue eyes boring into mine. "Do you think you can trick me and get away with it? What did you do to this Key?" He held it outstretched toward me like a sword, like he meant to skewer me with it.

I charged forward and poked him in his stupid, wrong-colored eyes. *"Get out of my mother!"*

He wheeled away, tears squeezing through his squinted eyes. When they opened, though, they were the right color.

"Thank God," I said. "Is he gone?"

In reply, Rosalee bashed my head with the Key. I crumpled, and a weight seemed to lift from her face as I hit the ground.

The pain was immense, but I could barely feel it compared to the pain of betrayal, of rejection. Rosalee had hit me.

My own mother.

"Don't look at me like that," she said. "It's better this way. This whole 'mother' thing isn't working out, not for either of us. If anybody asks, tell 'em I made you steal it. Or that Runyon did. It doesn't matter anymore."

She bent and hit me again with the Key, splitting my lip. "This is just so they buy it."

I wanted to say something, but there was too much blood in my mouth.

Rosalee turned her back on my agony and faced the doorway. "We should try this at your house," she said calmly. "You're stronger there, right? They say she can't control you there."

"That's true," said Runyon. "She had to sacrifice something in order to put that great a curse on me."

"Well, I figure if you can't make it work inside your own house, you can't make it work nowhere."

"You're right. We also have an ace up our sleeve as far as the Mayor is concerned." Runyon laughed. "One way or another, we leave for Calloway tonight!"

He made a different glyph shape in the air, and the view within the doorway changed, revealing the porch of a large white house.

I swallowed the blood. "Momma, *please.*" But she didn't look at me. Instead she went through the doorway and vanished.

I was alone.

I lay prostrate long enough for the stars swimming across my vision to disappear and a knot the size of a marble to sprout from my skull. I arose and staggered into the kitchen, a trail of blood running from my head into my eye. I was always getting blood in my eyes.

I removed the carving knife from the stand on the counter. I held the sharp blade to my wrist, and just as I'd known she would, Swan came barging into the kitchen, white wings spread, diving at the knife.

I whirled it away from her beak, slicing upward at the same time, and cut into her wing. Swan crashed into the wall behind me in a burst of feathers.

"Ha!" I screamed at her. "Not this time, Swan. It doesn't matter anymore. Rosalee said she wouldn't let anything happen to me. That I should trust her. *But you see what she did to me?*"

I slit my left arm open from elbow to wrist. The pain was immediate and hot.

"I *said* I'd paint the walls with my blood," I said, bleeding all over my dress, all over the floor. "Unlike *her*, I keep my word!"

I smeared my bloody hand along the white kitchen walls like a kid who'd gotten into the forbidden stash of watercolors.

Swan, bleeding and crippled, righted herself and hobbled

after me, her black feet clicking across the white tile, whooping mournfully, but at her pain or mine, I couldn't say.

I easily dodged her censorious beak and spread my art to the living room walls. I didn't feel on the verge of death; all things considered, I felt pretty good. So I slit my other forearm to speed things along.

I went all over the downstairs part of the house, even into Rosalee's room. Swan almost wrested the knife from me in the tight confines of the hall bathroom, but I eluded her with a few well-aimed kicks and an arsenal of Dove soap.

I shut Swan inside the bathroom, crawling on the floor by that point, tired from struggling with her and depleted by blood loss—more of it ran along the walls than inside my veins. I collapsed in the living room, almost directly on the spot where Rosalee had fled through the doorway. Fitting, since what was really killing me wasn't blood loss but rejection.

I whispered the words to "Gloomy Sunday" and thought of her, filled my head with her. I wanted to die thinking of her.

Death crept over me like cold water, nothing like what I'd imagined. I'd thought I'd feel a tingling or witness something visionary. Something prophetic or enlightening. But I only felt a need to sleep.

Sooooo sleepy.

"Hanna Järvinen?"

I had no strength to respond.

"Are you dead?" The voice seemed to be coming from miles away. From Seattle or Slovenia.

Something flipped me over and squeezed my cut arms. Something painful. "Stop it," I moaned. But it didn't stop.

"Now, now. I can't have you committing suicide in your *house*."

A sudden vigor and wakefulness filled me.

The hell?

I opened my eyes and beheld a tallish woman crouched over me. *She* was squeezing my wrists, squeezing the wounds closed, her face shadowy and wraithlike beneath a long, black hooded robe. Unlike Asher's costume party cape, this was the real thing.

"Are you Death?" I asked, looking for the scythe that would match the robe.

"No, transy," she said, an amused curl to her red lips. "I'm the Mayor. And you aren't allowed to die yet." She hauled me to my feet, then finally released my wrists.

But for a few smears of blood, the skin of my arms was whole and unblemished, pulsing with life.

I don't remember ever being as pissed as I was at that moment.

"Why did you save me?"

"Because, transy"—the curl to the Mayor's lips deepened as four burly Mortmaine stepped up beside her, flanking her—"you must be put to death *properly*."

Chapter Thirty-Two

The Mayor drew back her hood, heedless of my blood on her birdlike hands. From what I'd heard of her, I'd known better than to expect an old fogey in a pantsuit, but she rather exceeded expectation.

She was my height and striking, with golden Egyptian skin and strange Asian eyes with mirrored irises. My twin reflections gazed back at me as she faced me. I looked confused as hell.

I said, "You saved my life so you could *kill* me?"

"Killing yourself here alone where no one can see would be unsatisfying to too many people. Porterenes like to see for themselves that justice has been served."

"Justice?"

"You have a lot to answer for. You stole that cursed Key and gave it to Runyon, and for what? Do you think to free someone I mean to keep caged?" She tsked at me. "Is he such a charmer, then?"

"I was trying to get him to leave Rosalee. He's been possessing her!"

"Yet he didn't become a problem until you showed up. Why is that?" She licked my blood from her palm.

If I was the type to run away from things, I'd have run right then. She had a tongue like a snake. Not forked, but long and slimy, and now coated in my blood.

"Ah!" she exclaimed, excited, as though my blood had fueled the lightbulb that now burned over her head. "Because you smashed Rosalee's skull and awakened him! If not for you, she might have gone to her grave never knowing he was there."

"You knew all along that Rosalee was possessed?"

"How could I not know? Runyon hasn't been in that house for twenty years, and Rosalee was the last person to go anywhere near it. It's not exactly rocket science, Hanna."

"But if you knew, why didn't you do something?" I rubbed my healed arms. "With your power—"

"Why should I do anything for Rosalee? She disobeyed me. A person who messes her bed must lie in it. If I cleaned up after all my children, I'd never have time for myself."

"So why interfere now?"

Her mirror eyes narrowed. "Because this is personal."

The Mayor had her guards drag me out of the house and down the dark street in the cold rain—and me with no coat or any protection.

But I would be dead soon; catching a cold was beside the point. I should have been dead *already*. Why couldn't I ever die when I wanted to?

The Mayor didn't have to worry about catching cold. The rain seemed to part for her as she walked through it. Even stranger, when her billowing black robe passed over a dead armadillo in the street, it twitched to life and lumbered away.

I understood for the first time why everyone had been so impressed that Rosalee would cross someone like the Mayor.

What the hell had Rosalee been thinking?

The Mayor laughed softly at my expression. "Just for the record," she said, staring after the armadillo, "that wasn't one of your hallucinations."

When we reached the corner, the Mayor pulled me through

a hidden door. We went straight through with no unseemly sidestepping or falling, and when we came out the other side, we were in Fountain Square.

After the four Mortmaine came through behind us, we all walked to the colonnade beyond the lit amphitheater, in the space between the courthouse and the hotel where the last suicide door had been erected. I knew then that that was what she was planning for me. Wyatt had said only the Mayor herself could open a suicide door, and now she would open one for me. I felt almost special.

Several Porterenes stood beneath the colonnaded arches out of the rain, the gas lamps that lighted the square illuminating their grave faces as they watched us. The Mayor and I, and her coterie, joined a larger group of Mortmaine, about twenty in all, who semicircled me as I shivered in my pale shirtdress. Wyatt wasn't among them, nor any of the initiates, only tough folk all in green.

The Mayor stood next to me and addressed the waiting crowd. "This transient, Hanna Järvinen, took the Ortiga Key and gave it to our enemy Runyon." Her voice carried easily over the driving rain, to people I knew would soon be laughing in anticipation as they waited for a chance to squeal over my corpse.

"Runyon has possessed Rosalee Price these past twenty years, and when her daughter, Hanna, found out, she decided to steal the Ortiga Key and simply hand it over—"

"I didn't just hand it over," I shouted. I could barely get the words out through my chattering teeth, but if the Mayor was going to tell my life story, I wanted her to tell it right. "Runyon promised he'd leave Rosalee if I did!"

The Mayor smiled at me condescendingly. "And you believed him?"

The warm shame of my own näiveté chased away the cold.

"Why shouldn't she have believed me?"

Everyone turned and gasped to find Runyon in a doorway several feet behind the Mayor and me.

He was still in Rosalee's body, standing in what looked like a toolshed, I thought, noting the can of motor oil and a gutted electric drill on a shelf behind him. Rosalee's hair was peppered with sawdust.

Runyon smiled at the Mayor, blue eyes full of sardonic humor. "I've been told I have a very trustworthy face."

"Are you still here?" asked the Mayor, feigning surprise. "I thought you'd be long gone by now. Whatever could be keeping you?"

The bitter humor fled. "You know what," he said coldly.

"It doesn't matter how many Keys you make or use," said the Mayor with equal coldness. "You can never leave this town."

"Unless you remove the curse. Which you will." Runyon was supremely confident. "I'm not the bodiless eunuch you remember."

"I see the body, but the eunuch part is still relevant." She smiled cruelly. "You're much more attractive as a woman."

Runyon was unfazed and deadly earnest. "I can make things difficult for you if you don't reconsider what's more important: the lives of your people or a grudge. Think it over."

He stepped back from the doorway and a flood of stick figures took his place, pouring from the cutout door into the square. After the last one came through, the doorway disappeared.

They were literally stick figures, man-size with square blocks for heads and branches for ribs that curved tightly around what looked like beating human hearts. Their twiggy fingers clutched enormous wooden clubs that they immediately put to work, bashing unsuspecting Porterenes on the head and leaving them to bleed to death beneath the colonnades.

The Mortmaine converged on the stick figures in force, but

neither blunt trauma nor fire could stop or even slow their assault.

The Mayor and I were safe in a protective ring of her four bodyguards, but I didn't want to be safe. I broke through the bodyguards and chased after the stick figures, waving my arms for attention.

"Over here! Hey! If you want to smash someone, I'm totally available!"

They ignored me.

I raced over the slick stone and squeezed between a young Porterene woman and the stick figure about to knock her block off. "Come on," I whined as the woman took off, eyeing the stick figure's raised club as it cast a shadow across my upturned face. "Do it!"

The stick figure pushed me aside and tried to run after the woman. Tried, because as I reached to grab it, to *make* it attack me, my hand went through its chest and knocked against its heart, which rattled free of the stick figure's twiggy rib cage and smacked against the wet pavement at my feet. The heartless stick figure collapsed in a heap, like a mini woodpile.

One of the Mortmaine was nearby and saw the whole thing. "Go for the hearts!" he shouted to his comrades.

My soaked hair straggled into my face as I picked up the heart at my feet. It beat warmly against my palm a few seconds before it stilled. Glyphs branded the center of the heart, tiny pictures I didn't understand and one word I did: the word "purple" in a circle with a slash through it.

After the Mortmaine dispatched the stick figures, the Mayor and her bodyguards engulfed me once again; she snatched the heart from my hand.

"Where did Runyon get these?" she demanded. In the mirrors of her eyes, I saw myself, saw the baffled—and partially bogus—innocence.

"I don't know," I said. And I didn't, but I remembered that Rosalee had come home covered in blood to the elbow. I bet *she* knew where those hearts had come from.

The Mayor passed the heart to one of her bodyguards and addressed the three shell-shocked Porterenes who were all that remained of the huge crowd, most of whom had either escaped or lay dead on the square. The remaining three huddled together, shivering in the rain that washed their neighbors' blood past their feet.

The Mayor dragged me forward to face them.

"I need you three to bear witness to what her actions have

wrought. Now that the Key is once again in Runyon's power, now that he has returned to his home where no one, not even I, has dominion over him, he has all the time in the world to devise ways of using the Key to bedevil us all, merely for spite."

"It's not spite," I told her. "If you let him leave, he'll go to Calloway and no one will ever have to see him again."

"Runyon and your mother, gone away?" She shook me. "Shall I reward them for their disobedience?"

I tried to jerk away from her, but I couldn't; her grip was too tight on my arm. "Runyon was right. Your grudge *is* more important than the lives of your people."

The Mayor ignored me and addressed the three Porterenes. "Who would speak for her?"

Not one of them spoke. They looked so traumatized; they probably didn't even remember why they were there.

In the rainy silence, a door formed out of nothing. Black with a silver doorknob and hinges. A suicide door, just as I'd thought.

"Understand that this punishment is reserved for the lowest among us," said the Mayor. "There is none so low as a transient, except a coward, and you appear to be both. Suicide is, after all, the coward's way out. Shall you finish what you started at home?"

She was trying to shame me, but I was beyond shame. What did I care what this town thought of me? Everything I had was gone. I wanted to be gone too.

I opened the heavy black door, saw the gray within, the emptiness. I stepped inside and filled it.

Chapter Thirty-Three

It was gray and foggy within the door. Cold and wet. Numbness coursed through me as I waited for the end yet again.

I had barely enough space to slide to the floor and sit with my knees to my chest. It *felt* like a floor, but beyond the gray fog puffing around my hips, I saw nothing.

I waited for the end. I waited and waited.

How long did it take, for Christ's sake?

The man in the suicide door I'd seen had had a rope, at least. I didn't even have—

Something thumped against my head and dangled before my face.

A noose.

My eyes followed the swaying line of rope, but as with the floor, everything above my head was lost in fog. It was almost smoky, like a fire was—

Not that I wanted to burn to death!

I threw my hands overhead to protect myself from falling flames that never fell, thank God. I so did not want to burn to death. I wanted to die in a way that would make this gray space fill with blood, so much blood that when nosy Porterenes came to investigate, they would be drenched in a violent red flood.

Of course, such a stunt would only work once. It sucked that I would have to waste such an awesome effect on a lousy tweener-wiener. I wished I could be sure that Rosalee would be the first one to open the door.

I found myself wishing for *her* to fall down on my head like the rope had, but she didn't. Hell, she was probably already on another planet by now, or wherever the hell Calloway was.

Except she couldn't go to Calloway, could she? Not while the Mayor's curse was still in effect. She couldn't because *Runyon* couldn't.

Not that I cared. She'd hit me, after all. My head and mouth still hurt from it.

But then I had hit her, too. . . .

It would be weird if she'd hit me for the same reason I'd hit her—fear. It had to be way easier for her to go with Runyon than to risk caring for someone like me. *Love is a trap*—that's what she'd said. Maybe she was still trying not to get caught.

Well, to hell with that. I deserved better than that. We could work through fear. If she truly didn't want me, I wanted to know *for sure*. How stupid would it be to die over a misunderstanding?

The heat of resolution warmed me, circulated the feeling back into me, along with an unpleasant pins-and-needles sensation, especially in my elbows.

My elbows.

They were tingling. Almost painfully. I stood, dodging the dangling rope, raising and lowering my elbows as though they were antennae and I was trying to find the best reception. I went down on my knees. That was the spot that made my elbows zing.

A hidden door. A real live hidden door. But how to use it? I couldn't see it or even feel it except with my elbows.

Because I didn't have Wyatt's tattoo, that glyph the Mortmaine had inked into him: an eye within a door. If I could carve that glyph . . .

I spoke into the fog. "Spindle?"

It dropped onto my head, and I was almost set on fire after all. The spindle definitely singed my hair and burned my fingers. I dropped it, hissing, and it sank into the floor, vanishing into the fog.

I remembered then that Rosalee had worn gloves while handling the spindle she'd used on that boy's forehead.

I removed my purple tights, moving awkwardly in the small space, and folded them into a bundle, which I held forth. "Spindle!"

The long red, needlelike thorn landed neatly on my tights.

I lifted my dress and pushed down my underpants to reveal the smooth, creamy brown, unmarked, gorgeous curve of my hip. My hand, protected by my thick tights, trembled as I brought the point of the spindle close to my skin. I took a deep breath, then another, and another, and then I realized I was never going to have enough breath for this horrid mutilation, so I just did it. Touched the tip of the spindle to my hip.

If I were the type to scream in pain, my throat would have been hoarse by the time I finished that carving. But I couldn't afford to waste breath screaming. I could hardly breathe as it was—some leftover result of being kicked in the chest, no doubt.

I dropped the spindle and let it sink out of sight in the fog, and between one blink and the next, the hidden door appeared to me—a floating smile of darkness within the gray space, about the length of my forearm. I struggled and contorted and nearly dislocated my shoulders, but I finally managed to squeeze inside the hidden door.

It opened into a narrow, airless space even more dreary than the suicide door, a space without even fog to recommend it. I couldn't see a thing, but there was only space enough to go one way—up.

I stood gingerly in the darkness and reached overhead. My fingers poked through a yielding slit, and a splat of icy rain wetted my fingertips. I pulled myself up, feet scrambling for purchase.

Cold wind and rain engulfed the whole of me as I pulled myself out of the slit, which hovered about a foot over a gravel path. I dropped free and lay on the path, letting the rain cleanse me, breathing huge drafts of fresh air. My tights were gone. One of my ankle boots was missing. I was freezing. But I was free.

I sat up and looked around. The path twined around a pair of utilitarian tombstones set close together. In the light of a lamppost shining several yards from me, I could just make out the inscriptions: Richard and Mary Price. My grandparents. I was in the family plot, assuming Rosalee would have buried me here with the rest of her family and not shipped me back to Aunt Ulla in a crate.

I got to my feet, kicked off my remaining bootie, and wound barefoot and bare-legged through the muddy pathways and gravestones until I reached the street. Lamartine. My street.

I went home on autopilot and then stood in the empty house, soaked through and shivering, but still alive. Still with a reason to live.

A thump from the downstairs bathroom nearly sent me out of my skin, but then I remembered Swan, how I'd locked her in. I raced to the door to let her out and was rewarded by a series of sharp, beaky jabs to my knees. "Ow!"

I couldn't believe I'd expected to find her weak and bloodied and half-dead. Her wing was perfectly healed, and Swan was anything but weak. Her wings batting my head made me feel as though I were on the losing end of a vicious pillow fight.

"I'm sorry!" I yelled, hands up for protection. "I didn't go through with it! Look." I showed her my unmarked arms, the sight of which convinced Swan to stop pummeling me.

She alighted on the bathroom floor, hurt feelings ruffling her feathers.

I dropped beside her, kneeling in a nearly dried stipple of blood, and cuddled her. She was soft and warm; she was always more fun to pet when she wasn't wooden. "I don't deserve you, I know it." I checked the wing I'd slashed, making sure she was injury free, then bent my head to Swan's so that we were nose to beak. "I know it sucks having to look after someone like me, but karma's a bitch, Swanie. Now *I* get to see what it feels like to try to save someone from herself."

Good luck with that.

"Poppa?" I looked around the wrecked bathroom and then down the hallway. "Where are you?"

In your room. There's too much blood downstairs.

I picked up Swan, stroking her long neck, and as I went toward the stairs, I examined the walls. I decided that Poppa was too squeamish for his own good. The smears of blood were quite pretty, artistic rather than gory.

In my room I set Swan on the top shelf, curtsied to her, and turned to find Poppa lounging on my bed on his left side, his head on my pillow. Lying like that, no one could tell his face was all torn up.

"My life is in ruins and you're lazing in bed. Unbelievable."

I stripped out of my wet clothes in the bathroom and donned a purple terry-cloth robe.

"I like to let the words soak into me," said Poppa when I left the bathroom. "Even though she didn't stitch it for me."

I scraped my wet hair back into a bun. "What are you talking about?"

He sat up and folded back the pillowcase, showing me what Rosalee had stitched into the pillow: "I Love You Too."

I took the pillow and held it to my face, examining the tiny purple stitches. Purple. I remembered the word burned into that heart at Fountain Square. Had she burned the word into all those hearts? Had she made it impossible for the stick figures to hurt me?

I squeezed the pillow to my own heart. Poppa was right; the words seemed to soak into me, the knowledge that she loved me after all and that the time we'd spent together hadn't been a lie.

"Is she still here in Portero?"

"Yes. At Runyon's house. On Nightshade."

I brushed my cheek across the stitches. "What's Night-shade?"

"It's a street downsquare—darkside—where all the Mort-maine live."

Where the Mortmaine lived and the weird shit happened. Great. But somehow, I didn't feel worried. I squeezed the pillow. "Do you know the house number?"

"No, but it's easy to spot," Poppa said, as though he'd lived in Portero all his life. "It's the house at the end of the cul-de-sac. It's white and has pyracantha growing all over it. Plus, it has all the wards. There's no way you can miss it."

Now I was worried.

"The wards!" I groaned, and collapsed next to Poppa on the bed. "You mean the wards no one can get past?"

"Wyatt could."

I laughed, but it came out wrong, crippled and ugly. "Wyatt would sooner see me in hell after what I did to him."

My stomach growled. Crazy how your body insisted on making demands even when everything was circling the drain. I shot to my feet. "I'm going downstairs."

"I'm not. But . . ."

I looked at him, saw him eyeing the pillow still in my hands.

I ran my fingers along the words once more, and then I gave it to him and went down to the dark, bloody kitchen.

I know Wyatt's angry with you, Poppa said, continuing our conversation from the relative comfort inside my head, *but it's his job to be objective. That's why he was able to kill his own friend, because it was his job.*

"Would he consider it part of his job to help *me*?" I said, grabbing a handful of granola bars from the cupboard.

For the Key? What do you think?

"Maybe." But how could I get to him without alerting his folks? Especially his mom. I was not in the mood for another ass kicking.

I opened the fridge to snag a bottle of milk and saw the cherries. Dark red. Deliciously ripe.

Cherries.

Why didn't you think of me? said Poppa, distracting me.

"What?"

When you cut your wrists. When you lay there thinking of Rosalee and no one else.

I sighed and set the cherries opposite the blood smears on the counter. "Poppa, don't guilt-trip me. We know how we feel about each other. But Rosalee . . . ?"

It's okay. His words soughed desolately inside my skull. *My last thought was of her too. I didn't mean to pass it on to you, this obsession.*

"It's not an obsession; it's fascination."

The Price fascination, he said, as if he knew it well. *So powerful not even the devil infesting her will give her up.*

"He might," I said, fingering the container of cherries as a plan began to take shape. "For the right price."

Chapter Thirty-four

Carmona Boulevard was wrecked, the lights broken out, the traffic signs snapped in half. A crater-size hole dented the street; I knew because I'd driven Rosalee's red Prius into it and had to walk the last few yards to Wyatt's house. Just as well— the Ortigas might know Rosalee's car by sight.

Thin rain gleamed in the flowerless vines hugging the wrought-iron fence circling Wyatt's house. I slipped through the gate and crept to his backyard. Through the living-room window of his tall, skinny house, I saw Sera ranting from the couch as Wyatt and Asher sat nearby, listening. Asher nodded sympathetically after every word that left Sera's mouth, but Wyatt only looked empty, staring blankly at the floor.

I backed away from the window and searched until I found a jasmine-covered trellis; I climbed it, my French heels forcing me to be careful.

In the lit second-story window to my right was Wyatt's room. The body parts he'd stuck to his walls, the plaster legs and hands, now littered the floor, curled and shrunken like dead bugs, as if my theft of the Key had sickened the house. Or killed it.

But I couldn't fix that now. First things first.

On the left side of the trellis was Paulie's room. The blue glow of his night-light washed over him as he lay sleeping beneath his Superman bedspread, oblivious of the turmoil downstairs. Ragsie lay in his arms, wild orange hair spilling over the pillow.

I tapped at the window, and though I tapped gently, Ragsie immediately lifted his head. Carefully, trying not to pitch over backward off the trellis, I removed the plastic bag of cherries from my coat pocket and shook it in front of the window.

Ragsie scrambled out of Paulie's arms and hurried to the window, making quick work of the lock with his floppy arms. He threw open the glass and made a grab for the cherries, but I held them out of reach.

"Not yet," I whispered. "First I need you to get Wyatt for me. Can you?"

He nodded.

"Good boy." I held out the bag and let him take a cherry.

Ragsie opened his slit of a mouth and popped the cherry in whole, stem and all. When he reached for another, I again held the bag out of reach. Ragsie's shoe-button eyes regarded me reproachfully.

I leaned closer to the doll, close enough to see the creases in the woven cotton that he was made of. "Bring Wyatt out to the backyard, and make sure he's alone. If you do that for me, I'll let you have *all* the cherries. Okay?"

Almost before I'd finished speaking, Ragsie scurried off the windowsill and out of the room. I followed suit, scurrying down the trellis, hoping he hadn't run off to sound the alarm.

I kept watch in the shadow of an oak tree, water dripping off the scant red leaves and down the collar of my coat. I'd traded the hooded indigo for the fitted fuchsia coat I now wore, which, though hoodless and less warm, was much cuter and matched my shoes. Looking stylish always put a girl at an advantage, especially when she was in the wrong.

After some time, Wyatt came out to the backyard, Ragsie leading the way.

Good ole Ragsie.

"What is it, Rags?" Wyatt asked, his arms crossed over his T-shirt against the cold.

Ragsie scanned the yard, and when he spotted me under the oak, he ran to me.

"Good boy," I said. and patted his wild hair . . . and then cringed, taking my hand back. Ragsie's hair felt . . . human.

When Ragsie held out his arms, I gave him the cherries. He almost buckled under the weight of the bag, but managed to carry it back into the house on his strong cloth legs.

Wyatt, meantime, looked dazed as he came toward me, sleepwalker-slow. "Who's there?"

"Me."

My voice briefly stopped him in his tracks . . . then he marched under the tree and grabbed my chin, turning me so that the light from his bedroom window touched me. With his back to the light, I couldn't read his face, but I could read his touch, the ceaseless drift of his hands over my face.

"The Mayor opened a suicide door," he whispered. "Ma said it was for you, because of what you did." His warm fingertips pressed the pulse beating beneath my jaw. "Are you a ghost?"

I kissed him, and even though it hurt my mouth, I didn't mind; Wyatt's kisses were worth suffering over. I'd been prepared to never be this close to him again, and now I was breathing in his sighs. I wanted to inhale all of him, but he pushed me away, panting.

"Don't kiss me like that," he hissed. "Like you care when I know you don't."

He'd pushed me away, but he was still holding my arms, so I pulled him back into them. I could tell him I cared, but couldn't he feel it? He must have, because he stopped resisting me and let me kiss him the way I wanted to.

"How are you not dead?" he asked, when I let him breathe.

"It doesn't matter right now," I said, kissing his ears. The rain hung from his earlobes like delicate jewelry. "I'll tell you later. Right now, we have to save Rosalee."

This time when he pushed me, I went flying back into the tree trunk, nearly cracking my spine against it.

"So that's it," he said sardonically. "You came back here to use me. Again."

The self-disgust in his voice made me feel as low as the mud I stood in. I wanted to throw myself at his feet and beg forgiveness, I really did, but I didn't have time for that. "Wyatt—"

"I thought you could take care of yourself," he said, throwing my words at Evangeline in my face. "Remember? You don't need to be rescued."

"I don't. I'm trying to rescue someone else, and for that I do need help."

"Piss on what you need! How long you been planning to steal the Key, Hanna? Since the first day we met?"

"I wouldn't even have involved you if you hadn't interfered with me and Wet William!"

"Oh, I'm so sorry for *forcing* you to steal from me and my family!"

I pushed away from the tree, rubbing my back, but my pain didn't seem to bother him. "You said I never have to make hard choices, but I do, Wyatt. You think it was easy choosing between you and Rosalee?"

"Easy as hell, obviously!" On the verge of tearing into me, he paused, seemed to consider something. "Why would Rosalee need our Key?"

"Because Rosalee was possessed. *Is* possessed. Runyon's been hiding inside her for twenty years, and the only way to help her was to get him the Key. He promised to leave her if I did."

When he turned away, the upstairs light caught part of his face. He looked stunned. I guessed his Mortmaine mates hadn't clued him in. Maybe because he was still on the two-day vacation Sera had arranged for him.

"You didn't have to steal from me. Why didn't you tell me if you were in trouble?"

"Tell you that Rosalee was possessed? You killed Petra, and she was your friend. Who is Rosalee to you that you would spare her?"

He didn't say anything.

"I didn't take the Key to hurt you. I took it to save my mother. You understand about duty, right? Well, I have a duty to her. That's why I risked coming here, even though I knew you would hate me, maybe even tell on me. I had to try. Can you understand that?"

Still he said nothing.

"And it's not like we can't get the Key back along *with* Rosalee—they're in the same place—but I can't do it without you."

Nothing.

I got down on my knees on the soggy, leaf-littered ground.

Apparently, I was going to have to make time for this. "I'm sorry I stole your Key, Wyatt. I'm sorry I used you. I swear I'll make it up to you, no matter how long it takes. Even if—"

He pulled me to my feet, stood us both in the upstairs light. I watched a few worrisome emotions cross his face, mostly anger and shame, but strangely, they were all self-directed.

"You're wrong. I don't understand about duty. If I did, I would've told Elder to go to hell, would've tried to do something to help Pet. Anything before I just . . ." He sighed. "Your sense of duty is way less out of whack than mine."

He rubbed his hands over his face, to wipe away the emotion brewing below the surface. "I'm sorry about your ma," he said, when he had control of himself. "About her being possessed. But you gotta face the fact that no matter what I try, she might not—"

But I didn't want to hear that. "I can face facts later. First things first. I think I can convince Runyon to leave, but when I do, can you help her not to get sick and die? You said you'd try to think of a way."

"I did think of a way. I had just finished working on something that might do the trick when you stole the Key and all hell broke loose."

"So then that's great!" I said, ignoring the bitterness in his voice.

"*Maybe.* I never tried this before. I ain't tested it—"

"You can test it when we get her back."

"Do you even have a plan?" he asked, exasperated.

"We go into Runyon's house and get Rosalee back."

"That's not a plan! That's suicide. If the Mayor finds out—"

"Fuck the Mayor." I thought of the suicide door and shrugged. "Besides, who's afraid of suicide?"

He looked shocked . . . but then a species of non-high-minded admiration crossed his face. "If the Mayor ever heard you talking like that—"

His phone rang and sent Wyatt leaping almost out of his skin. He pulled the phone out of his pocket, cursing. "What the hell, Shoko? I thought I had the day off." He looked at the lit face of his watch. "Oh."

It was after midnight. Apparently, his two-day vacation was over.

"I have to go where?" He looked at me a long time. "I can't. I have to do something. No, for a friend."

I slumped against the tree, shocked that for once he'd chosen me over the Mortmaine.

"My friends *are* important, and I'm sick of turning my back on 'em just to uphold somebody else's moral objectives. You think I don't have my own set of morals? I don't care what she said. Stop telling me what she said. For the last time, fuck the Mayor and fuck what she said!" He snapped the phone shut and shoved it back in his pocket.

Then his legs gave out, and he huddled on the ground, shaking.

He looked at me, wide-eyed. "Did I really just say . . . what I said?"

I brushed the wet leaves off his shoulders. "Yes."

He shook his head, amazed at his own daring. "I'm so dead."

"You and me both. So why don't we go out with a bang?"

I waited while he staggered into the house to get supplies. When he came out in the green coat, he was much calmer, and he had brought something for me.

"I found her on the street after Shoko and me brought down that rock creature," he said, handing over Little Swan. "I almost threw it down the gutter, but . . ." He turned away, as if he couldn't bear to look at me another second, and stormed off.

I fastened Little Swan around my neck and caught up to him. "I'm glad you didn't throw her away."

"Whatever." He shoved his hands in his coat pockets and refused to look at me.

We left his backyard and went down the street, passing slits and circles of darkness, the hidden doors all around us.

"That phone call just now . . . are the Mortmaine looking for me?"

"Are you kidding? Nobody's ever escaped the suicide door. It ain't even crossed their minds that you could be out here talking to me. They're wondering why the suicide door won't open. It's never taken this long before. If the person doesn't decide how to die in an hour, she runs out of air and suffocates."

I remembered how difficult it had been to breathe.

"They called me because they want me there to see if I can figure out a way to open it. *Knowing* that you're my girlfriend, they want me to open the door, and never mind if the sight of your corpse drives me apeshit, just as long as I get the job done!"

Despite his ranting and raving and hurt feelings, I couldn't help feeling glad he'd referred to me as his girlfriend. Present tense.

"How *did* you get out?" he asked me.

I stopped and showed him my hip there on the street.

"Jesus!" he exclaimed, fingering the ugly glyph burned into my skin that was nothing like the elegant green tracery on his arm.

But he was more impressed than disgusted by the mark. Proud, even. I told him about the hidden door that led to my family's burial plot.

"Doesn't it seem to suggest," I told him, "that the hidden doors lead from one place to the other based on some sort of logic? If a person could figure out the logic involved . . . Why are you looking at me like that?"

He shrugged, trying to pretend his face hadn't just been awash in emotion. "Just thinking I oughta tell Elder about you. You should be one of us."

"No, thanks. Too much stress makes Hanna go crazy." I straightened my dress, rebuttoned my coat. "Look, Wyatt, I know you probably won't ever trust me again—"

"Let's not get sidetracked by all that now," he said quickly. "First things first, like you said."

A couple of streets over, Wyatt stopped at a tall hidden door—one so skinny it could only be traversed sideways. "After you," he said.

I squeezed through into darkness and squeezed out onto a quiet, well-lit street far away from Wyatt's house. The narrow houses and iron gates of Carmona had been replaced by gloomy Victorians with large, unmanicured lawns and ancient trees with thick roots that bullied the sidewalks out of shape.

"Where are we?" I asked Wyatt when he joined me.

He looked up and down the long, damp street. "Nightshade."

"Where the Mortmaine live," I whispered, remembering what Poppa had said.

"They're mostly gone this time of night, out patrolling." He pointed to the dead end of Nightshade, where the white house I had seen through the cutout doorway sat. "That's Runyon's house."

Weird squiggles bordered the house on every side that I could see, squiggles in midair that glowed eerie and green in the dark, as though the northern lights had strayed south and gotten trapped over the sidewalk.

"The Mayor wanted everyone to be able to see that the house was off-limits," Wyatt explained, "even at night."

We'd stopped close enough to the glyphs for me to see the dead birds littering the gutter.

"They fly into the wards," said Wyatt. "Feel." He guided my hand to the green air over the sidewalk, which was as solid as stone.

"How do we get past it?"

"Through the ground."

Wyatt removed a pale orange card from the deck in his pocket. He held the card between his palms and immediately liquefied from the feet up until he splashed into a puddle on the cul-de-sac. The green glyph-light twinkled over his liquid form as he streamed into a crack in the sidewalk.

I waited nervously in the street, eyeing the few houses with green trucks parked in the driveways, hoping none of the homebound Mortmaine decided to look out the window or take a late-night stroll.

One of the sidewalk's concrete squares rattled and turned orange, like Wyatt's card. The single section—more importantly, the *glyph* carved into the section—began to crack, then break into pieces. The green light wavering all around the house snuffed out, allowing darkness to press closer on the street.

A puddle arose from the broken section of concrete, like water from an underground spring; it lengthened and solidified until Wyatt was whole again, tall and straight in his green coat, beckoning me forward. "Come on."

I stepped onto the property, and Wyatt handed me two black cards, like the ones he'd used at Melissa's.

"One's for Rosalee," he explained, leading me across the lawn.

When we got to the porch, I unbuttoned the top half of my coat and lifted my chest at him. "Don't you want to put it on?"

He looked like he wanted to say no, but he did it anyway, put the card down my low bodice and pressed it below my breast. I stole a kiss while he did it.

"There's no time for all that," he said, pulling away.

"I know," I said, squeezing him. "It's just, in case something happens, I want you to know—"

"I know," he said impatiently, but when he saw the look on my face, he kissed me back and said it again, gently. "I know." He stuck his card to his own chest. "Now let's go get your ma."

"And your Key." I touched Little Swan for luck, as Wyatt turned the knob of Runyon's home.

Chapter Thirty-Five

Doorways perforated the air inside Runyon's house, dozens of them. In the walls, in midair, even diagonally. Wyatt and I had to inch around the one in the floor of the entryway, which provided a dizzying view of upside-down trees—dark peach trees.

All of the doorway views showed different areas of Portero—Runyon seemed to be having the same trouble as before.

Wyatt and I edged around the doors and entered a dusty living room full of great-grandmother-type furniture that only corseted women would enjoy sitting on.

Runyon stood in the center of the room, his blue eyes spitting fire as he slashed that same broken-down glyph into the air. He'd stopped opening random doors and was concentrating on the one before him. Every time he made the glyph shape in the air, the scene within the door changed, as if he were flipping through TV channels and nothing satisfied.

When my feet creaked against the floor, Runyon whirled, his dissatisfaction erupting into full-blown rage. *"What did you do to my Key?"* he shrieked.

"Don't take it out on me just because the Mayor cursed you. I kept my end of the deal."

But Runyon didn't want to hear it.

"What did you *do* to it?"

As Runyon advanced, wearing my mother's body like an ill-fitting suit, Wyatt stepped in front of me protectively. "You mean other than steal it from me?"

"Steal it from *you?*" Wyatt's effrontery stopped Runyon in his tracks. "*I* made this Key. I'm the one—" He considered us. "How did you get in here?" He looked at me. "Especially you. I thought for sure the Mayor would have killed you for helping me."

"She tried to," I said. "She put me in a suicide door. But I escaped."

"Preposterous." He was shocked, almost outraged. "No one can escape a suicide door."

"Maybe *you* can't. But I can do a lot of things you can't. I'm the one who released you in the first place. I got the Key when you couldn't. I got past the wards into your 'forbidden fortress.' What *can't* I do?"

Runyon smirked. "Get your mother back."

"Oh, but I can," I said, resisting the urge to poke him in the eyes again. "I'll make you a deal. If you give her back, I'll let you borrow Wyatt. He can use—"

Wyatt slapped me hard on the forehead. "I *knew* it! I knew I couldn't trust you—not when it comes to Rosalee."

I would have slapped him back, but I couldn't. I'd felt an immediate chill all over my body when he'd slapped me . . . and now I couldn't move. Not one inch. I couldn't even yell at him—it was like the dark park all over again.

"A freeze card," Runyon marveled, confirming what I'd already assumed Wyatt had slapped to my forehead. "Have the Mortmaine finally incorporated glyph cards into their fighting repertory?"

"Nope." Wyatt shuffled through his deck. "This is my thing."

"Your thing? Again, you have a false sense of ownership, boy. Those were my invention."

"I know," said Wyatt as he slapped a red card to Runyon's cheek. "Thanks."

The red card. The card he'd used on the lure and the flying leech. The card that made things explode.

"No, that's Rosalee's body! She's still in there!"

That's what I *wanted* to scream, but I couldn't. I couldn't even move.

As the red color seeped over Rosalee's body, Runyon knocked the cards from Wyatt's hand, the deck scattering colorfully across the floor. Wyatt dropped down to gather his cards, but not before Runyon darted forward and snatched up a green one, which he slapped over the red card.

Just in time. Rosalee's body, completely red now, had begun to roil and swell, hovering on the edge of explosion, but the green card settled her skin. It didn't get rid of the redness, but at least it kept her body in one piece.

"Red and green," said Runyon, admiring Rosalee's skin. "Such a festive combination."

Wyatt had ceased collecting his cards to stare in disbelief at Runyon.

"Never thought to combine them? Well, now you can thank me for that, too." Runyon flicked Rosalee's arms at Wyatt and a muddy red spray spattered against Wyatt and the blue wingback chair he'd been crouching near as he gathered his cards. The chair immediately exploded, filling the air with downy fuzz and bits of blue chintz.

The blast sent Wyatt rolling helplessly across the floor, but otherwise, he was unhurt. Or at least unexploded. He staggered to his feet, glaring at Runyon, and grimly removed his coat.

"And what card are *you* wearing?" Runyon asked. Some of the red color from Rosalee's skin had disappeared. "I see the anti-possession card peeking out of your shirt. But what else?" His eyes traveled shrewdly over Wyatt's body. "A shield card, perhaps? After taking that much damage, it's probably turned to dust. Let's see."

Runyon shot more of the explosive spray at Wyatt, who this time took a direct hit in the chest. He flew backward and fetched up hard against a curio cabinet, hard enough to break the glass doors. Yet unlike the chair, he didn't explode.

Runyon smiled at Wyatt, begrudgingly impressed. "I don't recall ever making a shield card that could take that much damage. Clever boy."

Wyatt's only answer was to spit up blood and then hurl a jagged bit of statuary from the curio cabinet at my mother's head.

This had gotten out of hand in a hurry. I had to do something before the two of them figured out a way to kill each other.

Poppa! Poppa, come quick!

Poppa appeared before me, Rosalee's pillow tucked under his arm. "Problems?"

Another explosion answered that question better than I ever could. *You've got to unfreeze me before they kill each other!*

Wyatt, now bleeding profusely from his nose, scrambled to one of the cards on the floor—a gold one—and hurriedly adhered it to his arm as dust sifted from beneath his shirt.

"Is that your last shield card?" Runyon exclaimed. Half of the red color had disappeared. "I have more than enough left to turn that one to dust too. Perhaps—"

Wyatt kicked him to the floor, but Runyon didn't stay down. He sprang to his feet, and they started boxing, Wyatt staying in close range, which made it impossible for Runyon to hurl the explosive spray at him.

"What's that boy doing to Rosalee?" Poppa cried, outraged.

Trying to kill her! You've got to remove the card on my head so I can stop them.

"Well, why didn't you say so!" Poppa ripped the card off my skin, and it turned to dust in his hand. "Hurry!"

And suddenly I *could* hurry. I ran forward and fell right on my face, crippled by an intense wave of pins and needles.

Wyatt and Runyon, meantime, were still in hand-to-hand combat, Wyatt jabbing repeatedly at Rosalee's face whenever Runyon let his guard down, not to punch him, but to rip off the cards. But Runyon was too good a fighter to let him get close enough.

Runyon managed to get a knee into Wyatt's belly and send him to the floor gasping for air. He stood over Wyatt and raised Rosalee's arms.

"No more shield cards, initiate. And no more stalling." Runyon flicked Rosalee's arms downward, and huge drops of the muddy red matter sailed from Rosalee's fingertips like water balloons, but Wyatt dodged them and heaved forward into Runyon just as the explosive spray tore a crater-size hole in the floor and sent us all flying across the room.

When I rolled to a stop, ears ringing, I spied the two of them wrestling near the window seat. I scrambled forward on my knees, near enough to see that the two cards had left a coating of dust on Rosalee's now properly colored brown cheek.

Wyatt rolled on top of Runyon and sat on him, push daggers in hand. "Looks like Christmas is over, asshole."

"Wyatt, don't!"

He looked back at me, and as a reward, Runyon flipped him overhead and sent him crashing to the floor.

"No!" I made it to my feet, tingling horribly from the aftereffects of the freeze card. I got between them. "Stop it. I mean it!"

They stared at me, twin expressions of bafflement on their faces, but it was Runyon who spoke, pushing Rosalee's hair out of his eyes. "How did you overcome the effects of the freeze card so soon?"

"It usually lasts thirty minutes," Wyatt added, his zeal to kill Runyon forgotten in the face of scientific curiosity.

"Because I wanted to," I told them. "And I know how to get what I want. And what I want right now is for the two of you to listen to me. This isn't just about me—I can get all three of us what we want. You get your Key, you get Bonnie, and I get Rosalee."

"How?" said Runyon, humoring me.

"Give Wyatt the Key."

"What?"

"Shut up and listen! He can help you."

"An initiate?" He gave Wyatt a disdainful once-over. "What would I want with one of the Mayor's young flunkies?"

"Doesn't he look familiar?" I prompted. "I don't know . . . sort of like the woman you raped and impregnated just so you'd have an extra set of bones to practice on?"

The disdain turned thoughtful as Runyon walked a circuit around Wyatt. I thought at any moment he might check Wyatt's teeth the way a horse trainer would. "I don't believe it," he murmured. "Anna's brood."

"Brood!" Wyatt exclaimed. "I didn't hatch from a chicken, *asshole!*"

But Runyon wasn't fazed by Wyatt's outburst. "I thought the Mortmaine killed it when they took my Key."

"Not *it*!" Wyatt rushed at Runyon and choked him. "*Her.* Your *daughter*!

Runyon backhanded him away. "*Bonnie's* my daughter," he snapped. "The only one who matters."

I had to get between them again. "Well, the only one who

can get you to your precious Bonnie is standing right here." I put my hand on Wyatt's shoulder, but he shrugged me off.

"Still trying to trade me, right?" He started reaching for his cards, so I grabbed his hand.

"No! You misunderstood me. I only meant that Runyon could use you—use your connection to the Key!—to get to Calloway."

"Yeah?" he said, as relief welled in his eyes like tears.

"Yeah." I squeezed his hand. "But we can work on our trust issues later." I turned to Runyon. "If you give Wyatt the Key, he'll open the door, and we'll all go through. On the other side, you leave Rosalee, and we'll leave you there with Bonnie. What could be simpler than that?"

I let them think it over. "So is it a deal?"

Runyon spoke first. "Deal." He handed Wyatt the Key, but then he hovered over him as if expecting us to go back on our word the way he had.

"What's the glyph?" Wyatt asked him.

"This is for Calloway." Runyon made a series of shapes with his hand that Wyatt copied, using the Key to trace them above the doorway Runyon had already opened. "And you'll have to write Bonnie's name over it," Runyon added.

Wyatt did, and for the first time, the shapes visualized, hanging goldly above the new scene that appeared in the doorway—the ocean shore at night.

Since Portero had no beaches, I knew this was a good sign.

Runyon knew it too. He gasped and hurtled through the doorway. Wyatt and I exchanged a startled look and then followed, needing to keep Runyon, and more important, Rosalee, in sight.

The disorientation I'd felt when I'd gone through the hidden door for the first time was absent, but as I passed through the doorway, I had to fight against an odd pressure, a resistance, as though plastic wrap covered the opening.

And then I was through, shoes filling with sand, greeted by the noisy rush of water.

I made sure the doorway was still open behind me, and when I'd reassured myself that Runyon's completely wrecked living room would still be there, waiting uninvitingly for our return, I looked around.

The stars were closer here and brighter, crowding the night sky as waves broke gently on the shore. The salt smell of the ocean was pervasive, the air softer and warmer than in Portero, too warm for my coat.

Wyatt had leaped through the doorway before me and had already caught a protesting Runyon by the arm.

"Let me go to her!"

"Go where?" I asked, struggling through the sand in my heels.

Wyatt pointed out a tiny hut way up on the beach, out of the tide line. The hut had been built among a sparse grove of lanky, palmlike trees. The pale, nubby bark that composed the hut had come from the grove.

A golden light passed before the glassless window of the hut, as though someone with a candle was moving about inside.

"Bonnie!" Runyon kept trying to break for the hut, but Wyatt had a firm grip on him and refused to let go.

"We had a deal, asshole," Wyatt reminded him, brandishing the Key in his face.

With a groan of impatience, Runyon left Rosalee's body. Strangely. Through her eyes. He billowed out like smoke as though the inside of her head was on fire. When the smoke cleared, Rosalee collapsed to the sand.

Runyon, after he solidified, looked as Rosalee had described him, two-dimensional and sepia-toned like an old photograph, a pudgy unimpressive man with muttonchop sideburns and an old-timey suit. He sped away toward the hut, moving as Poppa moved, gliding ghostlike over the sand.

I dropped to my knees beside Rosalee and removed the backing from the black card Wyatt had given me earlier, but when I tried to stick it down Rosalee's sweatshirt, she smacked my hands away.

"Momma, you need this."

"It doesn't matter where you put it." Wyatt said, trying to make peace. "Just put it on her arm."

"But you always put it down my . . ." I remembered how willy-nilly he and Runyon had placed the cards on their own bodies during their battle royale, how Wyatt had slapped the freeze card to my forehead.

I caught the knavish curl of Wyatt's mouth as I pressed the card to Rosalee's arm. "I *knew* you were being fresh," I muttered.

But Wyatt was too busy counting under his breath to defend himself—not that he could have. "Eleven, twelve, thirteen."

Runyon, who had nearly reached the hut, began to scream. I had no idea why until he glided back toward the shore where Wyatt and I waited with Rosalee.

Through the light fanning from the doorway leading back to Portero, I saw that, without benefit of a host or the Mayor's curse back in Portero to hold him together, Runyon was breaking apart. His arms had already disappeared to the shoulder, and more of him broke away as I watched.

He made a beeline for Rosalee, but he couldn't get near her, nor any of us as we huddled together on the sand, not while we wore the black cards.

Runyon howled, hovering in the air as whatever passed for his body disintegrated, dirtying the air like a mini dust storm.

"I can't fail now!" he cried. "Not after all these years!"

"Face it," said Wyatt coldly. "If Bonnie wanted anything to do with you, she'd've come out by now."

"But I came for you!" As Runyon turned and screamed at the hut, at his daughter hiding inside, even more of his body crumbled to dust, until he was just a torso with a head attached. "I'm sorry it took so long, but I'm here now! Bonnie, *please!*"

"Let her alone," said Wyatt. "Let her remember what you were like before you turned into a murdering rapist."

When Runyon turned to face Wyatt's stony expression, he was only a head floating under the stars, a desolate, grinless

Cheshire cat. "Tell her . . . tell her I'm . . ." His head blew away on the breeze before he could finish.

Wyatt fanned the swirling dust away from his face. "Good fucking riddance."

I agreed, not the least bit sorry that Runyon was gone. I don't think Rosalee was either, but since she hadn't looked up from her knees since Runyon had left her body, I couldn't tell. She hadn't even bothered to shake Runyon's dust out of her hair and clothes, but when I brushed at her shoulders, she jerked away.

"We ready to go?" Wyatt said, rising to his feet.

"What about Bonnie?" The light was still moving about in the hut. "Don't you think she'll want to come with us?"

"Hanna." Wyatt gave me a surprised look. "Bonnie went missing more than a *hundred years* ago. She's long dead by now. Runyon was off his rocker thinking he could find her all these years later."

"Oh," I said, feeling stupid. "But then . . . who's in the hut?"

Wyatt's scientific curiosity got the best of him. "Let's go see."

"I can't leave Rosalee alone. She—"

Rosalee lifted her head, eyes flashing. "Go with him, for Christ's sake. I don't need a keeper."

So I went with Wyatt to the window of the hut, even though all I wanted to do was bury my head in the sand. Apparently, Rosalee and I were back at square one.

Wyatt and I looked through the window and saw that the golden light was a many-winged bug with a glowing thorax—a baseball-size firefly. The bug gave off enough light for us to see that the crudely fashioned hut was covered in the hash marks of someone counting the days. Years.

That someone was on the bare wooden cot in the corner. Her bones were, anyway, neat and white and untouched.

"She must've died alone," Wyatt said, staring wide-eyed into the room.

I felt weirdly jealous of Bonnie. At least Runyon hadn't given up looking for her, even when he must have known in his heart that his search was pointless. Who would look for me if I vanished? Not Rosalee. Not the way she was now.

We walked back down to the beach.

Rosalee wasn't there.

I almost wasn't even surprised. As Wyatt ran up the dark beach in search of her, screaming her name, I tried to resign myself to the idea that she didn't want me, that the past weeks of kindness had been more about Runyon's feelings for Bonnie, not Rosalee's feelings for me.

And then I saw her standing in the starry surf up to her knees and realized I wasn't even close to being resigned.

I waded into the warm ocean water and grabbed her. "What are you doing?"

She wrenched away. "Let me go!"

"Come out of the water first."

"Don't tell me what to do!" She gripped her wild, curly hair in her fists and pulled it over her face. "God, he was right. He was so right. Love *is* a trap."

"Don't give me that shit! If love is a trap, so is fear. You'd rather send me away or be mean to me than take care of me. You'd rather beat me up and play errand girl for a fourth-rate demon than be a mother to me."

"Yes!" Rosalee got in my face. "That's it exactly. I'd rather be *dead* than be a mother to you."

"Liar! Why can't you admit the truth? *You're afraid.* You're afraid to love me!"

Rosalee slumped into the water, as if the current had stolen the strength from her legs. When she spoke, I could barely hear her. "He promised me I wouldn't have to be afraid anymore."

"And you believed him?" I hated throwing the Mayor's words to me in Rosalee's face, but about this, the Mayor was right.

Rosalee and I were a couple of dupes.

"He would have said anything to get his daughter back."

A wave rolled over Rosalee's head, but when it receded, she didn't resurface.

"Rosalee?" I reached into the water and pulled her up by the strands of her floating hair.

She shoved me away. "Don't."

"Well, I'm not going to let you drown yourself!"

"Then take me home! I just . . . wanna go home."

"So let's go," said Wyatt, startling us both.

He waded in after us and helped Rosalee to her feet, talking all the while to cover up the awkwardness. "I think there's a hidden door near Nightshade that leads to Lamartine. Or somewhere near there. I can have you home in a couple of minutes."

As Wyatt half carried Rosalee back to the shore, he said, "And you know I wasn't trying to kill you, right, Miz Rosalee? That stuff with Runyon . . . that was family stuff. You know?"

"I know," she said, as if she cared about Wyatt's family stuff or even that he'd nearly killed her. As if she cared about anything.

We tramped through the lit doorway, glaringly bright after the darkness of the beach, and back into Runyon's old house, tracking in sand and salt water. All the doors Runyon had opened had vanished, except for the one we'd come through, maybe because Wyatt had opened it, not Runyon.

Wyatt gathered his coat and the rest of his glyph cards, and when he used the Key to slash the hovering glyph, the door to Calloway vanished too.

Outside it was blustery, but the rain had stopped, if only temporarily. I was now happy to have the coat that had been such a burden on the warm beach, despite the wet hem dripping onto my freezing bare legs. But I wasn't happy for long.

Rosalee collapsed on the porch.

"Momma!" I dropped next to her, panicked to see her curled in a ball. It reminded me too much of Petra.

Rosalee shivered, coatless, as she'd gone from our house straight to Runyon's through the doorway. She was shivering, but not just from the cold.

"Don't . . . feel well," she said.

Wyatt draped his coat over her. "It's the spirit leavings," he told me. I didn't like the worry in his voice. "We have to—"

"Have to what?" But when I looked up, I saw why he'd stopped.

The empty street had filled with Mortmaine trooping onto the lawn of Runyon's house. The Mayor led them, striding forward, her robe swirling cinematically around her, mirror eyes flashing in the dark, full of Wyatt's reflection as she came to a stop and faced him.

"Fuck the Mayor?" she asked him, her voice low and venomous. "Is that what you said?"

Chapter Thirty-six

I stayed crouched beside Rosalee in the shadows as Wyatt stood to my left facing the Mayor, knees knocking together.

"I apologize, ma'am," he said, his voice steadier than his knees.

"You disobey my command to report to the suicide door, you insult me, and then you come here and break my ward, and all you can say is 'I apologize'?" The glint of her bared teeth was like light on steel. "What brought about this need to flagrantly disregard your duties?"

The mention of duties tightened Wyatt's mouth. "My duty to my family and friends, you mean? I haven't disregarded those, ma'am."

"To hell with your family and friends! Your duty is—"

"To follow blindly? To never think for myself?"

"Your duty is to the Mortmaine, initiate!"

Wyatt exploded. "I got the Key back and defeated Runyon and I did it *my way*, so don't tell me about my duty! I know what it is—it's to protect people who can't protect themselves."

"And who will protect you, Wyatt?" said the Mayor softly.

Wyatt's fire fizzled out. So did mine, and she wasn't even talking to me. Her voice carried a promise of ruin, like a tornado on the horizon. You knew there would be damage—the question was how much.

I rose and stood next to Wyatt; I couldn't let him take the damage alone. "*I'll* protect him. The way he protected me."

The Mayor's mouth dropped, the shock in her face spreading to the Mortmaine lined up in the yard, like the red card Wyatt had used on the lure; any minute I expected them all to explode.

"How did you get out of the suicide door?" Her disbelief was a living, pettable thing.

"Magic."

Her eyes narrowed. "There is no magic."

"Maybe not for you. But I'm from out of town."

"Is that how you were able to free that murderer?" she said, humoring me. "With magic?"

I thought about it. "I suppose death is a *kind* of freedom."

"You killed Runyon?"

The rain might have chosen that moment to fall in torrents anyway, but I think her voice called it down.

"I thought you hated him for what he did to Anna."

"Who cares about her?" she screamed, dry and untouched by the rain that drenched everyone else on the lawn. "She wasn't even from here. Runyon *was*, and he disobeyed me. That can't stand." She stalked closer, to the bottom of the porch steps, so close I could see my reflection in her left eye and Wyatt's in her right.

"The house needs a new occupant," she said, smiling angrily. "Maybe two. You like each other so well"—she pointed at us and we flinched—"why not spend eternity together?"

Behind us, the front door blew open with a bang like gunfire as the house turned into a vacuum. A selective vacuum—the only things it drew in were Wyatt and me.

My feet lost contact with the ground, but when Wyatt hurriedly grabbed the porch rail, I grabbed his outstretched hand and held on, parallel to the porch floor, the doorway behind me attempting to suck the wet French heels from my feet.

My arms hurt from the struggle to keep tight to Wyatt's hand, but my feet were my main concern: I'd be damned if I lost another pair of shoes today.

Without thinking, with no reason to believe it would work, I snatched Little Swan from my neck with my free hand, the plink of the silver chain snapping loud even over the roar of the storm. Her silver S-shaped form glowed in my cupped palm as I whispered to her, "Go get Swan. Please. Tell her the Mayor stuck me in the suicide door and now she's—"

But Little Swan saw no need to fetch Swan. Her diamond eyes flashed red as she unfurled her wings and flew at the Mayor, trailing her silver chain.

My own personal lightning strike.

The Mayor didn't know what hit her. She batted the air as though a bee were flitting about her face. Or a wasp. Little Swan moved so fast, even I couldn't see her.

When the house stopped sucking us in, I knew it was because the Mayor had started to panic.

"Get it!" she screamed, as Wyatt and I dropped painfully to the porch. "Get it off me!"

But the Mortmaine could only watch helplessly as their

Mayor danced around the lawn, slapping at her own skin.

"Get it off!"

"Little Swan hardly ever gets a chance to play," I said, as Wyatt helped me to my feet. "It wouldn't be fair to rob her of such a choice playmate."

The Mayor's mirror eyes narrowed on me. "Call it off," she hissed, less panicked now that she knew it was only me.

"Make me," I said. A dumb thing to say, but extremity always turned me into a toddler.

She turned to her army of Mortmaine. "Stop her!"

"Her?" I recognized Wyatt's elder. He recognized me, too. "The transy?"

The Mayor whirled on him, golden bits of her skin peppering the dark air. *"I said stop her!"*

As the Mortmaine readied their weapons and advanced on me, Wyatt hurriedly removed a yellow card from his pocket and slapped it on the porch post. Golden light flashed over the house, and when the Mortmaine stormed the stairs, they rebounded at least ten feet, as though they'd run into a vertical trampoline.

"Ha!" I screamed triumphantly, staring at the Mortmaine picking themselves up from the wet lawn. "That's why you don't like his 'nonstandard' weapons. Because they make him more powerful than you."

"How?" the Mayor screamed in frustration.

"Magic," I said again, because I knew it would piss her off. "You have it. Why can't we?"

"I'm a god!" she cried, like a brat who for once wasn't getting her way. "And this is my town!"

"The god of small towns? How silly! Anyway, gods have power only if you believe in them, and I'm not sure I believe in you."

The Mayor screamed as Little Swan shredded her skin at a faster clip. As more of her face disappeared, she began to look more like the Grim Reaper I had taken her for earlier. The Mortmaine, as one, backed away from the sight of her skull.

Or maybe they were backing away from me.

"Aw, don't be that way," I told them. "We *are* darkside, after all, where all the weird shit happens." I thought about it. "But I guess that would make *me* weird shit, wouldn't it? That's not too cool."

"How are you doing this?" The defeated tone of the Mayor's voice was encouraging. "I tasted your blood. There's nothing special about you!"

"Maybe you tasted the wrong thing. Maybe I'm like Wyatt—maybe the special part of me is in my bones."

"You can't do this to me!"

"Why not? You're not my god." The old bitterness rose in me, the feeling of detachment, of outsiderness. "I'm not even from here. I'm just a stupid horrible awful transy, right?"

But the sound of her screams was no longer fun.

"That's enough, Little Swan," I called. "Playtime's over."

Little Swan peeled a final layer of golden skin from the Mayor's cheek and dropped it into the grass as she flew back to me and settled into my hand. Her silver body blazed hot as an open flame, but I held her anyway and burned my mouth when I kissed her. The tang of metal flavored my lips as I tucked her into the pocket of my coat.

Everyone seemed stunned to realize that the Mayor had gotten her ass kicked by a necklace.

"Little Swan?" said Wyatt, incredulous.

"I used to hallucinate that Swan could rescue me whenever I was in trouble," I told him quietly. "Then I moved here, and now it's all real. And pretty damn convenient, wouldn't you say?"

"Hell, yeah," he agreed.

I turned to the Mayor and gave her one of my nicest smiles. "Look, I'm a simple girl. I'd rather not destroy a god, or whatever you are, just to prove I can. So why don't we make a deal?"

Even the storm had stilled, awaiting my pronouncement.

"If you give me a key and drop the grudge you have against Rosalee and Wyatt for disobeying you, I won't feed you to Little Swan for breakfast. How does that sound?"

The Mayor kept silent a long moment, as if she didn't trust herself to speak, tugging her robe over her face/skull to hide what Little Swan had done to it, but she stood tall as if unaware of how to stand any other way. "Only Runyon knew the secret to making Keys."

"Not that kind of key," I explained. "One of the little silver ones you give out to people who truly belong here. That's not too much to ask."

After a long breathless pause, the Mayor reached into her black robe and retrieved a key. She walked slowly to the steps and handed it to me gingerly, her mirrored eyes glowing strangely within the shadow of her hood.

"Perhaps now that you have a key of your own, you'll leave other people's alone," she said, gathering her dignity, even as the Mortmaine gathered bits of her face off the ground—an unnecessary chore, as her face was already mending itself.

Not even Poppa had been able to mend himself.

Maybe she *was* a god.

I curtsied, trying to help her save face. After all, I had to live here now; why be ungracious? "Thank you."

"You're welcome," said the Mayor grudgingly.

She turned stiffly to face the Mortmaine. "Never mind the rest. Leave them be." She walked off with her four bodyguards and vanished into the night.

The mood lightened considerably once she was gone. Wyatt even felt safe enough to remove the glyph card from the porch and wave it away to dust as the remaining Mortmaine regarded us.

"You'd better be glad you're so damn talented," Elder told Wyatt as he stepped toward the porch. "How the hell were you able to get Runyon to leave his host? Spirits never leave."

"They do if they want something bad enough," said Wyatt. He told them the story of our beach adventure, and then showed off his black cards. "I modified the anti-possession cards to get rid of the spirit leavings so Rosalee won't get sick from 'em."

"She's already sick." Elder was looking at Rosalee, who had risen to her feet and was holding herself upright against the porch railing, more by will than strength. I went to her, but she held me off with a glare.

"It'd be kinder to put her out of her misery now," said Elder reluctantly, as he stared at Rosalee. "We have no way of knowing those cards of yours'll work."

"That's why he needs to experiment," I said. "You just said he's talented. If his way works . . . wouldn't it be nice not to have to kill everything touched by evil?" I looked at Rosalee. "Wouldn't it be nice to know that redemption is possible?"

He looked Rosalee over, and even sick and exhausted, she coaxed a gleam of desire from Elder's eye. "Fine. Experiment. If Rosalee don't mind being your guinea pig, who am I to complain?" He jabbed a finger at Wyatt. "But you're on regular schedule today. Six a.m. sharp. We have more tunnels to dig."

"*Damn* those tunnels," Wyatt muttered.

"What's that?" said Elder sharply.

"Yes, sir." Wyatt sounded resigned, but I was close enough to see the light spark in his eyes.

The remaining Mortmaine left, into the houses lining the street or through the hidden doors.

I turned to Wyatt. "When can we use the cards?"

Rosalee let Wyatt sling an arm around her waist. "We already started," he said. "You put one on her in Calloway. Let's get her home and settled and I'll show you what to do next."

We walked in the dark and rain and had to go through two hidden doors before we made our way back to Lamartine. At the house, the blood coating the walls brought Wyatt up short. I blamed it on the Mayor.

"She was trying to scare me," I said.

He totally bought it.

We put Rosalee in her room, on her bed. I stripped Wyatt's coat from her and removed her shoes, trying to make her as comfortable as I could.

"Here." Wyatt handed over a bunch of those black glyph cards. "You put these on her, one at a time, and remove 'em every one to two hours, or whenever they turn white. The day the card stays black, you'll know she's clean. When you remove the card, it'll be gross, so expect it, but *don't let go in disgust*. And always burn the cards when you're done, down to the ash. I'll bring more when you run low."

I looked down at Rosalee, lying sick and bedraggled on the bed. "He's not entirely out of her, is he?"

"He is, but there's . . . residue."

I remembered then the black card still stuck to my chest. I removed it and then slapped from my hands the dust that its self-destruction left behind.

"It's bad," Wyatt continued. "The sooner we can get it all out, the better."

"How soon?"

"I don't know. It's never been done. We'll just have to wait and see."

He knelt next to Rosalee as I raised the sleeve of her sweatshirt. The card on her upper arm was completely white.

"Pull it," he said, but when I reached for it, Rosalee jerked away from me.

"I can do it!" she said. "I'm not some invalid." With considerable effort, she sat upright and pulled the card from her arm. It came free with a wet squish, trailing a tacky, semenlike substance. With a cry, Rosalee flung the card to the floor, wiping her fingers frantically against the bedsheet.

The residue clinging to the card molded into Runyon's face as it hit the floor across the room. It caterpillared toward Rosalee, dragging the card behind it as it scritched across the wooden floor.

Wyatt stomped on the card, holding it trapped against the floor, and dropped a lit match to the tacky substance. Flames brought it up short and engulfed the residue, which dried out and floated up and away like ashes.

Wyatt turned to Rosalee. "*That's* why you don't let go in disgust."

After he placed a fresh card on Rosalee's arm, I walked him to the front door and helped him into his coat. "Thank you. For everything."

"This has been the worst week of my life," he said, tucking the Key under his arm, "but right now, I don't think I ever been this happy."

"That's because you know the Mortmaine finally accept who you are. Must be nice." I started crying slow, quiet tears. I was too tired to cry any other way.

"I accept you," Wyatt said almost grudgingly, "despite what you did to me. You think I'm more accepting than your own mother?"

"Yes. You're a romantic," I said, sniffling into my hanky. "Not like Rosalee and me. We're not at all sentimental. You saw her in there. I saved her life, and she still won't let me touch her!"

"I'll make you a deal." He smiled. "You like deals, right? So listen: If Rosalee accepts you like I know she will, you come clean up the mess you made at our house and all down our street. If she don't accept you, you still gotta come clean up the mess, but you can stay afterward."

"You'd really let me stay with you?"

"You'd have to live under the bed and never, *ever* let Ma see you, but I can live with it if you can."

I laughed waterily.

He opened the blood-streaked front door. "Be there after church tomorrow. Around two—no matter what happens."

He'd reached the screen door when he changed his mind and came back and gave me such a hard squeeze, I couldn't tell if he was trying to crush the life out of me or hold me as close as possible. Maybe I *was* a little romantic, because I was sure hoping it was the latter.

When he was gone, I went back to Rosalee's room.

Poppa sat in the chair near the window, watching her. "She already looks better, doesn't she?"

He was right. She sat up in bed much easier than before, less gray and ill now that some of that gunk was out of her system.

She held the red box in her lap, gripping it so tightly her nails had whitened. She cut her eyes at me. "Were you afraid in the suicide door?"

I removed my coat and sat beside her, but despite the narrow bed, she managed to keep her distance. "Not afraid. *Hopeless*. But then I thought about you and how you needed me, and I knew I had to get out."

She opened the trickily hinged box and let me look inside.

On the red satin lining were two things. One was a picture of Poppa, Rosalee, and me—a tiny baby in her arms. Poppa was the only happy one in the picture. Rosalee and I had that sad mouth that made us seem like we knew something Poppa didn't.

I looked at him in the chair, but he kept his thoughts to himself.

I removed the picture and held it as though it might turn to ash in my hand. "I thought you didn't have any of you and Poppa."

"I don't deserve to. *This* I deserve to have." She removed the second thing from the box: a red pill.

It was made in the same style as the pill I'd received at the river, liquid sloshing temptingly within the capsule. "Did you get that from Carmin?"

"Yeah. The day after you showed up. I thought it'd be for the best."

"What does it do?"

"Guess." Her eyes bored into mine.

I didn't have to guess. I was my mother's daughter, after all.

"I told Carmin I wanted something to take in case I ever found myself staring a hideous death in the face. Something quick to put me outta my misery." Her smile was ironic. "I can't believe he fell for that shit."

"But why would you want to kill yourself?"

"If I was dead, you'd have to leave. If you left, you'd be safe. I meant to swallow it ten different times. I should have." She scratched her nails over the already gray card on her arm. "I feel so dirty. I'm sorry you were stuck with me as a mother." Her eyes were wet, but she wasn't crying. She was too much of a badass to really cry.

Not like me.

"I'm not stuck, Momma," I said, sniffling again. "I know you're not perfect. Neither am I. That's why I'm so afraid to go to therapy. If you find out how batty I really am, you might not let me come home."

"I should be the one going to therapy."

She considered the pill in her hand. "You called me a puppet, remember? You were right. When I let people in, they take me over. There's a neediness in me, and when you need people they use it against you. That's why I stay by myself."

"Wanting to connect doesn't make you needy—it makes you human. And anything worth having is risky. Like, I can't guarantee that I won't hurt your feelings or hit you over the head again. Those are the risks of having me for a daughter.

"But I won't ever call you a slut. Or lock you out of the house when you stay out all night. I won't make you kill anyone. And I'll always love you, no matter what you do."

I tried to take her hand, the hand with the pill, but she avoided my touch and cradled her fist to her chest like the pill was more important than I was. I grabbed her fist and pried the pill from it, ignoring her protests, and ran out of her room.

I raced upstairs and explained the situation to Swan, who whooped wisely and darted her hard beak at the pill in my hand, swallowing it so Rosalee wouldn't have to.

When I ran back to Rosalee's room, she gaped at me and at Swan nestled in the curve of my arm. I gaped too, not at her, but at Poppa, who was now at the foot of her bed, caressing her feet. "Stop that!" I said.

Poppa did stop, guiltily.

"You stop it," said Rosalee.

"You speak Finnish?" I said, happily surprised.

"A little. You're not the only one who knows Finnish, just like you're not the only one who gets to off herself whenever she feels like it. You think I bought that bullshit about the Mayor putting blood on the walls? *You* did that. Didn't you?"

She did her Easter Island thing, but I didn't cave. She didn't need to know everything, not that I'd slit my wrists, not that she was being haunted by Poppa's ghost.

"That's just it, Momma. I don't want to kill myself anymore. I don't want to, Swan doesn't want me to, and she doesn't want *you* to either."

My coat shifted on the foot of the bed as Little Swan arose from its purple folds, her broken chain rattling as she fluttered before my chest. Her wee talons caught the ruching of my dress, and she came to rest against my heart, like a silver brooch, wrapping herself in her wings. I smiled at Rosalee, who looked almost moronic with shock. "And neither does Little Swan," I added.

I climbed beside Rosalee on the bed and made the proper introductions. "Swan, Little Swan, say hello to Momma."

They both bowed their long necks in greeting, and Rosalee gasped.

"Swan's going to look out for you from now on."

Rosalee let out a little *oof* as Swan settled into her lap. The trapped look on her face worried me. She'd had to share her body with a jerk for twenty years, and now I was crowding her with all my baggage.

I reached for Swan. "Unless you don't want—"

"No!" Rosalee held Swan to her chest and stroked her downy feathers. When Swan cooed encouragingly, Rosalee smiled. "A gal like me's gotta take comfort where she can get it."

She stared at me when she said it, but when I pressed my hand over her heart, she winced like it hurt.

"Remember what I stitched into your mattress?" I said as her heart spoke into my palm.

She nodded.

"I wish I could stitch it right here."

Rosalee tickled Swan under her chin and pretended to think about it. "Only if the thread is red."

I lowered my hand and rested my head on her shoulder, gingerly, waiting for her to shove me away.

She didn't.